SWEET LOVE

MIA KAYLA

MAM BOOKS LLC

Visit my website at www.authormiakayla.com
Cover Designer: Najla Qamber Designs
Editor: Jovana Shirley, Unforeseen Editing, www.unforeseenediting.com
Developmental Editor: Melissa Shank, booksmakemegiddy@gmail.com
Proofreader: Julie Deaton, Deaton Author Services,
www.jdproofs.wixsite.com/jddeaton

ISBN-13: 978-1-953370-98-3

 Created with Vellum

To my BFFs (Book Friends Forever),
Thank you for bringing this book and characters to life.
There are so many books to read out there, but yet you read mine.
And for that I will be forever grateful.
xoxo
Mia
This book was born in my reader group - Mia Kayla Book Friends Forever

CHAPTER 1

CHARLIE

MY FATHER HAD ALWAYS SAID, "Love what you do and love the job you choose."

I wished I had taken him up on his advice because as a computer tech, my job was okay at best, but today, my view was quite interesting.

Milk chocolate bars. Chocolate-covered almonds. Hazelnut bars. Sour candies. Gummy candies.

This was every little kid's dream—a real-life candy wall. And it was right in front of me.

I would have been in heaven if I actually liked chocolate, if it didn't leave a bad taste in my mouth, if it didn't remind me of things I'd rather forget.

When I had walked in through the pink glass revolving doors on my first day of the job at Colby Chocolates and Candies corporate office, I had known I was in for a treat. Literally.

Unlimited sweets was one of the perks for working for

one of the biggest manufacturers of candy and chocolate in the nation.

I wrung my hands together, waiting for the cute, short girl who was giving me a company tour to come back from the restroom, when my eyes widened at the guy right next to me.

Sweet, sinful, dark chocolate male brown eyes stared down at me.

"You look like a candy cane," I said. The moment the words left my mouth, I smiled, all teeth, because ... awkward. Immediately, heat rushed to my cheeks because what kind of introduction was that?

"It's a pretty impressive outfit. I wish I could say I'd designed it myself." His voice oozed with masculine sophistication, opposite to the white pants and his candy cane–striped red and white shirt and suit jacket.

It was as though I were on a candy commercial—or a bad porno. Right next to me, in front of this candy wall, stood the finest guy I'd ever laid my eyes on—tall, insanely handsome.

Whoa, de whoa.

I blinked and then double-blinked. Then, I shut my mouth because it'd slipped open.

Six foot something. Smoldering chocolate-brown eyes. Chiseled chin. Dark brown hair. Face of a god. Smile of an angel.

I looked around me as though a cameraman were going to walk in, following this guy, taping a commercial in front of the candy wall.

I gave him a once-over again because I couldn't for the life of me stop staring.

"It's not Halloween. Why are you dressed like that?" I

bit my tongue before some other stupid thing flew out of my mouth.

"How do you know I don't dress like this on a regular basis?" He quirked an eyebrow, his gaze traveling languidly up my body. "Pretty impressive ..."

I swallowed.

His gaze faced forward. "Pretty impressive wall, right? It's good candy. Especially the signature Colby's Chocolate Bar."

When he smiled, my stomach flipped and flopped and flopped and flipped again.

"That one's the worst. Their candy is *eh* at best."

The smile slipped from Mr. Candy Company's beautiful face.

He reached over me and plucked a Colby bar from the wall. This one had nuts. "You know, if anyone caught you saying that"—he wrinkled his nose—"they'd throw you in one of those machines that melted the chocolate."

I shrugged. "The truth hurts. And plus ..." I plucked it from his hand—maybe because I wanted to touch him, maybe because I was flirting. Yes, very much flirting at this point. "Why is the biggest thing on the packaging the company's name?" I was just rambling, trying to spark conversation. "Like, oh, it's not enough that *Colby's* is written on the factory walls and the company cars and vans. It must be written on the candy bar too, in big, fat letters. It just has to. Why couldn't they have called this bar the Nutter Bar or something more interesting? I don't see Hall's Chocolates branded this way. It's mostly to the actual feel of the chocolate. Or if you are branding to Colby's, I feel like it should be branded to the essence of family, but you can do it without using the family name in giant letters."

Colby's was the biggest candy and chocolate manufacturers in the nation, and Hall's was its direct competitor.

Candyman paused, his smile slipping. In the next second, he composed himself and then tapped at my temple, touching me.

Maybe he is flirting back? Or maybe it is wishful thinking on my part.

"You're right. The other candy companies don't do that. They have weird candy names, and their family logo is branded smaller on their bars."

"And this packaging ..." I scrunched my nose. "I think it's the same original packaging. They need to brand to future generations too, cater to families. I swear that's why only old people eat Colby's."

He looked at me as though I'd offended him in some way.

I bit my lip from talking any further.

After a beat, our gazes went back to the candy wall.

"Sweet, tart, or chocolate?" he asked.

Candyman was staring at me as though the answer to this question would unlock some deep, dark secret. I thought about it. I preferred gum. Gum kept me from saying too much or falling asleep on a job, and it caused me to stop binge-eating when I was just plain bored and not even hungry.

"Neither. I'm not really into any of this."

He tilted his head and assessed me. "That's crazy. Why would you work for a candy company if you weren't into candy? And I have never met a woman who doesn't like chocolate. You don't even like chocolate?"

"Nope. Not even the ones with caramel and nougat inside."

Plus, chocolate didn't bring back the best type of memories.

He reached on the shelf and grabbed another candy bar named Goodlicious. When he tore it open, I peered around me. It felt like I was opening a candy bar without even paying for it yet. He broke the piece in half and extended it my way, and nausea slapped me in the face.

The smell of cleaning solution mixed with chocolate hit me in the nose, causing me to relive a memory.

I pushed those thoughts aside and forced myself to straighten.

He didn't have to literally shove their product down my throat.

"No, it's okay. You have it. And to answer your question, why can't I just be here for a paycheck?"

He reeled back, actually shocked.

Because that was what it came down to. This job was just a means to an end. Money to pay for the space for my exhibit.

"Tell me you love your job as the spokesperson for Colby Chocolates." I lifted my chin and quirked an eyebrow, curious. "Like, really love it and that's why you do it and you wouldn't mind *not* getting paid."

He could very well love being the pretty-boy face of Colby's.

"How do you know I'm the spokesperson for Colby's?" He popped the chocolate bar in his mouth and began to chew, and momentarily, I was stunned and fascinated at how he chewed, staring at his lips.

I blinked back into focus. "Because you'd sell more in that candy outfit than dressed up in your regular uniform." And now, I was definitely flirting and had no filter. What was wrong with me?

Someone should've told him he could be modeling instead of working here. His mother and father had definitely failed him.

He sported this evident smirk, and the longer our eyes locked, the hotter my cheeks flamed. But for the life of me, I couldn't look away.

"Connor ... Connor." Casey, the woman giving me the company tour, ran toward us at a full-on sprint, almost knocking into the wall.

As awkward went, Casey—the mousy girl with the thick-rimmed glasses—embodied all of that.

I was thankful for her interruption.

"So, I guess you've met Charlotte." Casey bent over, placed her hands on her knees, and breathed deeply as though trying to catch her breath.

"No, not formally. But I guess I have now. Nice to meet you, Charlotte."

"Charlie." I placed my hand in his extended one.

His handshake was firm, strong, masculine. Mine was clammy and sweaty as though I'd washed my hands and forgot to dry.

"I have to get going, but I'm sure I'll see you around." He held my hand and my stare for far too long until I exhaled and finally extracted my fingers from his.

"See you around."

Then, he turned and walked farther down the aisle. My eyes were glued to his figure until he turned a corner and was gone.

"I've never seen a man as fine as that one," I huffed out. Because if you couldn't be honest with another woman about admiring the male species, who else could you be honest with?

"Who? Connor? Yeah, ew." Casey's face pinched.

"Negative. Never. Ever. Not even if he were the last dick on earth. We grew up together. He's like my brother."

I laughed. Okay, duly noted. Casey wasn't attracted to the Connor kind.

My head flipped back toward her direction. "What was the matter? You ran out here like the company was on fire and this was the safe zone."

Thank goodness she hadn't face-planted into the candy wall.

"I was afraid I'd left you for too long. Sorry, when nature calls, it calls." She smirked.

I grabbed another Goodlicious bar and handed it to her. Someone should enjoy some chocolate if it wasn't going to be me. "Thanks for the tour. Can you lead me back to my desk now?"

"Sure." She placed the bar back on the wall. "I'm diabetic."

"You are?" My stomach sank. "I'm sorry."

"It's no big deal. I was diagnosed years ago, but I have it maintained. Anyway, come follow me." Her flats with cute little bows tiptapped against the pink tiles. Every other tile had Colby's logo etched on it.

"Casey, which department do you work in again?"

"I'm a manager in quality and assurance. In charge of the people who taste-test the candies for consistency and flavor."

I nearly tripped mid-step. "And you're diabetic. Can you taste-test the candies?"

"A little. But not too much."

"I'm sorry."

"Don't be. I'm not. I love my job. I love this place, and it helps with my figure." She slapped her nonexistent hip and gave me a cheeky thumbs-up.

I wondered how that even worked. This woman was employed in the quality and assurance lab. She managed the Q and A specialists, whose main job was to chew candy and determine the peak of the taste and consistency.

Man, if I thought my life was unfair, so was hers.

CHAPTER 2

CONNOR

I WALKED into the office and shut the door behind me.

Kyle, my brother, was seated at my desk as though he worked here, throwing a ball in the air and catching it. His feet were plopped up, as though it were his desk.

Floor-to-ceiling windows highlighted the Chicago skyline behind him, which had been my temporary view over the last few weeks. All big cities seemed the same—tall buildings, condo high-rises, city lights. Looking over at the skyscrapers reminded me of my permanent office in New York.

"What did people think of your outfit?" Kyle smirked.

"They actually loved it," I deadpanned.

"Nice," he drawled out.

"Especially the stripes on my shirt. I think we should add a bonnet to this ensemble."

He threw me the ball, and I caught it mid-flight and placed it on the desk.

"This is the last time I bet you on anything. Why can't

we be like normal people and bet money?" I unbuttoned my shirt, slipped off my clothes and slid on my regular button-down, navy blue slacks, and striped tie.

"It's more fun this way. Maybe you should learn never to bet against your little brother."

Once changed, I kicked Kyle off my chair and motioned to the seat in front of me. Like a good boy, he moved but not before grabbing the ball from my desk and tossing it up in the air again.

My chair swiveled back and forth, and I took in the city, which I used to live in, where I had grown up in. I wouldn't call this home because home was where the heart was, and there was no heart in Chicago.

"Three more months until this is over." My voice was distant, and so were my thoughts.

When I'd left this place and gone to college, I'd told myself I'd never be back again. The only things that had brought me home were Nana and to see Kyle. Not even my parents begging had brought me back here. I was back because Nana had asked me to help my parents' dying company survive.

"Well, hell, it's not gonna be me, big bro. I'm not going to be the one to lead this company."

"Then, why are you here?" I wrinkled my brow, watching the people below us, like little ants on an ant farm, doing their daily jobs.

The ball hit me directly on the side of my head, and it dropped to the floor, which forced me to turn around and look at him.

"Don't be a jerk. You're not here long, so don't blame me for wanting to spend time with you," he said, shooting me a look.

"It's not what I meant. I mean, why are you here, at the company, when you don't work here?"

"I'm always here. Even when you're not. Because our parents are always here. And Nana is here." He stood and walked to my side of the desk, leaning a hip against it. "And most of all, I want to see you save our parents' company."

I noticed how he hadn't said *our company* because neither of us considered this our company even though our parents wanted to make it our legacy.

Everyone wanted to see me save this company. The profit margins had been dwindling for the last year. My parents had had consultant after consultant in to try to turn things around, but each and every one had failed. They'd all turned to me as their last hope. I had come here with no ideas, only a determination to analyze the issue and to save the company. But the aha moment had hit me when I talked to Charlie.

I rubbed at my day-old stubble, noting that I would have to shave tomorrow. "I've figured it out." It was as though a light had switched on in my brain just minutes before, showing me how I was going to save Colby's. "We have to totally rebrand. We can't just turn things around with new products. We need a total rehab from top to bottom."

The new girl had hit the nail directly on the head with her comments.

Kyle knocked my desk twice, and then he pointed at me. "And this is what you're good at. You're good at taking a company that's failing and making it rain money again."

Wasn't it the truth though? I'd moved from New York City back to Chicago, leaving a job that I loved, a place where I was appreciated, and a place that paid well.

I was the executive director of the Commercial Loan Workout Division at Financial State Bank in Manhattan.

For companies not making a profit and were about to be kicked out of the bank, I would help them by either cutting expenses or getting rid of their line that was no longer profitable. That meant firing employees if I needed to. I knew how to get the company from the red and back into the black. That was what I did, and I excelled at my job.

I knew I could do this. There was no heart in this transaction. It was simply a favor to my nana, the woman who had basically raised me by herself because my parents were never home, working to build this company up.

I'd do this job, like I'd promised Nana I would, just as I did my job at Financial State, within the allotted time period and get back to my life in New York.

"I met a girl." It was so random, yet it had everything to do with branding. "She hated the name Colby Chocolates, hated the packaging and how our original chocolate bar tasted."

"*Hate* is an intense word," Kyle scoffed.

Maybe I was exaggerating. A chuckle escaped as I thought of her face when I'd opened the candy bar and torn off a piece.

"She actually doesn't care too much for candy and chocolates. But she does think the branding is off."

Kyle rolled his eyes. "Tell me you're not dating this girl because that would be an interesting dinner conversation topic, especially when you invite her to meet the parents."

I laughed without humor. "Maybe she has a point though. *Colby's* is everywhere. It's the name of every candy bar instead of embodying the candy bar itself."

Kyle shrugged. "Well ... yeah. Dad grew this company to where it is today, and I'm sure he is pretty damn proud of his name and believes it should be plastered everywhere. On our uniforms. On trucks. On all the candy bars. A logo on the back of our other branded candies. Anyway, I don't see him changing it up anytime soon."

That was the problem.

"He has to think of what is best for this company, not feed his ego." I moved my mouse to fire up my computer.

I had gotten her first name but not her last. All I knew was, she had started recently, and Casey knew her. I wondered if she worked in our marketing area, and if so, that would make sense because she had an eye for things. If I had trouble locating her, I could always ask Casey.

Kyle peered over on my screen as Charlie's picture popped up. "She's cute. Big bro, why are you stalking the new girl?"

"I'm not stalking the new girl."

Interesting. So, she was our new computer tech person. I would have never guessed that.

When I shut my screen, Kyle reached for my mouse and moved it, so her picture would pop up again.

"So, what are you gonna do? Are you going to ask her why she doesn't like our chocolate?" Kyle asked, breaking me from my thoughts.

It hadn't crossed my mind, but that seemed like the brightest idea my brother had ever come up with—to pick her brain a little more.

"I think I'll do that." My voice was soft, reserved, as my eyes took in the woman on my screen.

Charlotte Grayson had the brightest smile I'd ever seen on a company photo. Two dimples were set deep in her cheeks. It was the first thing you noticed about her. That, and the green in her eyes, the lightness in her wavy, blondish hair.

"Big bro. Connor!" He waved a hand in front of my

face, and then his smirk widened like he'd caught me doing something inappropriate.

"What?"

"What's that look?" With a little shake of his head, he poked me. "Man ... I think you might like this woman who hates our chocolate."

"That's ridiculous." I was simply here to turn this company around.

My leave of absence at Financial State Bank had an end date and start date back to work. My job and my life were in New York. There could be no distractions. Especially not the green-eyed, blonde-haired beauty.

CHAPTER 3

CHARLIE

CASEY PULLED BACK her brown hair over her shoulder. "This is where we eat. Not very fancy, but it's okay." She motioned around the area. "What I like about it is that the coffee room is separate from the break room."

Casey, being the good hostess that she was, led me to the vending machines that outlined the far end wall of the break room, specifically pointing out what each vending machine sold, which was not Colby Chocolates. I guessed that made sense, as chocolates were free.

There were five round tables that could seat maybe six people each. Vending machines. A sink. A fridge and a microwave. A water dispenser at the far end.

"Did you bring a lunch, or should we buy lunch? But if we buy lunch, we'll have to go out." She waved a hand in the air. "That's fine with me, but that kinda cuts into our time, so in the summer, I usually just bring a lunch. Not like we can't go out and bring our lunch. If that's what you decide to do." Her mouth was like a nonstop machine gun but with less noise.

Part of me wondered if she needed a drink of water or if her throat was dry because I always needed a drink of water after speaking too fast in a short period of time. Also, I wondered who "we" was.

"No ... it's fine. I brought my lunch and plan to bring my lunch every day."

I didn't mention the fact that I was broke. Hence this job. Hence I also needed to save money within a short period of time because I had plans of my own. I wasn't here because working as a tech girl for the largest candy and chocolate manufacturer was my dream job. It was by far not my dream job. This was simply a job to pay the bills, and I had bills to pay.

"Okay. If you do, don't keep your lunch at your desk. This location carries smells. One time, someone had curry at their desk, and chocolate and curry and ... yeah, no." She scrunched her nose.

"No ... I already put my food in the fridge."

She peered behind her at the only fridge in the room. "Oh. Did someone give you a tour of the break room this morning?" Her voice was tinged with slight disappointment.

I linked my arm through hers. "No, Casey. I found it on accident."

She smiled then and patted my hand. Then, she almost skipped us to the table.

There was an aura around Casey. A joyful one, a cheerful one, and one I needed in my life. Especially now.

We were seated at a table when Casey jumped to a standing position and waved her hands in the air like we were at some big gymnasium-style cafeteria. "Alyssa, Alyssa, Alyssa. Over here ..."

Alyssa—a sophisticated woman with sleek, straight Pantene black hair, warm olive skin tone, wearing very high heels and a form-fitted suit—strolled toward us at a leisurely, not-in-a-rush pace.

She dropped to the seat next to me and extended her hand. "Alyssa, as you know already. And you are Charlotte, also known as Charlie. You're an implant from Wisconsin. Your mother just got married, and you are living in the elite town of Inverness with your new family. You have an evil stepsister, who in all aspects of the term is evil, and a doting stepfather, who is perfect. The end."

I blinked up at her. *Is this woman psychic?*

Alyssa laughed. It was one of those worldly laughs that sounded perfected and practiced in front of the mirror. "Casey told me all about you. As you can tell, she can't shut up."

Casey slapped Alyssa's side. "You're so rude. I can shut up, and I can keep a secret very well, especially if the secret means life or death."

I hadn't even realized I'd talked about my family life to Casey. She did check on me the whole morning, and I did let little snippets of my life slip through. I hadn't known my little snippets equaled my entire life story.

I took my sandwich out of my paper bag. "Since you know so much about me, why don't you tell me about yourself, Alyssa?"

"Alyssa Brighton. Born and raised here in Illinois and currently working as CPA and head accountant for this company. Went to Columbia Business School. Graduated summa cum laude. Father is a successful lawyer with his own firm here, and my mother is the head of a nonprofit organization for blind children. I'm the youngest of four children. The only girl. You can imagine my pain." She unpacked her own lunch from a square Louis Vuitton lunchbox. Even her lunch containers looked expensive.

"No offense, Alyssa. What the hell are you doing at this factory?"

She should be working at some high-powered accounting firm.

I unwrapped my plain ham and cheese sandwich from the Saran Wrap. I'd made it myself this morning. It seemed a little grade school—compared to Alyssa's steak, potatoes, and carrots and Casey's fancy salad with radishes and almonds and kale—but this was me, and I loved my ham and cheese sandwiches.

"Honestly, I needed to get away from my parents and my overprotective brothers. I couldn't exactly sow my oats with the secret service of brothers following me everywhere I went. Plus, I swore I would never work for corporate. I like this company much better. A family-owned business is where I need to be." She squirted some sanitizer on her hands before unwrapping her silverware from plastic wrap.

Casey smiled big, her eyes squinting to the point where I couldn't see her pupils. "She doesn't need the money." Her voice was whisper-soft, so only I could hear. "She works here because she loves it, and she hates rich people."

Well, I guessed there were some people who worked because they actually loved their job and didn't give two craps about a paycheck. Unfortunately, I was not one of those people.

"Nothing is a secret with Casey." She stuck the fork in her cut-up steak. "I don't hate rich people. I hate corporate America."

As I sat there, taking everything in, I realized they were

opposites in every term of existence, but it was as if they'd known each other for years.

"How do you guys know each other?" I said, mid-chew.

"We room together," Casey squealed.

I almost choked on my sandwich. I coughed and then grabbed for my water, taking a long gulp down. Room together? Being as they seemed to be on opposite spectrums of the universe with their personalities and what they wore, I couldn't exactly see them as rooming together. Nor could I see them as actually eating lunch together, but yet here we were, three mismatched peas in a pod.

"We do," Alyssa said without emotion.

I didn't know if she regretted her current living situation or just didn't care. Looking at the diamond infinity ring on her right hand, I doubted she needed a roommate to make ends meet.

"I know what you're thinking." Alyssa waved a hand in the air. "But it's hard not to love her. Overbearing and nonstop chatting are a little bit annoying at times, but she makes it up in her caring and cleaning ways." Alyssa's voice was smooth, like one of those older movie stars who spoke with an air of authority, which made you believe that everything she said was true and there was no room to question her.

Casey pushed her shoulders to her ears, grabbed Alyssa's hands, and shook them within hers. "I love you, BFF. I wish you'd wear that necklace I gave you."

"Don't make me take my words back." She nodded toward Casey's unfinished salad. "Eat."

I found out that Alyssa and Casey lived in Presidential Towers, a high-rise in the West Loop of Chicago.

Alyssa was the head of the accounting department. She managed five people and was damn proud of doing it.

When our lunch was finished and we were about to say our good-byes, Casey took out this little contraption from her lunchbox. "I hope you don't mind. I have to test my blood sugar."

Immediately, I stood and took two healthy steps back. "I do." Sweat beaded across my forehead and on the back of my neck. "Um ... um ... you can't do that here." I placed both palms against my chest and closed my eyes, tightly feeling the ground sway beneath my feet. "You know what? I'm going to go." I about-faced, my eyes still closed.

"Honey ..." Alyssa gripped my shoulder. Her voice was meant to soothe me, but it did the opposite to my raging, beating heart. "You look a little green. Maybe you should sit down. Casey, baby, put that away, please."

I gripped Alyssa's forearm, and she led me back to the table, where I sat down.

"It's put away," Casey said.

Slowly, I opened my eyes, my breathing and pulse still ragged.

Casey placed one soft hand on top of mine on the table. "You have an aversion to needles or something like that? Because I get it. My roommate was like that. And my mother, she can't be around when I have to check my blood sugar. When I was younger, my father did it—"

"Casey ..." Alyssa's stern voice stopped the chatty box from chattering.

I dropped my head in my hands and rubbed at the temples. After a beat, I found my voice again. Taking a deep breath and slowly letting it out, I said, "I have an aversion to needles—to blood mostly. Any blood. Even if it's a paper cut, I faint at the sight." I inhaled deeply and exhaled slowly, practicing my calming techniques.

Alyssa patted my back. "Well, it's really good we know

that now. I wouldn't want you to inadvertently faint or something like that, especially not on your first day of the job."

It took a few seconds to get my bearings and for my breathing to even out.

Casey smiled. "Are you okay? Do you need some water?"

Alyssa had ahold of one of my hands, and Casey had ahold of the other.

I shook my head. "I'm fine."

And for a tiny bit, the first time since I'd moved into this new town, as these two new girls held my hands, I knew that everything was gonna be okay. At least here, at work, it would be.

"You know what is better than water?"

I peered up at Alyssa.

"Alcohol." She smiled. "Happy hour tonight, and we're not taking no for an answer."

CONNOR

It was funny how time went by so quickly when you were on a deadline.

I breathed through my next few seconds, peering at the sea of little people walking to their destinations below me. At this height, looking down, it seemed like I was on top of the world, but looks could be deceiving.

I'd been racking my brain on new concepts for the rebranding initiatives, working through lunch at my desk, trying to think of new ideas I could have my marketing team work on, but other than what Charlie had said this morning, my mind was coming up blank.

Maybe I could outsource, hire another marketing firm.

But the reputational risk was too huge. It couldn't get out that Colby's was struggling.

Leaning closer, I rested my head against the floor-to-ceiling window. *It didn't matter, right?*

I never considered this my company. It was my parents' company, not mine.

If I'd had it my way, I'd rather they have worked at regular jobs, be home at regular hours, and then they would have had more time for us.

I don't care about this company.

I don't care.

But the more I said it, the more I knew it wasn't true. Then, all of it—all those long hours, all my bitterness to my family, their time away from me and Kyle while we were growing up—would have been in vain.

This company needed to thrive. More than the livelihood of my family depended on it. Other families depended on it.

The door opened behind me, and Kyle strolled in. I almost groaned out loud.

"You're still here?" I deadpanned. "You need a job."

He plopped down on the seat in front of me. "I have a job. I sell socks."

Socks. A socks company that was failing. My parents had given him enough money to start his own online company. After graduating with a business management degree, he'd decided that he wanted nothing to do with Colby's and he wanted to start something of his own.

From a young age, my brother had gotten everything he wanted. That was how I saw it anyway.

By the time he had been born, money had been less tight, and business had been booming.

Although my parents had never been around for me,

they had been more present for him. Still busy but at least there. You'd think I'd hold a grudge against him, but I loved the bastard.

"You need to look for more retail stores to sell your socks."

He needed to branch out from just his website. He needed business to drive traffic to his website, but I'd already told him this multiple times.

"Yeah ..." He kicked up his feet and placed them on my desk, his ankles crossed. "I'm going to a sock convention."

I shot him a look. One day, he'd grow up. Something or someone would knock him on his ass, and he'd get his shit together.

"Hey, is Claire out there?"

Claire was my temporary secretary.

"I didn't see her."

She was most likely hanging out with Nana, eating cookies in some corner.

"I need her to set up another meeting with the marketing team. They need a reset." I couldn't outsource, so my marketing team needed to step up and revise their vision for Colby's until we were on the right path.

"Call Nana. She's probably with Claire."

I laughed because I had thought the exact same thing, them being around the same age. There were people who loved this company so much that they would work here till their dying breath—and that wasn't an exaggeration.

"I've got to get back to work." I turned back to my computer, ready to fire it up. "Did you need something? And your feet, off my desk."

He sat straighter in his seat. "Yeah, Casey, Alyssa, and that new girl are going to happy hour later. I'm heading to O'Malley's after work. Want to join me?"

I perked up. "Charlie's going?"

Kyle's smile widened. "So, the new girl's name is Charlie?"

"Yeah. Why?"

He pushed out of the chair and stood, smirking. "I'll see you at O'Malley's."

I stared blankly at the screen. "I didn't say I was going."

"You didn't have to. I know you are. It is written all over your face."

My eyes met his as he walked to the door.

"Charlie, huh?"

I shook my head. "Shut up."

"See you at five thirty."

And the door shut behind him.

Desperation settled deep in my gut. I didn't have time to mess around.

Maybe I didn't need to meet with the marketing team just yet. Maybe I just needed to pick Charlie's brain on what she'd said earlier to get a better direction on where we should be going.

"Charlie, Charlie, Charlie, I think I need to buy you a drink tonight."

CHAPTER 4

CHARLIE

O'MALLEY'S WAS a small bar in the South Loop of Chicago. TVs surrounded the main area, and circular leather seats outlined the bar in the center of the room. Autographed pictures of sports stars I didn't know hung on the walls. Except for Michael Jordan. I knew that much.

"And here, darlings, are your Miller Lites, as requested." Alyssa settled by Casey in a booth, handing her a drink and sliding my bottle across the table.

"To new and ever-lasting friendships. Cheers!" Casey lifted her bottle to mine and then clinked her bottle against Alyssa's wineglass.

O'Malley's wasn't a wine place, but she'd insisted that it was. Business professionals were dressed in work attire but with undid ties, suit jackets placed on the back of their chairs, indicating that this was an after-work bar. And after work meant hard liquor or at least a cold bottle of beer.

Their conversation continued about the company, and I simply listened.

"All I know is that if we do not think of something soon, layoffs are going to be made because the profit margins are thinning." Alyssa placed her wineglass to her lips, and a line creased in between her eyebrows.

My stomach sank at the news that Colby's was struggling. "I had no idea. Why are they still hiring then?" I asked.

"You're the only person they've hired on in months. They were in desperate need of a computer technician in Chicago since Bert, our former tech, retired." Alyssa tipped back her glass, almost draining all of her wine.

"I just don't get it." Casey ruffled her silky brown hair and rubbed at her temple. "Are people all of a sudden not buying candy? How does that even make sense? Seriously, who doesn't love chocolate or candy? It's a staple food, like mac and cheese. But better because you have to have a piece of chocolate after every meal." Her mousy voice was animated and echoed through the room.

Alyssa pursed her lips, leaning toward her in their seat. "Quiet down, Casey. If everyone knew about this dilemma, there would be an uproar because thousands will be losing their jobs if the company goes belly up." She straightened and placed the wineglass at the center of the table, her fingers sliding up and down the slim, thin neck.

"Plus, I hear that they are working on some new products and an improved look, and it's gonna be great," Casey said, pride heavy in her tone, sitting taller.

"Yeah, I'd work on the overall look first. The fact is, the branding is outdated. The packaging is something out of the '80s, which I get. It should be out of the '80s because Thomas Colby started the company in the '80s." I reached into my purse, plucked out the black leather-bound notebook that my father had given me, and placed it on the table.

I remembered the day he'd brought it home, wrapped in thin silver gift-wrapping paper. It was an actual sketchbook —not the normal lined paper from school, but my first actual sketchbook.

My father had been the first to point out that I had an innate talent to draw. Not only did I love to draw, but I was also good at it.

During the last days when he had been sick, I remembered him looking up at me from the hospital bed and simply saying, "Draw me something, Charlie." It was like him saying, *Sing me something.*

I pushed the memories back to where no one could touch them, where they couldn't hurt me, where I didn't have to think about them anymore.

My hand did what I always knew how to do—sketched. "This is what I'm talking about, guys. It's all about the packaging, the feeling, the look." I lightly tapped the pen against my chin, thinking.

"Maybe it's the color. This brown is outdated. We need something neutral that would appeal to the older generations but also kids." I sketched a rectangular box and then did little strokes inside of the box. "Let's think of the name of an imaginary candy bar that we own." I twisted the pen within my fingertips. "It can be ... Chewy Caramel, and then in tiny lettering, we could have the signature Colby name."

I drew horizontal lines inside of the box, my mind twisting with new ideas. "I think their Crunch Bar is the most popular ..." I sketched little bite marks on the inside of the rectangle. "Funch," I said without a second thought. "A fun approach to crunch. It could also mean, family with crunch." I lifted my head and shrugged. "It's a Funch bar."

I placed the name on our imaginary chocolate.

Alyssa turned my sketchbook around, toward them, and shrugged. "That would work. That would actually work. You can always say, *I'm gonna Funch you in the face with this Funch bar.*"

Her statement caused Casey to laugh.

"What do we have here?" Casey flipped to the next page of my sketchbook, to a picture of the beach and some seagulls.

The beach was one of my favorite places to go. It reminded me of my youth, of family times. When I had been younger, during the weekends, we'd have a picnic in the sand and build sand castles.

I stared at the sketch for a long while, nostalgia hitting me directly in the chest.

"You, Charlie, have talent. Shit ..." Casey flipped through each and every page, breaking me from my thoughts, and confidence filled my shoulders, forcing me to straighten. "I didn't know you were an artist."

I threw my beer back and smiled, my gaze dipping down to the table. "Thanks."

There was nothing like getting validation through compliments about your craft, nothing like it on earth.

"Chin up. Take it like a woman. Say thanks and acknowledge that you're good at what you do." That was what my father always told me because I had a hard time with taking compliments.

"Let me see what you have there." Alyssa pulled the sketchpad away from Casey, and both of them leaned over my drawings, flipping through the pages—the abstract figures, one of a billboard I'd passed on the train, the Chicago skyline. The one they were currently gawking at was a naked figure ... a male naked figure ... a very attractive male naked figure.

"I think I will have to take up drawing really soon." Alyssa's sultry voice was tinged with amusement. She grabbed the base of the wineglass and took another sip. She smiled, assessing me. "You're definitely in the wrong profession." Her tone was matter-of-fact, as though she were saying the sky was blue and the grass was green or that this beer was wonderful.

I wished she could speak to my mother, who thought art was just a hobby and that my drawings were simply there to entertain myself.

I could hear her words loudly in my ears. *"Pretty paintings are not gonna make you money, honey."*

I'd show her that Daddy was right. That I had a gift that needed to be shared with the world. That I could unveil my paintings and drawings, and people would actually buy them. I would definitely show her that other people enjoyed my creations. Sometimes, I believed that this exhibit I had planned was for her more than me.

I shook my head, not wanting to think of it that way. I wanted to showcase my talent. I was just sad that my father wouldn't be here to see what I'd done.

Casey's eyebrows furrowed. "Why are you a computer tech?" She stared at me as though I'd committed a crime.

I wanted to tell her I didn't know. I wanted to tell her that, if anything, I hated my job, fixing computers. But I couldn't. Not when my mother had paid my college debt and worked two jobs to do it. Not when my mother had told me computer science or engineering was the best thing I could do for my future. That, with those career paths, I'd never be without a job because someone would always want to hire me.

When I didn't answer, Alyssa answered for me, "We all eventually end up where we are supposed to be without thinking about it. Do you think I dreamed of being a CPA at a candy manufacturer when I was younger? How about you, Casey? You work for quality and assurance because you love candy and you like to watch your employees eat it and taste it and stuff their faces with it, right?" She tilted her head and looked at her. Really looked at her.

Casey lifted her chin with pride. "Because I love this company. I believe in this company. And I wanted to do what my dad did, and I'd like to think I'm a good manager."

"Well, well, well, what do we have here?" A guy with an arm tattoo and hazel eyes rested his elbows on our table, his beer in his hand.

Right behind him, strolling in, looking too handsome to stare at, was Connor.

"Hey, Pigtails," Tattoo Guy said.

Casey scoffed and reeled back. She threw him, I swore to goodness, the dirtiest look that I'd ever seen her throw at anyone. *Holy crap, one person who Casey didn't like.*

"Get away from me, Loser." Her words burned like acid, but the guy didn't flinch. "Anyway, who invited you here?"

Alyssa raised her hand. "Sorry." But she didn't sound sorry.

"I'm Kyle." He extended his hand toward me in greeting.

"Charlie," I said, introducing myself.

"Oh, I know." He sported an all-knowing smirk, which had all of me curious.

I took his hand and gave it a little shake. Connor

remained silent behind him. But his eyes were burning a hole on the side of my face, just simply watching me.

"Do you work for the company?" I asked.

"Nope. I'm just this jerk's brother." He tipped his chin toward Connor. "And I'm Casey's special friend."

Casey pinched his shoulder, and he yelped, rubbing at it.

"Hey!"

"Shut up." Casey motioned between Connor and me. "And you have already met Connor."

I waved at him from my seat.

Kyle tapped Casey's shoulder with his pointer finger, purposely being annoying. "Scoot over, Pigtails. I want to sit down."

"The hell you are," Casey screeched. "Sit over there." She pointed to the other end of the room. "There's no room here."

"But I want to sit by you, cutie." He lowered his tone to an overly flirty voice, and Casey's scowl deepened.

Alyssa and I shared an amused glance.

Alyssa moved over and forced Casey to move closer to her. "Kyle, sit down. Casey, you behave."

I was by myself in the seat, and there was only one place where Connor could sit. But he stood there, watching me, like a statue, utterly still.

"Connor?" Alyssa lifted an eyebrow and motioned to the empty space beside me. "Sit down. You're making all of us nervous here."

I scooted over, and Connor slipped in right beside me. He was like a heater. His closeness radiated warmth, and the warmth spread all through my body. I couldn't look at him, so I sipped my bottle. I stared at my chipped nail polish. I stared at the lines on the table. I stared at everything, except for him.

They talked about work and about Helen—a coworker of ours I hadn't met yet—and all I could do was sit there and listen and notice every single quality in Connor. The way he laughed in a deep baritone, that oh-so masculine intonation of his voice, the beer that he was drinking, the way his fingers tapped on the table. His woodsy scent of either his aftershave or his shower gel was so enticing that it had me leaning over, wanting to sniff him.

And all of a sudden, I turned mute, too shy to speak, too shy to do anything other than steal glances his way.

I was acutely aware of his thigh brushing next to mine, and I could not breathe. And it felt like the bar had turned into a sauna. I pulled all my hair to the side, trying to give my neck some air to cool down.

The only thing that broke me from my thoughts was him reaching for my sketchbook.

"Did you draw this?" His voice was full of wonder but then also full of shock.

I placed my hand on top of the sketchbook, as if to block him from seeing anything further.

Before I could even say a word, Casey piped up for me, "Yes, she drew it. We were imagining our very own Colby's candy bar. Charlie is multitalented. Not only is she Superwoman, who can fix computers, but she is also a talented artist." She embarrassed me further and flipped to the next page. "There's more here. Charlie, show them your drawings."

My ears turned unbelievably hot—super hot, as though someone were lighting a torch against my lobes.

"It's nothing. It's nothing really. Just a hobby." As soon as the words left my mouth, acid burned the back of my throat. Because wasn't that what my mother always said—that it was just a hobby? I hated that word—*hobby*. As though I didn't have passion for it, as though I did it just to pass time, as though it didn't burn inside of me and I didn't have this need to wake up and draw every day to express my artistic ability. As though everyone could do what I could do. "It's just something I do in my spare time."

"You have talent. Accept it." Alyssa tipped back her wineglass and lightly slapped the table with one palm. "Don't be shy. You have to show your abilities off, not dim them."

I didn't fight it any further because she was right. I needed to own it, so I lifted my fingers from the pages.

Immediately, Connor reached for my sketchpad. He opened it and flipped through the pages, slowly taking in each individual sketch of art.

He didn't say a word. Not a single word. And his silence was deafening.

I watched his reaction. The widening of his eyes, the way his mouth slipped ajar, the way his finger ran down the paper in appreciation.

Kyle pointed at me. "Charlie, what the hell are you doing, fixing computers?"

The whole table laughed—well, everyone, except for Connor, who just simply stared at the sketches.

"That's exactly what we were trying to tell her," Casey said.

Kyle bumped his shoulder against Casey and then smiled. A dimple popped on one of his cheeks. "See, Pigtails, I told you. We don't disagree about everything."

She scowled and lifted her nose, bumping her shoulder against his. "Just stop talking."

"Why does he call you Pigtails?" I asked.

"We went to grade school together ... well, high school too. She wore the same pigtails to school every day."

Ah, now, I got it. The way he teased her reminded me of little boys teasing girls because they had a crush on them.

"Shut up." Casey pushed at his shoulder, but he didn't budge. "Get out of my booth!"

I'd have to ask Alyssa about this later. Casey seemed to be the type that was slow to anger, and he wasn't even doing anything annoying other than just being there.

"You've got pure talent, Charlie. Absolute pure talent." Connor's words were soft, but they seared through me. There was no humor in his tone or his features.

He'd said it just like my dad had said it years ago. Dad would repeat it over and over and over again.

"Charlie, there are few people who can do what you can do. Not everyone can sing. They can be trained to sing, but some are born with a voice to sing. God gave you this gift. You were born to share your art with the world."

"Thanks." I took a sip of my beer, letting the cold liquid cool the warmth inside of me.

I averted my gaze because looking at the beauty of this man made my body heat tick up in temperature.

"I don't know about you guys, but I'm hungry." Kyle raised a hand, waving over a waitress, and ordered a bunch of appetizers for the table.

"You didn't even ask what we wanted to order," Casey snapped, her voice harsh.

She was like Jekyll and Hyde in one person, and the flip of her switch was this Kyle guy.

"I ordered you chicken strips without the breading. I thought you'd like that."

"Who eats chicken strips without the breading?" She

leaned into him, eyebrows scrunched, her lips pursed, and an absolute scowl taking over her features.

"Well, you know, with your condition and all, you should monitor your carbs."

It was like watching an old married couple on TV argue. It was quite comical. I bit my tongue to prevent laughter from seeping through my lips.

"I have diabetes, and it is controlled. I eat normal food, you know."

"Chicken is normal food."

Alyssa leaned over, so she could look at them both. "Do I really need to sit in between you guys? Can you behave for the next few hours?"

"Can't you see it's him?" She poked her finger into Kyle's shoulder, and he jumped.

"You're hurting my feelings, Casey." And when she went in to poke him again, Kyle grabbed her hand and intertwined their fingers. "Seriously, I'm just looking out for you."

She shoved at his shoulder and pushed him so hard that he slipped out of the booth. "Get out. I'm playing pool while we wait for food. I can't sit here by you because you are so annoying."

Instead of getting back into the seat, he followed her to the pool tables. "I challenge you to a match. If I win, you eat my chicken with no breading, and if you win, I won't say a single word throughout dinner."

"You not talking? Impossible." Her smile turned glorious. "Fine, I might be little, but I can play pool."

"I can't miss this." Alyssa slid out of the booth and headed to the pool table at the far end of the bar.

And then there were two.

"Are they always like that?" I gripped my bottle a little

tighter, focusing on my friends on the opposite side of the room. Having Connor this close to me made my pulse tick up in tempo and the inside of my palms sweat.

When I lifted my head, Connor was staring directly at me, and I immediately slid my stare back to the trio at the pool table.

"Yeah. Casey, Kyle, and I grew up together. They are more like siblings who don't get along. I think Kyle gets a kick out of annoying her. At one point, it was his hobby of sorts."

"That's pretty cute." When my eyes flittered back to his, I noticed his business-casual blue button-down, opposite to what I had seen him wearing this morning. "So, where's the candy-cane uniform?"

"It's at the dry cleaners."

That smile. It was actor beautiful, and curiosity ate at my insides.

"Mmhmm, sure." I waved a hand in the air. "If you aren't the spokesperson for Colby's, what department do you work for?"

His eyes widened right before he said, "I'm in charge of the marketing team." He coughed, and the coughs kept coming until he took a sip of his beer, most likely to take care of the tickle in the back of his throat.

Marketing? I wouldn't have pegged him for working in marketing. Maybe research and development.

"That's pretty impressive. Sometimes, I wish I had taken that route instead of the path I took."

If I'd majored in marketing, I could have been unleashing my creativity somehow, using the skills I loved to use on a daily basis.

He leaned into me, his face so close to mine that my breath caught. "Charlie, the girls are right. You're definitely in the wrong field." His stare was all-consuming and heated everywhere he took me in. "You're talented, Charlie."

I couldn't help but smile because of the way he'd said it. He barely knew me, yet there was so much power behind his words.

"I can guarantee you that my marketing team would not have thought of this." He plucked the sketchbook, opening the page to the Funch candy bar. "How did you come up with this?"

I laughed. "We were just messing around. I mean, if you look at the current branding, it's outdated, and it kinda sucks, doesn't it? Be honest."

After a beat, he spoke, "You're right." His eyebrows pulled together, his gaze so intent on mine. "But where did you come up with the idea?"

I shrugged. "It just came to me." Having a highly creative mind, even as a kid, an endless amount of ideas filtered through my head. "The girls were talking about the company coming up with new products in the following year and a new look, so ..." My ears felt impossibly hot at his stare, and when he inched closer, I moved further against the wall, giving myself some room to breathe.

His finger jabbed at my sketch. "This would have taken my marketing team weeks to come up with, just this simple concept, yet you came up with it in a few minutes."

"Thanks." My voice was shaky, soft, even to my own ears.

"Now, tell me"—he angled even closer—"this morning, when we were by the candy wall and you said we should brand toward the essence of family, can you expand on that further?"

I pulled at the collar of my shirt, feeling my body temperature heighten.

"I'd love to hear your thoughts. I can take them back to my marketing team and implement them."

His eyes burned with this fevered passion that made me shift in my seat. Good God, was this man serious about his job.

"Um ..." I blew out a breath and reached for my beer to take a sip, but the bottle tipped over. "Shit!" I jumped, the bottle rolling off the table and dropping to the floor but not before the liquid spilled everywhere—on the table, on Connor's shirt, and on his pants.

"I'm so sorry." I grabbed the napkins from the table, wiping up his shirt and the liquid at his waist.

"I'm fine."

Fine? That was an understatement. He was the finest man I'd ever laid my eyes on.

I swallowed, noting the way his blue button-down firmly hugged his arms, as though his muscles were cold.

"I'm such a klutz. Seriously, I'm so sorry."

When I grabbed more napkins, he reached for my hand, stilling me in my spot. I could feel the sexual magnetism that made him so self-confident.

"I'm fine. Really."

Our eyes locked again, for what seemed like forever.

One ... two ... three seconds passed by until he let out one heavy breath.

"Hey, guys."

Our faces flipped to Kyle's.

"You guys wanna join us? Alyssa doesn't want to play."

I swallowed hard, already scooting out of the booth, giving Connor a playful shove. "Yeah. Let's play." I needed out of this booth before I passed out from heat exhaustion.

"Connor, let the girl out."

Connor threw his brother a look, clenching his jaw, and then he slowly moved out of the booth.

"Who wants to make a little wager?" Kyle's smile widened.

"No. I'm done making bets with you," Connor snapped.

Kyle threw an arm over my shoulders, wiggling his eyebrows. "He's a sore loser. But heads-up, don't make a bet against me. I always win."

"Let go of my friend, you womanizer!" Casey yelled, walking toward us. "Charlie, stay away. You'll catch his STD, just standing by him."

Kyle held both of his palms up, almost running toward her. "Don't worry, Pigtails. I only have eyes for you."

Her scowl was comical, and I stifled a laugh in my throat.

Connor bumped his shoulder against mine. "You know how to play?"

I nodded. "Yeah."

"You're on my team." The way he said it brooked no argument.

"Okay."

His eyes appraised me, and he was doing that little intense-gaze thing that made my cheeks flame.

"Is there anything you can't do, Miss Charlie?"

Yep. I can't stop staring at you.

That little tidbit I kept to myself.

CHAPTER 5

CONNOR

THE MARKETING PLANS were lying in front of me, scattered on my desk.

A few nights ago, I hadn't exactly lied to Charlie. I was indeed the head of marketing while I was working at Colby's on a temporary basis. But I didn't include the fact that I was the head of all the other departments as well. My words had flown out as though I'd been born a natural liar.

But I knew why I'd lied. I'd lied because the attractive, talented woman didn't have preconceived notions about me, being the son of the CEO. There was a natural ease between us that I knew wouldn't be there if she found out. Though I didn't want to admit it, I'd also lied because of selfish reasons. I'd wanted to pick her brain, get more ideas on where to take this new look for Colby's rebranding initiatives.

I'd already met with the marketing team, laid out my plans for the rebranding, and they'd come up with a few specs this morning.

Charlie's original idea was spot-on. I wanted something clean and that spoke to families and children and future generations.

Our brand could be our family, given that we were a family business. Even if we weren't on the best of terms, the rest of the world didn't need to know that.

I wanted a modern, good brand, which meant new packaging and a new logo. We needed a new brand that people could relate to, a feeling related to Colby Chocolates.

If we were going to spend money on marketing, we needed a good slogan, a good logo.

The meeting that I'd had with the marketing team ended well, and I thought I'd conveyed what I wanted to do with the rebranding initiatives of Colby, but when I'd received the new potential marketing materials ... they were okay at best.

Maybe it was because they were all about to retire and were not with the new trends.

Most of our employees had started with Colby's years ago. There was very little turnover because my parents treated their employees well, even better than their own family members.

I rustled through the papers one more time.

"No." Flipped paper. "No." Flipped another piece of paper. "No!"

I slammed a palm against the desk and ran the same hand through my hair. I needed this right. Time was running out. I needed to solidify the changes to the brand, sell the changes to my father, and then put the changes into motion. I couldn't possibly extend my leave of absence at Financial State any further. My current employer would let me go; I knew that much.

"I feel like it should be branded to the essence of family, but you can do it without using the family name in big, fat letters."

Charlie had been exactly right. But even with giving her original bar sketch to my marketing team as inspiration, they had gotten the concept all wrong.

I hated that our conversation at the bar had been cut short by a game of pool.

After leaving the bar, I'd realized one thing: I needed her on the team, needed her to work on these rebranding initiatives. I wouldn't take her from her regular job, but I could get her overtime approved for helping me. Problem was, would she even agree to that?

I'd have to talk to her today to try to convince her.

The buzzing on my phone broke me from my thoughts.

I pressed the button on the intercom.

"Mr. Colby, your father is on line one." It was my secretary.

"Thanks, Claire."

We were all Mr. Colby—my father, me, and Kyle. It would get confusing at the company if I worked here permanently. I ticked off another reason I needed out sooner than later.

"Dad."

"Hey, I'm scheduling an impromptu meeting in the boardroom at one. Please make yourself available."

Great. Has this man ever heard of a schedule? No one appreciated impromptu meetings, especially when their schedules had been planned out for the day.

"I'll be available."

There was a long pause before he spoke. "Are you coming home tonight or at least stopping by for dinner?"

I'd been renting an apartment within walking distance

to work. Tension between my parents and me was at an all-time high, and I didn't want to say something in the heat of an argument. Keeping things strictly professional was the best way to deal with them right now. It'd been that way ever since I left for college.

"Not tonight." *Or any other night for that matter.*

"Nana requested you for dinner."

I huffed audibly loud. "I'll talk to Nana."

When they used the word *Nana*, it was as though I couldn't say no. Maybe she'd settle for alone time—with just us going out to dinner.

"Okay, son. I'll see you in a little bit."

Son. I rolled the word in my mind. If only they had raised me and treated me like their son.

———

My father paced the front of the room, near the whiteboard, as everyone in the office filed into the boardroom. My mother sat at the head of the table. Her short hair was pulled back in a sleek brown ponytail. She had aged well and looked half my father's age with his pepper-gray hair.

I watched the interaction of the employees greeting my father as they walked in. Almost as pals, more than coworkers or acquaintances for sure. Some of these people had been here since before I was born. I stood, flushed against the back wall with a few other employees, trying to blend in. No matter what others thought or said, that was what I was. I'd act like an employee, here on a temporary assignment.

"Connor." Elise from accounting pinched my cheek. "Glad to see you're back."

She'd known me since I was a little boy, eating the candy directly from the conveyer belts.

"Hey, you." Logan from quality and assurance patted my shoulder. "You're back."

"Just temporarily."

"I hope not," Jenny from production said. "We miss you at the company. We really want you back."

I smiled down at the woman who used to set up a scavenger hunt around the office for my brother and me when we were younger.

"They need me back at Financial State Bank pretty soon." My voice was polite, respectful.

In a way, these people who had worked for this company for so long were the ones who had raised me.

A long mahogany table sliced the boardroom horizontally, and chairs surrounded all sides. But as people filed in, they occupied the chairs backed up against the wall. Some people preferred to stand while other people preferred to sit, and most of the people seated at the center table were VP level or above.

As more and more workers filed in, thoughts raced in my head. I'd been here before but in front of a different company, not in front of my family's company. As sales decreased and expenses stay the same, soon, profit margins would dwindle down to where layoffs were needed. A sinking feeling hit the pit of my stomach, and I thought of Elise, Logan, Jenny, and many others I knew closely at Colby's. I didn't want to do that. Lay people off, people I knew, people who had watched me grow up. My father didn't want to do that. He'd raised this company from the ground up, working nonstop, my mother right alongside him. If anything, these people had seen my father more than Kyle and I had.

There were multigenerational employees, such as Casey, where her father had been the head of quality and assurance before her. My father might not have known all of the factory workers, but here, at corporate, he knew them all by name.

Even though I didn't want this to be personal, it was. Those companies that I tore apart for Financial State were nameless faces, but everyone in this room knew me by my first name and vice versa.

It'd kill him to fire any of them, and my stomach churned at the thought of if we'd have to come to that.

Alyssa and Casey were the last to enter the room, Casey laughing, as always. They staggered in, and beside them, Charlie strolled in, smiling. Her dimples were set deep in her cheeks, her most endearing quality. It was almost child-like, but when you took her all in, you knew she was no child. She was all woman with her slim waist and the nice curvature of her ass.

I cleared my throat and swallowed. *Yeah, can't go there.*

Casey and Alyssa made their way to their regular spots at the table, but Charlie backed up against the wall.

Casey swept her hands over to the seat next to her, but Charlie adamantly shook her head and inched further away, almost at the corner, as though she didn't want to be seen.

"Charlie, get over here," Casey hissed.

My father peered up at Charlie as the room quieted to a hush. With one look, she meandered to the seat.

And then my father started his spiel. "As we close out this quarter, I want to personally thank each and every one of you for all you do. For all your hard work, day in and day out. I'm so very proud of this team and where you've taken Colby's."

I stood, stone-faced, thinking of when I had been

younger and how many times I'd wished he'd said he was proud of me, proud of what I'd done in school or how I'd made it to varsity football when I was only a sophomore. I'd never once heard that from my parents' mouths. I'd been a good kid—gotten good grades, excelled in sports—but just once, I'd wished I had been acknowledged for my hard work.

My father knocked on the table twice. "And despite the talks about canceling the company party this year, it will still be on."

All of the muscles in my back tightened. We'd discussed this. We couldn't afford a big holiday party at the Ritz again. *Didn't he understand that this company was not doing well? That every single dollar counted?*

"But Grace and I will host it at our home this year."

When his eyes made it my way, I relaxed, just a tad.

"It won't be a grand event, as it has been in the past, but we'll be all together to celebrate our accomplishments. Since it will be at our house, you can bring your families."

He motioned to me at the far end of the room, beckoning me forward, and I pushed myself off the wall. Automatically, my eyes met Charlie's, and I swallowed. Her face lost its color, and she openly gaped.

Great. Just great.

My mother pointed at me. "Connor, why don't you tell them about the things coming down the pipeline?"

I inhaled deeply and smiled. "Well, I wasn't exactly prepared to talk about our pipeline, but since you put me on the spot ..."

The crowd laughed, and my eyes made it back Charlie's way. She averted her gaze and dropped her stare to her hands in her lap.

Come on, green emeralds. Look up.

"In regard to the new products that we plan to launch, we're in the early stages, but in addition, we'll be focusing on branding this year and introducing a new and improved logo along with a new slogan and feel for Colby Chocolates and Candies."

My eyes flickered toward her, but she was notably focusing on her fingers. Maybe even picking at her nails.

"I've been diligently working with our marketing group to come up with this. We'll have to finalize plans within the next month to get things printed and advertising set." For the life of me, I wanted to meet her eyes, see the speckle of deep green in them, green as a newly manicured lawn. "We're going to start off by rebranding our infamous Colby's Chocolate Bar. Start off with the packaging and then advertising, eventually rolling it out across all the other lines, across the whole company."

Still, no reaction from Charlie.

But my father spoke up, "What's wrong with Colby's current packaging?"

I hadn't informed him yet of my plans. I'd only told him that there were new products in the pipeline, not a brand-new rehaul of everything.

"It's outdated. The packaging specifically. One might think that it's a little conceited to brand our name on the chocolate bar rather than the name of the actual product."

The room laughed again, but my father was not at all amused.

"That's how it has been branded since the inception of this company," he said.

"I feel like it should be branded to the essence of family, but you can do it without using the family name in big, fat letters," I repeated Charlie's words from the first time we'd met. "Brand to connect with future generations."

Now, her gaze lifted from the hands on her lap to the table, as though something interesting were written on the mahogany.

Frustration hit me in the gut, not being able to see her eyes, read her reaction.

"Charlie." I cleared my throat, realizing I'd called her name out loud. "Charlotte is a new employee at Colby's. She works as a computer tech at corporate." I smiled and motioned for her to stand.

Her face was beet red, so red that it seemed as though her cheeks would explode. She sucked in her bottom lip, and for a moment, I was mesmerized at her bottom lip being fuller than the top.

I swallowed. Hard. "Tell me what you think about our current branding."

I had no idea why I had called her out. That was reckless of me really. But I wanted her to voice her honesty, and more than that, I wanted to see her face.

"I-I think ... I mean ... there's always room for improvement in everything, right?" She smiled, all teeth, and wrung her fingers in front of her, her face turning all shades of red, her eyes teetering between me and my father's.

"I totally agree."

When I crossed my arms over my chest, her jaw clenched, and a tiny bit of me felt a little guilty for putting her on the spot.

"So, if you were leading this relaunch, what would some of your suggestions be?"

The smile slipped from her face, and if looks could kill, I'd be dead on the ground.

"I don't have expertise in that area."

"But you know what you like, and above all, you are a consumer, so let's just entertain this idea, shall we?"

I was pushing this way too far. At this point, Alyssa and Casey were shooting daggers my way.

When Charlie sat silent, I prompted her to continue, "We'll start by what you like about the current packaging and what you think needs improvement."

"It reminds me of my childhood."

"That's the thing though, how old are you? Twenty-one, twenty-two?"

"Twenty-five."

Hmm. Interesting. She looked younger. I would have never pegged her being only four years younger than me.

Judging by the look on her face, I couldn't push her further. I'd ask her to join in this rebranding initiatives at a later time, when we were alone, but not now.

I walked the room, making it around the table, speaking to the employees, "This type of branding will only appeal to those like Charlotte and myself, in their late twenties or our parents or grandparents. It won't speak to the children currently. And who is buying chocolate or asking their parents to buy chocolate?" I walked right behind Casey, Charlie, and Alyssa. Everyone was staring at me, except for Charlie, who had her sights on something very interesting on the table as she planted her butt back on the chair. "Children." I tapped her chair twice. "Right, Charlotte?"

She turned and shot me the meanest of looks, and I bit my lip to suppress laughter.

She cleared her throat, her voice firmer this time. "Not sure what the current children like or want, but yes, I can see your point."

"Connor." My father's voice was stern, firm, and not one bit amused. Not surprising. "We'll have to discuss this at a later time." My father broke the staring contest I had been having with Charlie and dismissed the group. "We'll be sending the company party details by the end of the day. Thank you all."

Charlie was the first to stand. She moved past me and out the door, not waiting for Alyssa or Casey, who stood to follow her.

"Nice job in getting the new girl to turn fifty shades of red," Alyssa commented.

Casey shoved a finger into my chest. "What's the matter with you, Connor? I know it was just a question, but why did you have to put her on the spot? Sometimes ..." She threw me one dissatisfied look. "Sometimes, you just don't think, and you're supposed to be the more sensible brother." Then, she stormed off, followed by Alyssa, to go after Charlie.

All of my muscles tightened because that was exactly what I'd done, hadn't I? I hadn't been thinking; I had simply reacted.

I rubbed at my brow, frustrated. I owed someone an apology.

"Connor," my father called out as everyone filed out of the room.

I turned to face him, his full head of pepper-gray hair, his brown eyes so similar to mine, his chin held high. His suit had been pressed to perfection, not a wrinkle in place. This was my father in his truest form—to the world, to his company, to me.

My mother patted my shoulder before walking out. Her little gestures indicated that she'd been trying since I'd been home. Trying to be the mother she never had been— because Nana had taken that spot.

Automatically, I straightened to meet my father's stance.

"Rebranding?" One word heavy on his tongue.

I nodded. "It's a way to give the company a new look while capturing new clients."

"I don't know."

"I've seen this done time and time again with struggling companies. This was their one game changer to bring them back to the black."

"So, you have a plan in place?"

"Yes. A solid plan," I lied through my teeth, but this was where I was going to fake it till I made it.

"Okay. We'll see what you come up with." My father nodded. "When you're ready, you can present it to the board, and we can go from there."

I nodded. "Okay. Sounds good."

He about-faced, and I almost saluted him as though he were a general.

When he was out of my vicinity, I rubbed at my temple, letting out a long sigh.

Shit, I had a plan, but it would only work if Charlie was on board.

CHARLIE

My ears burned unbelievably hot, the heat spreading to my forehead. My cheeks warmed, and I could imagine what my face had looked like at that meeting. I stormed out of the conference room and back to my desk. I fired up my computer and logged in, diving back into work because that was what I did.

Job. Job. Job. I need money, money, money.

"Hey, Charlie," a mousy voice piped up behind me.

I didn't have to turn around to know who it was. It was Casey. I was sure Alyssa was right behind her.

"Connor is Connor Colby?" I gritted my teeth.

I didn't know if I could forgive him for embarrassing me in front of all of management. My fingers tiptapped against the computer. Maybe I could call in sick—but for the rest of the month. I wanted to pretend that this didn't bother me, but it did, especially after everything I'd said about his company, about his chocolates and the branding. And not only had I said these things multiple times in front of him, but today, I'd also said them in front of Thomas Colby, the CEO.

"Connor is Connor Colby," I repeated, mostly to myself.

"Yeah ... Connor and Kyle Colby. I kind of grew up with them," Casey said.

I peered up at her and then set my gaze back to the computer. Why hadn't I put two and two together? She had mentioned that at the candy wall on my very first day. But she'd also introduced me to Connor and not mentioned that he was the CEO's son.

It was like Casey could read my thoughts. "By the time I came back for you on your first day on the job, you'd already introduced yourself and seemed comfortable around him. Plus, since it was your first day, I think I was just too worried about making sure that you were okay and that you knew where the break room and the facilities were that I didn't even bother to mention that he was *the* Connor Colby, not just Connor in a weird outfit."

"Casey"—Alyssa's voice was heavy with disdain—"details matter, baby. This is what I've been telling you. The smallest details matter."

I rubbed at my forehead and placed my fingers back at the computer and keyboard. "Why was he wearing that candy-cane suit?"

Unless all CEOs and upper management wore those suits for no reason.

"Kyle and him always make these stupid bets. And we'd just gotten the factory uniform. I'm assuming, for whatever reason, that Connor lost a bet." Casey sat at the end of my desk, her ankles crossed. "It's weird. He never puts anybody on the spot like that. That was really out of character. I mean, I don't know why he would even do that."

"I have my ideas," Alyssa said, which forced Casey to stare at her. Casey paused, waiting for more, but Alyssa shrugged and simply said, "But I'll keep my suspicions to myself. What did you exactly say?"

"That I hated chocolate and candies and that the packaging for Colby's chocolate bars was outdated," I groaned and rubbed at my temple.

Goodness, why did I have to be so honest at times? Why couldn't I keep my thoughts and ideas to myself?

I turned to face them fully and placed both palms over my eyes, rubbing them as though I were just waking up from deep slumber. Casey and Alyssa laughed, and deep-seated humiliation prickled my skin.

I stared at them, my look incredulous. "It's so not funny, guys. I need this job." I jutted out my chin, the anger straightening out my shoulders. "He didn't once tell me he was *the* Connor Colby, the son of the CEO. He told me he was the head of marketing. And why did he put me on the spot and force me to say all those things in front of Mr. Colby? I'm so annoyed." I could feel the vein at my temple pulsing.

Alyssa placed a consoling hand on my shoulder and squeezed. "It's fine. He's leaving eventually, and you won't have to deal with him."

"Leaving?" As soon as the word left my mouth, my shoulders slumped.

"Yeah. He came back to turn Colby's around. This isn't his permanent job. He has a hotshot bank job in Manhattan that he has to get back to."

"Oh ..."

Alyssa waved a hand. "Anyway, this calls for drinks again after work, on me."

Casey slid up beside me and frowned, pushing out her bottom lip. "Details do matter. I'm sorry."

There was no way to be mad at Casey. Unless you were the Devil himself, but even the Devil, I assumed, could be won over, especially by this cute, little, mousy girl.

"It's fine."

It wouldn't be fine, but I'd just have to get over it. And I would ... eventually.

"I'll just drink my embarrassment away tonight," I sighed.

Casey laughed, pointed at me, and shot her finger like a gun. "After work, five thirty, at O'Malley's."

"Yes. Be there for happy hour. All right?" Alyssa patted my hand. "Don't worry. Everyone will forget what you said in the morning."

Doubted that, but I smiled for her benefit.

Work had been my safe haven recently. Especially when I preferred staying at Colby's and working late and hanging out with my friends at work over going home to my mom and her new family.

I just hoped I wouldn't see Connor around. Not today. Not tomorrow. Not a week from now.

CHAPTER 6

CHARLIE

I'D FINISHED HOOKING up ten desks to the new network, and I'd done it by skipping out on lunch with Casey and Alyssa. I was way ahead of schedule and pretty damn proud of myself. I'd pat myself on the back if it wouldn't look hella awkward.

It was two in the afternoon when I finally sat down in the break room by myself, eating my plain ham and cheese sandwich. It was a lunch made for grade-school kids, but it was also a staple lunch my father used to prepare me all the time.

My father. Talented guitar player. My hero, and I was his princess.

I missed him. Badly.

When he'd died, he had taken a big part of me with him, the part that believed that I was good enough, that I was worthy, that I was perfect. Now, there was no one left to cheer me on, push me to do my best, and remind me that I was talented and just how I had been made to be.

My chest ached at the absence of him. He used to make my lunch every day before he went to work. He'd leave me little notes in my lunchbox or in between my notebook. Funny quotes or terrible drawings, just to make me laugh during my long school days.

Before the sadness took me under, I focused on the task at hand, at eating lunch, but the ham and cheese sandwich suddenly lost its flavor.

After taking another bite of my food, I flipped the page of my book—the latest book by Piper Rayne, *Sexy Filthy Boss*. It was a romantic comedy that had me laughing before melancholy thoughts filtered through.

Just like my father, I loved drowning myself in a good book. It was my favorite thing ever.

I took another bite of my sandwich and dipped my nose back into the pages. I was almost on the next chapter when a deep baritone stilled me and forced my head up. Immediately, heat rushed to my cheeks again, and my heart pitter-pattered in my chest.

Damn it, betraying heart.

I needed to remind that stupid thing that Connor was the one who had embarrassed me in front of everyone in the boardroom.

"Having a late lunch?" He had a steaming cup of coffee in his hand, and his smile was actor beautiful.

"Coffee so late in the afternoon?" I shot back.

He lifted his cup, smiling. "I haven't been able to sleep lately. Can I join you?"

His cool, aloof demeanor after everything that had happened irked me. Something about me was that I lived for comfort. Never did I like to put myself in a situation that would make me uncomfortable. Parties? Nope. Clubs? Nope.

Sitting and talking to one of the hottest guys I'd ever met, him being the CEO's son. I'd rather not. I'd rather walk on coal, eat the coal, and burn my throat and all my intestines with it.

I should say no. I should say I was done with lunch.

"Sure," I choked out, mouth full, not making eye contact. My right cheek puffed out, chipmunk-style, because I hadn't swallowed the last of my sandwich yet.

He embarrassed you, remember? He embarrassed you.

Then, I decided I was done, and I didn't have to sit here in discomfort. I gulped the last bite down. "You know what? You can have my seat. I'm just about done, and I have a ton of work to do."

There wasn't an occupied seat in the whole room. Why couldn't he have taken one of those, so I could finish my lunch?

I stuffed my empty sandwich container in my brown paper bag. I still had my chips and cookie left, but I wanted to leave.

"Charlie, can we talk for a second?"

My expression pinched, and I smiled a forced, pained smile. "I actually have a lot to do today."

"Please. Just give me a few minutes,' he sighed, his eyes soft, almost pleading.

For a moment, I debated on denying his request. I did have a lot of work to do, but more than that, I was irked at him.

But after a long beat, I nodded.

He took a seat in front of me, tapping his fingers against his coffee mug. "About the meeting today ..." His gaze dipped to the cup within his hands before meeting my eyes. "It wasn't cool. It won't happen again."

My ears burned while agitation seeped deep in my skin

as I remembered how he'd put me on the spot at the meeting. "Why did you lie to me?" I snapped.

My irritation seemed to amuse him because his eyebrows shot up and he smirked. "Lie? I didn't actually lie."

I rolled my eyes, his small smile aggravating the crap out of me. "You could have told me who you were."

"But where's the fun in that?"

I gritted my teeth and jutted out my chin, ignoring his comment. "Like I said, I have a lot of work to do today." I stood, already done with this conversation and annoyed that he'd interrupted my lunch.

When I turned to leave, he gripped my hand, stilling me. "I'm kidding." His hold tightened on my fingers and my eyes narrowed.

"Not about the sorry part because I obviously meant that part."

When I didn't say anything, he clasped his other hand over mine, where it looked like he was praying, my fingers sandwiched within his. "I'm sorry, Charlie. I know I should have told you who I was, but ..." His eyes searched mine. "But I didn't want you to filter your true thoughts about our products or, more importantly, act differently in front of me." His voice was soft, genuine, almost begging.

"Why would I do that, treat you differently?"

"Because of my last name. Because of who I am." He shook his head, and his eyebrows furrowed. After a long sigh, he said, "People tend to act differently around me when they find out who I am."

His last name was a nationwide name, so I understood this part, but still, it didn't make me feel better.

"Honestly, would you have been able to tell me what

you thought about our products if you had known who I was?"

My eyes drifted to his hands clasped over mine, and I shook my head. "Still ... you should have told me."

"I know. I should have. Please sit, Charlie. I need to ask you something."

Being so close to him, I drowned in his chocolate-brown eyes and read the sincerity in them. I should hear him out. I could do that much. I debated on it, but after a beat, I sat down.

He released my hand, and his gaze dropped to the table. Clearing his throat, he said, "This rebranding initiatives is Colby's last effort to save this company." He visibly swallowed and met my gaze. Despair and concern reigned in the span of his brown irises. "Our profit margins have dwindled, and we've sustained substantial losses for the last year. I need a concise, strategic, and actionable plan to save this company, and my main focus is a brilliant marketing vision."

I could feel his utter determination oozing out of him. "I've seen my marketing team's initial specs, and it's not going to cut it. My gut tells me that it won't take us out of the red, and I need help." Desperation was heavy in his tone, which matched the intensity in his eyes. "We're not going to spend hundreds of thousands of dollars on a marketing plan that I don't believe in." He leaned into me and rested his elbows on the table. "What you said the other day ... about branding to the essence of family, I think that's the direction we need to take, and I need you to help me."

It took me a few seconds to register what he'd just said.

When his request finally sank in, I blinked up at him and reeled back. "What?"

"I need you to help me with the rebranding initiatives."

"I heard you. But why?"

"Do you even have to ask? I've seen your work."

I shook my head, unbelieving. "Okay, yeah, I drew one half-assed picture of a pretend candy bar for fun. That doesn't mean I'm qualified to help you with the rebranding initiatives. That's crazy."

He ducked his head, his gaze alert and intent on me. "If that's your half-assed idea, then I can't wait to see your real vision."

Sweat beaded on the back of my neck. *Hundreds of thousands of dollars?*

"I'm not qualified," I repeated, the shock of what he was asking me, hitting me full force. "You're not talking about just a candy bar wrapper. You're talking about a whole revamp."

"That's right. Packaging, logo, commercials, all of it. I know you can help me get this company to where we need to be."

"No." I blinked up at him, feeling a heat wave hit my body. "I'm an artist. I'm not some sort of marketing expert like you think I am. I've never been to school for that, and I don't have any experience in that field."

There was power behind his tone when he spoke. "We'd need my marketing team too, but what I need is fresh, new ideas. You could bring that in bucketfuls. Some of this marketing stuff is all about creativity. You can go to school, yeah, and learn tricks of the trade or whatever marketing gurus learn, but sometimes, it's as simple as knowing what people want, what people like. And you know what looks good."

I pressed one hand to my chest. "Listen, I'm flattered. Really. But I just can't accept this offer."

"I'd pay you overtime."

Tempting, really tempting, as I needed the money, and if I were sure I could do the job and be successful at it, I'd take him up on his offer. Though overtime would be really nice, that wasn't the issue. Simply said, I wasn't qualified to take this position when so much was riding on the line.

"I just can't."

He pinched his chin, never breaking eye contact. After pressing his lips together, he tipped his head, nodding. "Okay, I know this is a lot to take in, and I understand where you're coming from, but from our brief conversations and the little that I've seen of your work, I believe you can really help us."

His compliment made my stomach flip and then flop.

"Thanks," I said, shifting in my seat, hating his fierce stare locked on me.

After a beat, he picked up his cup. "I have to get to a meeting, but, Charlie ... please don't deny me just yet. You're talented, Charlie. Don't try to hide it. And I'm sure it's just not me. I know some artists who would think the same thing. I know quite a few people in the industry that I could introduce you to." His gaze was firmly fixed on mine. "Just think about it, okay?"

The idea of helping Colby's with this rebranding initiatives was tempting but scary as hell. "Okay."

His smirk had me looking at what his eyes had flittered to.

"*Sexy Filthy Boss*?" He lifted a curious eyebrow.

Great. He had seen the title of my book.

When he reached for the book, I grabbed it and chucked it into my lunch bag.

"It's a romantic comedy by one of my favorite authors.

Okay, I guess I'll see you later." I waved a hand and tried to tame the heat on my face.

"Give it here ..." He motioned with his fingers, beckoning me, my diversion tactic failing.

"What?"

"Your book. I want to see it."

"Are you into romance novels now?" The heat of my cheeks rushed to my ears.

"Come on. I want to see it. I promise I won't make fun of you."

My face scrunched, and I pulled it out of my lunch bag. With a big pout, I plopped it on the table. When he reached for it, he flipped to the back cover to read the blurb. And I wanted to crawl under the lunch table and die a fast, easy death.

His eyes seared through me, and we were locked in this sort of no-blinking contest. "Do you fantasize about this sexy, filthy boss?"

The heat on my face turned from tamale hot to *caliente* hot. If I'd had any doubt I was beet red, there was no doubt now. I widened my eyes.

Honest to goodness, this could be classified as sexual harassment. But I knew he was just trying to get a rise out of me.

"I'm totally kidding. I shouldn't have said that." He pushed the book back in my direction and rubbed at his brow. "I've taken enough training to know that was totally inappropriate. That was actually random." He tilted his head from side to side as though there were a crick in his neck. "I'm sorry. I couldn't help it."

He locked eyes with me, and I swore it was as if he had secret powers because it stilled me in my spot, to the point where I couldn't even move, let alone breathe.

"You just turned bright red. It's ... cute." He shook his head as though he were clearing his focus and cleared his throat. Then, he rubbed at his brow again. "Anyway ..."

Is Connor flirting with me?

But there was no way. He was beauty, and I was the blonde beast. I couldn't fathom him actually flirting with me.

"Yeah, that's my God-given talent. My face can turn so red that I look like one of those cartoon characters with their heads ready to blow. It's a gift of mine that I've had ever since I was younger."

He laughed. "You're funny. I like that." There was that weird staring contest happening again until he cleared his throat for what seemed like the millionth time and stood.

I wonder if he was coming down with something. *Did he need a cough drop?*

He knocked on the table twice. "I have a meeting in about ten minutes, so I'll let you get back to your book. But let's talk later about your decision."

"Sounds good."

He turned to leave, but then he stopped and turned back around. "Charlie ... let me know what happens."

"With what?"

"With the sexy, filthy boss. You know ... if he gets the girl?" And then he winked and walked away.

Shit. Oh, shit.

I could've ignored all the little signs before, but now, I thought Connor Colby had been flirting with me.

CHAPTER 7

CHARLIE

I WAS one of five people who serviced Colby's for the Chicagoland area that experienced computer problems. Mostly, I'd field calls and walk people through their issues on the phone, but there were certain times that I couldn't solve the issues, and I'd have to do desk calls.

Nancy had called to tell me that her computer wasn't working. She must have been close to eighty, which was past retirement age with her set of all-white hair and reading glasses, so I wondered why she was still here. I grouped her with the Alyssas of the world— those who worked because they believed in the company.

I pressed the power switch off to power down her computer, then pressed it again to turn it on. Sometimes, all a computer really needed was a reset. Didn't we all?

"So, it's your first week on the job?"

Her sweet voice reminded me of my own grandma, and a pang shot straight to my chest at the absence of her. She'd died when I was only a teenager, but still, we had been close.

"It is."

"And you like this company so far, dearie?" She opened one of her drawers and pulled out a box of cookies. "Want one? Sometimes, all this candy is too much, and I want something sweet but not chocolate."

I nodded with understanding. "No. It's okay." I patted my nonexistent hip. "Trying to watch my figure." I winked.

"So, you didn't answer my question." Her eyes crinkled at the sides as she took a bite of her cookie.

"Oh, I like it here. I do. So far, everyone has been nice to me. And you can't complain about the perks." I leaned in closer as though it were a secret. "Especially unlimited candy and chocolates." Even though it was a perk I didn't care about, I was sure I was the minority. This made her laugh again. "How long have you been here?"

"Forever. I was here years ago when Colby Chocolates first started, and now, I can't believe how fast and large it's grown. We're a nice little family here." She took another bite of her cookie, and crumbs fell down her chin. She stuffed the cookie in her mouth and immediately grabbed for another one like a little kid.

Must be that good.

"Are you from around here?" she asked.

I reached toward the back of her computer and powered it up. "No, originally from Wisconsin. My mom got remarried a few months back, and so we're living here now."

"So, how are the new surroundings ... the new family?"

"It's been an adjustment," I said. "The best thing about moving so far has been this job, to be honest."

My newfound friendships with Alyssa and Casey made it easier for me to come to a job I didn't care too much for.

These connections I'd made were the reasons this job was enjoyable.

"I'm glad to hear that, dearie. The longer you're here, the more you'll find out that we're one real-life family."

"Keeping busy I see." Connor's deep baritone had me flipping forward, almost knocking my head against the screen.

The broadness of his shoulders and his tall height were overpowering, intimidating.

Pitter-patter. Pitter-patter. There went my freaking racing heart, betraying me.

Goodness, my poor, fragile heart couldn't take another episode like the one during lunch the other day, and plus, it'd made me overthink way too much. *Had he been flirting or not?*

"And you ... shouldn't you be working harder?" I sassed, reaching for the back of the computer, doing nothing in general because, shit, I wasn't sure what was exactly wrong. It was either pretend to know what I was doing or go blind. Because looking at him made my eyes hurt. Like, physically hurt. Like, I had looked directly at the sun for far too long.

Nancy laughed at my comment.

"Nancy here couldn't figure out why her computer wasn't working."

He reached for Nancy's cookie box in her lap and tucked it under his arm. "I think you've had enough cookies." The muscles in his jaw tightened, his gaze alert, as though Nancy were going to be grounded in the next hot minute.

Nancy crossed her arms over her chest, giving him the nastiest stink-eye.

Well, that was quite rude.

I snatched the cookies from underneath his arm and

extended the box back to Nancy. "I think she's old enough to decide when she's had enough cookies. Don't cookie-shame her."

"Cookie-shame?" He plucked the box from Nancy again and tucked it back under his arm, giving me a firm, steady stare.

I openly gaped at him. *Really? The nerve of this man, telling a grown woman what to do.*

Nancy interrupted our staring contest, "I'm not into technology nowadays, but I think I know what it is. Maybe this is it." Then, she turned on her computer monitor.

My gaze moved from Nancy to the computer to Connor and back again. *Why didn't I check that first?* "Well, since that's settled"—I wiped my hands in an exaggerated effect —"I think I'm done here."

Nancy stood and gave me a full-on hug, arms around me so tightly that I was surprised by her strength, given her size. "Thank you for coming by."

I froze. It was a little excessive, since I hardly knew her, but still oh-so nice. She was right. There was a family feeling with this company. I'd known that the first day I walked in here. My arms slowly wrapped around her but not as tightly because I was afraid to crush this little cookie destroyer.

I patted her back twice, and then when she released me, Connor stepped up to her and planted a kiss on her cheek.

Stunned, I reeled back. I knew this company was a close-knit group, but ... shit ...

"Bye, Nana. And no more cookies for you."

Nana?

He turned to leave, and I followed him down the hall.

"She's the cookie monster. She will eat a whole box of

cookies within a span of five minutes if you don't monitor her."

"She's your grandmother? But her name plate said Nancy Knicklebocker."

He nodded. "She's my mother's mom. She's my only living grandmother left."

He reached for my elbow and guided me to the side, into the corner of the hall. He was so close that I could smell the mint on his lips, too close in a boss-subordinate situation, and I was a nano-second to hyperventilating.

"We need to talk." His voice was firm, meaning business.

Can't think. Can't think with him being this close.

My breathing turned shallow, and I exhaled through my mouth.

"To talk about how I don't like the branding of your signature chocolate? But we already had that conversation in front of the whole boardroom and CEO." My tone was sarcastic, meant to lighten this mood between us.

He leaned in, his gaze alert. "I already apologized about that, and ... actually"—his eyes flickered to my lips, and I held my breath—"that's exactly what I want to talk about. Have you thought about my proposition?"

He was talking about me joining the rebranding initiatives, but my mind went straight to the gutter.

"I-I just don't know. I don't know if I can do what you want me to do."

When a few workers passed us by, Connor took a healthy step away from me, running his hand through his caramel-brown hair. "Meet me in my office." It wasn't a question. It was a command, based on the tone of his voice.

He turned to walk down the hall, and I followed right behind him.

Why did I feel like I was a student walking into the principal's office?

"Am I going to get fired if I say no?"

He turned around and gave me a quizzical look. "No. Why would you think that? I wouldn't ever do that."

Crap. I hadn't meant to say that out loud. *Where the heck was my brain-to-mouth filter when I needed it?*

And of course he wouldn't fire me. That would be a lawsuit waiting to happen. At least I hadn't said anything that would have embarrassed me, like how his shirt today brought out the brown in his eyes or how just looking at him made my mouth dry and my heart palpitate.

I bit my inner cheek and reminded myself that I'd wholeheartedly decided that I shouldn't think of him that way because, one, he was my boss, and, two, I needed this job.

Remember. Remember. Remember.

But it was hard to remember, especially when I was looking at a face like his.

We entered his office, and he shut the door behind me.

"Charlie, can you have a seat?"

As I walked to his oversize desk in front of a breathtaking view of the Chicago skyline, it was easy to remember who he was—the son of the owner of one of the largest chocolate companies in the nation. I could hear his feet pad toward me, but I didn't turn around. I stayed, feet planted on the floor, until Connor swung around his desk, sat down, and steepled his fingers by his lips. I fiddled with my hands in front of me, walking slowly to the chair in front of his desk as though I were walking the plank of a ship.

"Have you made a decision, Charlie?"

"This is the thing: what if I can't do what you want me to do?"

"All I'm asking you to do is try. Brainstorm with me, sketch up some initial plans, just do what you were born to do and give me ideas with that original vision you had in mind."

I sighed, unsure.

He reached into his desk and pulled out the sketch of my imaginary chocolate that I'd drawn out at the bar. "I'm sorry. I stole this from you. But this is something I can work with. My marketing team can proceed this with vision." He waved it in the air and smiled so beautifully that it made my heart hurt. "If you help me, we can work together to save my family's company. We employ thousands of employees nationwide, and I can't fathom failing them, unable to pull through. We need to give this company a fighting chance to succeed in this market and against our competitors. To do that, we need a whole new look, a whole new vision. Charlie, I'm asking you to help me."

It was the kind of speech that took place on top of a podium in front of thousands of people, and it hit something deep inside of me—family.

I had to admit, it would be fun. It had been a fun thirty minutes at the bar, thinking with the girls on branding this imaginary chocolate bar—what the name would be, what the packaging would look like, what the logo would be. I hadn't seen it as work because it was enjoyable.

When I didn't say a word, he walked to my side, sat at the edge of his desk, and crossed his ankles, facing me directly. "Charlie, seriously, I need you."

When I still didn't speak, he stood and dropped a little, getting in my line of sight. With the lightness of his fingertips, he placed one hand on top of mine. My skin was set aflame at his touch, and a jolt of electricity surged through

me. I decided if he were the sun, then what I had just experienced was solar energy.

"Charlie, please." He paused, mulling something over in
his head. "I'll make it worth your time. I know people in the
industry. I have connections in New York with influencers
who can get your work noticed. Just help me save my family's company."

I rolled his words over in my head. *Shit, this could be
huge. One major blast, and I'd be all over social media.* I'd
seen it spiral for other creatives. I could possibly be the next
big thing, but that wasn't my next thought.

"Why do you call it your family's company? You are the
son of the CEO. Doesn't that mean it's your company too?"

He reeled back, seeming surprised by my question.
After a long sigh, he stood, anchoring himself against the
desk again. "It's complicated."

It's complicated. Wasn't that the saying of the century?
Life was complicated in general.

Curiosity ate at my insides, and I pressed him further, "I
was talking to Alyssa and Casey. You are temporarily
working here. So, you're leaving?"

He sighed and rustled his hair with one hand. "The
relationship with my family is complex. Beyond complicated. I knew the company was failing, yet I wasn't gonna
let it fail. The selfish part of me is very bitter toward this
company. See, you don't become this successful"—he
paused, looking past me, above me—"without giving something up in return. Without sacrificing something."

I wanted to press him further, but I knew now wasn't
the time.

The mood turned somber.

He stared blankly above me and slowly shook his head.
"I really don't want to get into it, but pushing all that selfish-

ness aside, because my brother, because of Nana, because of the thousands of people we employ and their families and how they are so dependent on my family's company to survive, I'm determined to save Colby's. Not for my legacy, but for them."

I wanted to cry. It was a heart felt speech with utter and gut-wrenching feeling.

It was then I decided I would help him.

After releasing a slow breath, I said, "If there is anything I can do that will make a difference, I'll help you."

His eyebrows shot to his hairline, and without thinking, he brought me in, squeezing me so hard and so fast that I nearly fell over. I for sure would've fallen over if I wasn't sitting down.

He cleared his throat and backed away, visibly embarrassed, but not before our eyes locked in a gaze so intense that I could feel it, taste it, bottle it up.

"Thank you," he said, his voice shaky and so soft that it vibrated like silk against my skin.

I nodded, unable to breathe for a second as goose bumps pebbled along my arms.

He ran one sexy hand through his hair and stood, turning to go back to his seat. "We can start this weekend."

Holy mother heat wave.

I placed a trembling hand on my neck. "Okay, this weekend."

CHAPTER 8

CHARLIE

I DROVE SLOWLY in the right lane because I didn't want to go home to Mommy dearest and my super stepdad.

As far as stepdads went, he was pretty perfect—for now at least. He was smart and owned his own company, and he doted on my mom left and right. But part of me wondered how long this facade would last. I mean, they had known each other and dated for six months, and then they had gotten married.

Or maybe they'd last forever. Maybe he'd make her happy. Maybe I was thinking the worst because he simply wasn't my dad.

My father had died right before I graduated high school, right before I'd made the decision that would change the trajectory of my life—going to computer tech school. I knew that if my father had been alive, my career path would have ended differently.

When my father passed years ago, my mother had been devastated. We both were, but for once, she turned into someone I had to take care of, as she went through bouts of depression. One thing that my parents had instilled in me was the importance of family, and because of that and because I loved my mom, I had known that wherever she went, I'd follow.

After going around in circles, I entered the new McMansion that I now called my home. Richard had bought my mom this house, so they could start a new life together even though his paid-off, older mansion was in the same city.

They'd bought the place months ago, wanting to start a new life together. Now, here we were—me, mom, my new stepdad, stepsister—all in one big, fake happy, blended family.

It was odd, driving to this place. Given my parents had been blue-collar workers, we'd only been able to afford a modest home with two bedrooms and a one-car garage. It was as if I had gone from rags to riches overnight.

My new place of residence was huge. My temporary room had its own bathroom and walk-in closet fit for a queen. When I'd mentioned that I wanted to move out, my stepdad had hired construction workers to remodel the pool house as my own personal apartment. Currently, it was my art room, where I was working on my pieces for the exhibit.

The maid, Elsa, greeted me when I entered. She tried to take my laptop bag, which I refused to give her because what idiot didn't know how to put their own stuff away by themselves?

The door chimed behind me, and I turned. In stepped Sandy. All of my muscles tightened, and I wanted to stomp back out, get into my car, and go over to Casey and Alyssa's. Sandy with her sandy-blonde hair and her crystal blue eyes and a figure that only belonged on the cover of a magazine.

Sandy, my evil stepsister. Evil personified. When she spoke, I pictured her breathing fire through her nostrils.

She dropped her bag on the floor and handed Elsa her jacket. Remember what I'd said about what idiot couldn't put away their own belongings? That was my evil stepsister.

I'd been determined to be nice to her because we were finally family now, but after the tenth time of her being bitchy to me, I'd had enough. I wasn't even trying anymore. I treated her like the bully she was. I simply ignored her.

"Charlie, how have your first few days at work been? Did you happen to not offend anybody in the first week?" She brushed her hand through her perfect locks, and I swore the curls bounced like they would in a shampoo commercial. "Do me a favor and try not to get fired, okay?"

"Don't worry. I won't," I deadpanned. "Actually, I love this job. This is the first job I've had in a long time that I feel like I can retire here." I clenched my teeth into a tight smile, lying like my life depended on it.

Did I love work? No. But I loved the people I worked with—my newfound friends. I'd upped and left my life in Wisconsin, friends and all, so it was refreshing that Alyssa and Casey had made me feel part of their girl group.

"Well, thank goodness I own a recruiting firm and that Daddy insisted I help you find a job."

More like my stepdad had forced her into finding me this job.

She lifted her shoulder to her chin. "Like I said, let's hope you won't get fired. You've never once in your life since you've graduated from college held a job for more than a few months, so I guess only time will tell."

I wanted to wipe her sassy smirk off her face.

"Girls." My mother flowed effortlessly into the foyer. Her flowery skirt hugged her hips when she walked. She had her arms outstretched, and her smile was big, wide, and inviting.

This was Olivia Grayson, now Buckingham, in her normal form. There wasn't a curl out of place from her long, flowy blonde hair, and her clothes had been pressed to perfection. That was where our similarities ended—in the color of our hair and our emerald green eyes. Where she was curvy and beautiful, I was not. Where she was tall, I was average. Where her clothes were always immaculate, half the time, I looked like I'd pulled my clothes from the wash and thrown them on.

My mother brought me into her chest, fiercely hugging me, just like she had when I was a little girl—her little girl—and I melted into her arms. I lived for her hugs. With my mother, she showed how much she cared outwardly, but what she thought and what she said were opposite to her actions.

When she turned toward Sandy's direction, her whole face lit up, and mine sank. She brought her in and hugged her as well—a gesture usually meant for only me—but now, I had to share her.

"Sandy, I like the haircut." She pulled at the end of Sandy's blonde locks and walked around her to see the back of her newly cut hair.

I wanted to tell my mom I had gotten a haircut last week, but she hadn't said a word about it. But I wasn't gonna bring it up. Because I wasn't about to be "overly sensitive"—as my mother often labeled me. I missed it when it was just us—and Dad.

"In this suit, you look like a model." My mother ran her hand down Sandy's sleeve as she admired the tailored fit.

My jaw clenched, and my gaze flickered to my own suit.

"Oh, Olivia, I need to hook you up with my tailor. She

makes the best suits. Anyway"—she waved a hand—"how's Granny? Is she okay today? Do you think she'll join us for dinner, or do you think she's worn out?" She peered behind her toward the double staircase that led to our rooms.

Her grandmother was elderly in her nineties. They'd transferred her from the nursing home to the house for home care.

There were very few times Sandy seemed human, and it was with her interactions with her grandmother that I was able to experience this.

My mother patted her shoulder, consoling her. Only I didn't know why because it wasn't like her granny was gonna die anytime soon. She was old but not bedridden.

"Why don't you check on her, honey, and ask her how she's feeling? We can have Elsa bring her down if she needs to be helped."

With an upward tip of her chin, Sandy headed down the hall and up the stairs, and once she was out of my vicinity, I exhaled deeply and relaxed my shoulders.

"So, how was your day at work, honey?" My mother's eyes gave me a once-over, taking in my suit. She didn't comment on it.

Did she like it?

I gritted my teeth because this was my issue not hers, wasn't it?

I was only perfect in my father's eyes. A pang shot straight to my chest, long and hard and endless, when I just thought of him.

Good God, I missed him. I missed the way he'd called me the perfect princess. I missed the way he'd made me believe I could do no wrong.

In my mother's eyes, I was anything but perfect. I had inherited my father's bone structure, his lanky frame, his green eyes, but I had my mother's hair and her full lips. A combination not stellar enough to even be noticed.

"It was fine, Mother ..."

Fine. Fine. Fine. A word I used often with my mother, even when things were not so fine.

━━━

We were all seated at the kitchen table. Granny—or I should say, Sandy's Granny—wasn't feeling too well, pushing around her food on her plate.

Sandy sipped her wine and leaned back against the chair. "It's just getting so busy. I had to hire two more people to keep up with demand."

I focused on my food, trying for the life of me to block her out. If I had to hear about Sandy's job one more time, I would bang my head against the table until I knocked out and they had to call 911. This was the thing: it wasn't jealousy that caused me to want to gouge my eyes out every time she talked about her recruiting firm that she owned; it was the fact that she would brag nonstop about it, as though using it to tell me, *Look at what I can do.*

"Soon, you won't have anymore room in that office you rented out." Richard Buckingham III sat right by my mother, feeding himself with one hand and holding her hand over the table with the other.

They were always touching affectionately, like the newlyweds they were. Each time I witnessed it, I'd think of my dad. It wasn't like she was cheating—my father was dead—but I couldn't help but picture how they had been together, how much love they'd shared, just with one look. As though they hadn't had to even touch to witness their overflowing passion for each other. Just how they stared lovingly at each other proved it.

Sandy's gaze made it my way. "The economy is high therefore, everyone needs a job nowadays, and people want to be placed, which puts my recruitment agency on the top of every company's list when they're trying to fill positions."

She had gotten me the job's at Colby's, yes. Was I grateful? Yes. Did she have to remind me that she had gotten me the job every second? No. Come to think of it, if the request for her to find me a job hadn't come from Richard, then I doubted she would have helped me. My gratitude should go to him.

My mother smiled at her stepdaughter. "We're just so proud of you. You've taken your company that you just started a little over a year ago, and you've expanded it to where it's overflowing with opportunities. It's just ... awe-inspiring."

This was the part where I wanted to gag, possibly throw up all my mashed potatoes and meatballs onto the kitchen table, and feed it to Sandy.

I doubted that would do any good because my mother would just have me clean it up, and I didn't want to do that. There was no reason to add another point on why she was so embarrassed of me.

"This family was meant to be. Look at that, Charlie. As soon as we moved in, you needed a new job, and lo and behold, your sister owns her own recruitment agency." My mother clasped her hands together like this was a good thing.

If I only didn't need this job, need it for my end game—my exhibit.

"I hear you can get and eat all the candy that you want. Must be one of the greatest perks at the job," Mother added.

Richard lifted his head from his plate. "You're working for Colby's?" He eyed Sandy from his spot. "I thought you didn't do business with that company anymore."

My stepfather didn't pay attention to little details that involved me because if he did, he'd have known I had been hired last week.

Sandy waved a hand and exaggeratedly rolled her eyes. "Dad, if they're paying, I'm not about to deny their money. It's a win for them and a win for me."

"I don't know. It's not a company I want you dealing with. Especially since I heard it's going under."

I guessed what the company had been trying to keep a secret wasn't so top secret anymore.

I decided to tune out the family for the rest of dinner. I tried to think of when I could get back to finishing my latest project—an abstract oil painting. I'd stored my painting supplies and set up my own little studio in the pool house. That way, it wasn't in the house, and no one could bother me when I was in the deep zone of creating.

Soon enough, construction would be complete, and I could permanently move into the pool house. I'd had plans to move out, be on my own, until we moved here. But now, with this exhibit, I couldn't afford a place of my own, not when I'd had to pay a substantial amount of rent to lease the spot for my show.

When dinner was over and everyone headed to the living room, I helped Elsa clean up. My mother had told me I didn't have to do so, but I did. Sandy merely scowled without saying a word as though it were beneath her that she shouldn't and couldn't help.

"Miss Charlie, you're fine. You can go in and spend time with Richard and your mother." Elsa took the plate from my hand, and I frowned. "Ms. Sandy doesn't come home often, only since Granny came back from the nursing home."

I sighed. I knew she was right, but I didn't want to socialize. I wanted to drown in paint and canvas and oils, not interact with my new blended family.

But I did the right thing and trekked toward the living room. Richard sat next to my mother on the worn brown leather couch with his drink of choice—scotch. Sandy was in the opposite lounge chair with her dry martini. Granny sat next to Sandy in her wheelchair.

My drink of choice was none of the above because liquor made me tipsy, and it made me say things that I couldn't take back, so I wasn't about to get drunk, not in front of my new family. Liquor made people honest, me especially.

Just as I sat down, Sandy stood, ready to go, like always whenever I was around. She put up a show just in front of the family—but not for me.

"Charlie, why don't you follow me to the door and lead me out? I'm not sure where my jacket is."

I fisted my hands at my sides and gritted my teeth in a tight smile that screamed, *I don't like you, but no one is able to tell because I'm smiling*. She knew exactly where her jacket was. I wouldn't hate her so much if she didn't have this undying need to make my life uncomfortable.

Richard and my mother eyed me from their seats, probably wondering if I'd cause a scene for a simple request.

Nope. Not playing this game, Sandy. Not looking like the bad guy. Not today.

I followed Sandy out of the living room, down the hall, and to the foyer where she opened the closet and plucked out her jacket.

"Now, since you've found your jacket, I guess you don't

need me anymore." I smiled. "Unless you want me to help you put it on." *And wrap it around your neck in a double knot.*

She slipped on her coat and fixed her sleeves, never bothering to look up. "It took me a lot to get you a job at Colby's."

"I know, and I can't thank you enough," I snapped.

She reminded me every time she saw me, like a broken record. Her look told me that, in appreciation, I owed her my firstborn child.

"I've got a little bird on the inside, and it looks like you're not making a good impression thus far." Her laugh was cynical, high-pitched, and annoying, like a witch—the Wicked Witch of the West.

Who the hell did she know? How far could her claws reach?

"So, do me a favor and don't embarrass me and get fired, okay?" She adjusted the strap of her designer purse over her arm, pulling it further up her shoulder. Only then did she meet my eyes.

She gave me a once-over—from the top of my baby hairs on my head to the toes of my fuzzy socks. With one last sour look, Sandy fixed her collar and was out the door without saying good-bye.

All of my muscles tightened.

I hated her more than I hated Brussels sprouts, and damn, I hated Brussels sprouts really bad.

I pushed back my shoulders and lifted up my chin. Results set deep in my gut, I would excel at this job and do my very best to help Connor with the rebranding initiatives, so whoever Sandy knew in the inside could tell her that I'd had a hand in helping save the company. *Take that!*

CHAPTER 9

CONNOR

WE WERE MEETING for our first brainstorming session.

I was excited to get this started because we didn't have that much time left to get this done before I had to leave and go back to New York.

The stirring from the door had me adjusting the Chinese food cartons on the long boardroom table. Charlie's hair was in a bun on the top of her head, messy but in a sexy way that made it seem like she had gone to the salon to get it done.

"Hey."

"Hey." She brought in her laptop and a big sketchpad, which dropped on the long mahogany table that cut the boardroom. Then, she frowned.

And I laughed because her face had just transformed to one of a five-year-old. "What's the matter?"

"I just ate."

"Oh." I realized what had upset her, and then I

mentally slapped myself because I should have told her earlier that I would be providing dinner.

We were working late. The least I could do is pay for her dinner.

"Well, if we're here late, trying to figure stuff out, we can eat it for a late-night snack."

"You think we'll be here late?" Her brow furrowed, and she teetered in her spot. "If so ... I might need to call an Uber."

"Where do you live?"

"Inverness."

So, she came from money.

"That'll be a fifty-dollar car ride. I'll drive you."

She shifted, looking visibly uncomfortable. "I ... I don't know ..."

I opened the takeout box of fried rice and the rest of the food. "How about I eat, and you tell me about your ideas? Later, we can figure out how you're going to get home."

"Uh ..."

"Charlie, sit down." I used my authoritative voice, the one that I used in the boardroom or in a liquidation scenario at the bank.

"When did you get here?" She unbuttoned her light jacket and hung it on the back of her chair. She was wearing jeans that nicely hugged her frame and a red V-neck knit top that accented her—

I swallowed and forced my eyes up to her face.

"I've been here all day. So, I've been going over the numbers that Alyssa gave me yesterday." I undid the collar of my shirt just a tad, wondering how the hell the heat index had jumped a few notches in the room.

"So, how is it looking?"

I stood up and moved to the thermostat just to check that it was set at a reasonable temp. Sixty-eight degrees felt like eighty today.

After a beat, I sat back down. "Not looking too good. The rate of expenses does not match income. It's the fall season, which is one of our busiest seasons, but our sales numbers are not meeting what they did last year." I grabbed a plate, and started pouring the rice and the chop suey onto it. Then I plucked an eggroll and placed it on my plate.

"Well, we're going to turn that around, aren't we?" Her cheery voice almost broke me from my sullen mood. *Almost* because I knew that nothing was a guarantee.

"We have to, or layoffs will begin in February."

It was a hard conversation I'd had with Alyssa today, and one of Alyssa's strengths was her no-bullshit attitude. This would hurt her as much as it hurt my father. Alyssa had grown to know the employees at this company.

"All righty then, we have to get started." She opened her sketchbook, which was a different sketchbook than the pocket-sized one she'd had in her purse at the bar. Opened, it occupied a good portion of the table. "Should we just start writing ideas first?"

"Sure." My mouth was still full with food, so I placed my plate on the table to concentrate.

"I was telling Alyssa and Casey that when I think of Colby, I think of the family feel, the way you guys treat your employees like family, how you invite them over to your house. I feel like we need to brand to that." She wrote down one word on the top of the pad. "*Family.*"

Her eyebrows scrunched as she searched the word for some underlying meaning.

"*Family*. It's such a heavy word, don't you think?

There's so much meaning behind the one single word." Her voice was full of emotion, and I had an underlying need to know about her family.

"Tell me about your family."

The question—or more like a command—startled her, and her eyes met mine.

"What do you want to know?"

Everything.

"Whatever you want to share. Do you have any siblings?"

She laughed, and one hand flew to the top of her bun. "Well, I have an evil stepsister." The side of her mouth crept up. "She's beautiful, absolutely beautiful, but like the saying goes, *Beauty is only skin deep.*"

"How about your parents? Tell me about them."

I didn't know how the branding/marketing session had turned into a me-wanting-to-get-to-know-her session. Yet here we were.

Her smile slipped, and she inched back, shrinking smaller into her chair.

"My mom remarried. And ... I guess I like him. The new guy."

She was almost the color of her red shirt. "I didn't mean it that way. Richard is a nice man."

After waving a hand she pulled at her neckline, and I shifted in my seat because my eyes flew back to her fingers ... which were near her exposed creamy skin by her collar-bone. I tore my gaze away and focused on her face.

What the hell is wrong with me? It was as if I were a teenage boy going through puberty and had never seen breasts before.

"My stepdad treats her like a queen, and she deserves to

be treated as such. She's not used to anything less because my father treated her like a queen all the way down to his last dying breath. I mean ..."

My heart seized.

Charlie dropped her stare to the table, and I couldn't read her eyes. I placed a hand on her fist, my thumb brushing against her knuckles. Only then did her gaze flicker up to meet mine.

"I'm sorry about your dad. What happened?"

"Cancer." Her tone was heavy with sorrow, and my heart sank.

I released a deep sigh, and I had this undeniable urge to hold her. But I kept steady. As I'd grown up in a no-parent household, it was my grandmother who had taught me about kindness and sympathy toward others. It was how I'd helped raise my brother. My parents had been too busy with raising a business instead of raising us.

She pulled her hand from under mine and rubbed at her brow, her fingers trembling. "He was in hospice toward the end, and that was really, really tough. Quite honestly, it's still really, really tough." Now, both her hands made it to her temples, as though reliving the memory was too hard for her to handle.

"You want to know the real reason I don't care for chocolate?" Her shoulders dropped, and when she lifted her head, I saw all the emotions swimming in her green-as-emerald irises. "It's because"—a slow, heavy breath escaped her—"when we were in the hospital, I'd go to the vending machine and grab a chocolate bar while waiting for his results or when he got his treatments. Almost every day, I'd go and get a chocolate bar, and now, I just can't do it anymore. It brings me to a part of my life I want to forget."

Silence stretched between us. It was as though I could tell her mournful misery came off her in waves, and it sucked. Life sucked sometimes. Out of everyone, I knew that the most.

"I'm sorry," I found myself saying again. "About your dad. About your hate for chocolate now. About everything." I decided to focus on the positive then. "Your mom is so lucky to have you."

"Thank you." Her eyes briefly met mine before her gaze fell somewhere over my shoulder, seeing nothing. "When she found someone, even though my life was set in Wisconsin and I had a job and my friends, I just wanted her to be happy, so here I am. Implant." She ended that sentence with a smile, but it was a forced smile that didn't meet her eyes.

"That's selfless of you. Really. Given that you could have stayed back in Wisconsin. It's not like you're seventeen, not legal, barely out of college, and you need your parents."

She shook her head. "I'm far from a saint, let me tell you. Half the time, I'm trying to think of ways to secretly torture my stepsister." She laughed at her own joke, and it was a beautiful laugh. "But honest to goodness, my childhood and family mean everything to me. My childhood was filled with laughter—like, I'm talking belly laughs till I couldn't get up—and on the daily. How many families can say they're like that? We were one unit. Even though I didn't have any siblings, I never lacked a thing." Her smile widened, and it was natural this time. "At times, my dad was a big, old kid, constantly joking around."

I wished I had memories like that. Endless laughter with my parents? It never happened. But I did have laughter in my memories. They consisted of Nana and Papa and Kyle. Memories of them playing board games with us, going to the movies, taking us to football practice, and sitting in the front row to watch our games. But in those memories, my parents were not present.

"You're lucky, you know that? Having my parents present is what I lacked in my childhood. We had a ton of toys and we got whatever we wanted, but they were never around."

Our gazes locked, and there was no pity in her eyes, but I could read a deep curiosity on her face as she tilted her head.

So, I answered the unspoken questions, "See ... my grandfather—my dad's father—had a dream. I was never close to that side of the family, just my mother's side. My grandfather started that dream, and my father, he's the one who brought that dream to reality." A tightness formed in my chest, as it did every time I thought of what they had sacrificed to get here. "My dad and my mother hustled and worked endless days and nights, selling their products to whoever would take them. Going from store to store to manufacturer to manufacturer to meeting and meeting after meeting, begging for a chance to be sold. Then, they were. And their success snowballed." There was a sour taste in my mouth, the bitterness spreading to my gut.

Because behind every success story, there was a downfall and liabilities, and the outcome of my parents' success was my bitterness toward them for just not being around when I had been younger. At times, I felt like I had been adopted by my nana because I hardly ever saw them.

"I think they only had Kyle because they felt sorry for me, that I didn't have a playmate." My voice was tinged with sarcasm as I shook my head. "I shouldn't say that."

I cleared my throat to get down to business. I pointed to

the sketchpad and underlined the word *family* with my finger. "It's all about perception, you see. Dad's perceived to be the perfect businessman and perfect father even though he didn't raise us himself." I bit my tongue because at the end of the day, my childhood was what it was. It was what I accepted it to be. As an adult, I made my own path now.

Still, hearing Charlie's story of her happy family had brought all this history back to the forefront.

"I think we should expand on this word. I do believe that my father loves his employees and cares about them deeply. I mean, some of the people on the management team helped him get to where he is today, so if anything, they are more family than I am." I stood because I'd lost all self-control and just had a case of diarrhea of the mouth. "You know what? Excuse me. I'm just gonna use the restroom real quick." I smiled. "I'll be right back."

CHARLIE

I turned Connor's words over and over in my head, and I realized one thing: no one family was perfect. Everyone played their part, and people had their flaws. At the end, one thing remained: love. Connor had a deep bitterness toward his parents, but he wouldn't be here, trying to save their company, if he didn't love them.

It was hours later. Papers had been strewn everywhere, tossed on the floor, on the desk, and in a couple of chairs. So much time had passed that I had finished the rest of the Chinese food.

And still, it came down to one word: *family*. We were in agreement with that; otherwise, we had nothing. No slogan. No idea on packaging on the rebranded chocolate bar. Nothing.

"Why don't we get the marketing people involved? Why aren't they here in our brainstorming sessions?" Because obviously, I wasn't any added help.

Connor was hunched over, hands threaded through his hair, elbows on the table, staring intently at the paper in front of him. I didn't think he'd heard a word I'd said.

I wanted to tell him this was a bad idea, getting me involved.

"Connor? Anyone home?"

I knocked on the table twice, and his eyes shot up to mine.

His hair was a disheveled mess. It was probably because he had run his hands through his hair a million times. But man, oh man, did he look sexy. His hair kind of reminded me of one of those guys in those underwear commercials, jumping around with nothing on other than the boxers that they were advertising, with bedhead that screamed sexy.

"I think we need to include the marketing team on our brainstorming session," I repeated.

He leaned back against his chair, running his hands through his hair again. Then, he placed both hands on the top of the table in a prayer-like motion.

"No. We need new blood for our revamp. That I'm sure of. Not saying that their ideas aren't great, but they're not stellar. It's not good enough for what we need."

He said *we* like we were one team and it was only us who could save this company. Honestly, it was too much pressure for me to handle. But I empathized with him because I knew how much was riding on this.

"How about we continue next week then? I mean, it's late. It's already ..." I reached for my phone in front of me and nearly dropped it on the table. "It's two a.m. It's two o'clock in the morning." I had to repeat it twice just to hear myself. "Oh, Colby, crapola, it's over." I stood.

Connor laughed, and it was a full-on body-shaking laugh.

He was laughing so much that it was like he had this contagious laughter. The more he cracked up, the bigger my smile became.

"What's so funny?"

"I don't know." He swiped at his eyes. "I think I'm just going crazy, but you said, 'Oh, Colby, crapola,' and then I was just thinking about chocolate and melted chocolate and crap and ..."

It wasn't funny, but I blamed it on it being so early in the morning and that we were way past delirious.

I pointed and shook my finger at him. "It's a thing, you know." And then I began to laugh again. "My dad would use that, and I got the saying from him. When I was in a mood, he'd take a chocolate, chew it in his mouth, and open his mouth for me to see, which was kinda gross, but as a kid, I thought it was funny because chocolate and crap."

We were at the point where we were all giddy and laughing for no reason, and practically anything could set the giggles off.

"Your dad sounds like he was a fun guy."

"He is. You will love him." Those words flew out of me so fast that it hit me directly in the chest, and I paused. "I mean ..." My gaze dropped to the table, and my eyebrows pinched together. "I mean, you would have loved him. I did."

All humor erased from the room, vanished as though a vacuum had sucked it up, sucked up all the laughter because of memories.

Sometimes, talking about him and reliving memories

felt so real, so tangible that it was like he'd never left this earth.

Connor broke me from my thoughts when he leaned in and got into my line of sight. "Let's go. We've worked hard enough, and it's been a long night. I'm driving you home. No arguments."

CHAPTER 10

CHARLOTTE

AS ALL CARS WENT, Connor's car was fancy. It was evident by the leather seat that warmed my butt. I pressed a button on the dashboard, and it pushed the seat forward. I pressed the back button and the forward again just because I was fascinated by the functions. Then, I amped up the seat warmer. I was acting like a little kid, but all we'd had when I was growing up was a rusted Toyota Camry until it died and we had to buy another beat-up car. And this car had not only its seat warmers, mini fridge built in the center console, the iPads built in the headrests for each passenger in the back row, but it also had a heated steering wheel.

A heated freaking steering wheel.

He laughed beside me, but I ignored him.

"Thanks again for driving me home." I was undoubtedly thankful, given that it was raining—and not just pitter-patter rain, but typhoon rain.

"It's not a problem, Charlie. Plus, you wouldn't want to get caught up in this."

His hands were on ten and two on the steering wheel, and I didn't blame him because I could barely see through the windshield.

I thought of today, what had transpired by trying to help Connor figure out this new launch.

I wished I had gone to school for something I liked. I wished I'd trusted my dad and not listened to my mom's nagging voice, spouting off about important career choices that made money because we didn't have any.

Maybe if I had gone into marketing, I could have been some sort of help.

What a wasted day. What a wasted night for Connor.

"I think you need to bring a professional in," I said.

"What are you even talking about? We have the *family* concept. You thought of that, all on your own. It's brilliant. We just need to expand on that."

His eyes flipped to mine and then back to the road in front of us where his windshield wipers were going wild. "I don't need anyone else. I have you. Raw, uninhibited talent. What you have in you is innate. I already have my marketing team. You're just the missing piece." There was a lightness in his tone, and it filled my heart.

I was so used to my mother telling me that my art was just for fun and that no one would ever take me seriously. But I would show her. This exhibit would show her.

"You sound just like my dad." Nostalgia hit me full force, and I swallowed down the lump in the back of my throat. "He ... he had me believe that I could do anything. Absolutely anything. Like my paintings would be in the Louvre or some museum where they would pay top dollar to showcase my work." I waved a hand, dismissing my comment because, really, it sounded ridiculous. Me? At a museum. How crazy and absurd, and yet it was totally my daddy.

I exhaled a heavy sigh, one that was audible, and it had Connor gazing in my direction again.

"You should believe him," he said, voice soft. "I want to know more about this incredible man."

"Why?"

Sometimes, little glimpses of my dad would push through my thoughts. I didn't really have anyone to talk to about him. And I missed him terribly. I thought about him on a daily basis, and there were times when I was drinking a caramel latte, and his face would push through my thoughts. I'd picture him sitting opposite me on the kitchen table with his black coffee in hand. We used to have regular coffee dates. It was everything. We'd even taken a class on how to work as a barista for a day.

"I'm sorry. I've just been talking about him way too much because I've been thinking about him way too much recently. I can't help it." Honesty seeped out of me.

It felt nice for once, not having to put up a front, not having any pretense. I wished I could talk to my mom about him, but she had Richard now, and it wouldn't be the same.

"I want to know about him. Don't be sorry."

"Why?" I asked again because, seriously, why would he want to know?

"I wouldn't call my family the conventional family. I mean, yeah, I have a dad and mom, and they're married, but if we are branding toward family ... we should use your family as an example, not mine." He swallowed and tried to tame the bite back from his tone.

"I'm sorry." Because I was. Because I felt bad for him.

"Nana says I shouldn't blame them. That they worked

hard, so we could have everything and not worry about money. But there's this part of me that wishes they had just been around. Every game ..." His voice softened. "I used to play football. And at every game, I would look at the stands, hoping they'd surprise me and just be there." This time, his laugh had an edge. "Way to set myself up for disappointment. And that was why I decided that I wanted out. After college, I upped and moved to Manhattan, never looking back."

I understood where he was coming from. I needed that affirmation from my parents. My dad had always been proud of me, and there was never a time that I doubted his love for my work or his love for me. I was Michelangelo or Picasso in his eyes. But in my mother's eyes, that was a whole different story.

And maybe Connor accepted their relationship, but me, sometimes, I was still vying for my mother's approval, for acknowledgment.

"I know how you feel. My mother is the opposite of my father. In high school, I had all these art fairs. My teachers would showcase my work and tell her and my father that I had talent." I fiddled with my hands in my lap. "She'd always let me know what she thought of my work. 'She does that for fun. It'll never be a good job for her. *How can one paint for a living? Do you even know anyone that paints for a living?*'" My voice reached a high-pitched, motherly sound, mocking her. "And when my father died, my mother only reiterated how much was riding on the line, and that's why I went into computers because it's a good-paying job.

"We didn't have a lot when I was younger. They both worked blue-collar jobs. My mom was a secretary, and my father worked for a printing company, fixing the printers." I bit my bottom lip. "We struggled a bit, and I got that she didn't want me to feel it."

And I had felt it—with my thrift-store clothes and my worn-out gym shoes, compared to others who had more. It was fine though. I'd had my own group of friends who didn't care what the latest trend in fashion was. Most of all, I'd had a happy and full childhood.

"That's a shitty thing to say. And absolutely false. I know a handful of people in your industry. I know Nui Cavinchi."

I stared at him, mouth agape—like, seriously, I could fit a ping-pong ball in there.

"The painter, the art dealer, and the social media queen–slash–influencer, who has over a million followers on Instagram?" My eyes widened.

"When I told you I knew people in the industry, I wasn't kidding around."

I freaked. Inside though. Because it wouldn't be cool to start screaming like a banshee.

I stalked Nui on social media, on her blog, on her podcast. I knew the names of her animals and her favorite burger joint. It was bad. She was a painter and also a buyer because not only did she have talent, but she also had a good eye. One post from her, and you would be a viral sensation.

"How do you know her?" My tone was even, but inside, I was freaking the heck out.

Connor was basically famous by association, given her status.

"We went on a date." There was a lightness in his tone.

I jerked back and pointed to him, unbelieving. "You? You dated Nui Cavinchi." This time, my face didn't hide a thing.

Why was I so surprised? They were both wealthy and

insanely good-looking. They had that in common, as all things went.

"I did. It was one date, and I think I bored her to death. We'd met through mutual friends." He laughed. "I actually didn't really know who she was until our date, until she showed me her artwork. Pictures on her phone. And then I looked her up, and to say I was blown away would be an understatement."

The rain pounded harder against the windshield, and Connor slowed his pace. At this point, we were going ten miles an hour with no one on the streets.

"What happened?" Curiosity got the best of me, and I had to know.

"We weren't compatible. So, there wasn't a second date, but we've remained good friends."

I blinked at him and then blinked again and again.

He caught my stare and laughed. "Which is another reason you should help me. I meant it, Charlie. I'm going to introduce you to people who will acknowledge your talents and tell the world about them."

My heart sped up in my chest, and all I could do was stare at his side profile as his eyes remained glued to the road in front of us.

"Okay." My voice sounded unsure because, for a little bit, it was like a dream, a *too good to be true* dream.

For once, it seemed like everything was falling into place for me. A job that wasn't horrible, new friends, an upcoming exhibit, and possibly—if everything worked out—I'd get noticed for my talents, and maybe this would be the start of something grand.

"If you help me, I promise I will introduce you to Nui."

Little did he know that I'd decided to help him anyway.

"Okay."

"Okay? You could sound a little bit more enthusiastic." He pulled into our gated community and followed his navigation down the winding road.

"I'm still in shock. You could've told me you knew Brad Pitt, and I wouldn't be this excited."

Seriously ... Nui Cavinchi.

The navigation led Connor to the McMansion I now lived in. He parked in front of the driveway and turned to face me.

"There's no doubt that she'll agree that you have talent. You just need to help me with this, and I'll make the introduction. Easy. The only thing I ask is, you never doubt or question your abilities to do this, to help with this launch. Because I know you can." There was such conviction in his tone, in his words.

In that moment, I wanted to kiss him. Kiss him because I was so grateful, because he was so hot, or because I simply wanted to see how he tasted.

"Okay." My voice was more confident this time.

"Stay put."

The rain pitter-pattered harder against the windows, but before I could tell him that I'd give him his umbrella back at work, he stepped out of the car, taking the umbrella with him and moving to the passenger side to get me.

When he came to my side, I opened the passenger door, and his arm went around me to bring me underneath the umbrella. The scent of him, the masculine smell of this man, hit me directly in the nostrils, and all my lady parts were awakened. He smelled divine. I wanted to sniff his shirt, take it off, and sleep on it later. *What was his aftershave?*

"This is crazy. We'll have flooding if this doesn't stop

soon." He walked up the driveway, but just then something by the garbage can made me pause, mid-step.

My heart stopped beating in my chest, and it felt like I had been punched in the gut because my breath literally got knocked out of me, and I couldn't breathe.

I didn't think. I reacted. I ran, chest heaving, heart pumping, arms swinging.

"Charlie!" Connor yelled, but I ignored him.

I ran down the driveway, leaving Connor under the umbrella and getting sopping wet.

My worst fears were confirmed. I lifted some of my canvases into my arms that were by the garbage can. Six or seven paintings, all ruined. My arms were full because the canvases were too large to carry on my own.

Tears flowed down my face, like a dam that had burst, coming faster down my cheeks than the endless rain.

How could my mother do this? How could she treat my artwork literally like trash and throw everything out?

I'd worked on these for weeks. And it would take me weeks to work on more. I wanted to showcase at least thirty paintings at the art exhibit.

All those wasted hours. All that wasted time.

Tears blended with the rain and flew down my cheeks effortlessly.

"Why? Why? Why did she do this?" That was all I uttered to myself like a damn broken record.

"Charlie ... you're getting soaked."

I ignored him and felt this unbearable rage bubbling under the surface. "She hates my paintings that much? She knew this would hurt me, so why would she do this?" I tried to lift more paintings into my hands, but they slipped and fell, the reds, blues, and oranges blending into one massive mess of color down the driveway.

"Let me help you." Connor abandoned his umbrella, tossing it on the ground.

He reached for the remaining four paintings, and I led us back past the house to the backyard, past the massive pool, and to where my studio was—the pool house. I stepped in and turned on the lights. The rest of my paintings were everywhere. Stacked on the floor, some stacked on the couch. I had a painting mat at the far end of the room. Brushes, my watercolors, my acrylic paints were all on the side table by a blank white canvas, ready to be drawn and painted on. I sighed with relief.

These paintings—the ones ruined—had been in the garage, but when and, for the love of God, why had she thrown them out?

I swiped at my eyes, staring at the soaked canvases and the paintings ruined. This was ridiculous. I couldn't help how she felt, but I couldn't help my feelings either.

Why couldn't she just respect me and my art? Why couldn't she just be the mom who encouraged me instead of trying to change me? Why couldn't she be like my dad?

The tears were hot and heavy as they ran down my face, and although I tried to suck it in and stop crying, the tears wouldn't stop falling.

"Hey," Connor called out.

I turned to face him. "Why would she do this?"

I blinked up at the lights above me, but the tears wouldn't stop falling, heavy like a waterfall.

"I'm sorry." His voice was soft, sincere. His clothes were soaking wet, his hair flat.

But it was as though I didn't see him or hear him. All that filtered through me was this overwhelming anger that threatened to take me under. I wanted to scream and yell for all the wasted effort in my ruined paintings. I wanted to call Gene, the person that owned the studio, and tell her I was no longer going to lease the storefront to showcase my work. Most of all, I wanted to cry because if my father were here, I wouldn't feel so utterly worthless.

And then ... without warning, Connor pulled me into his arms.

CHAPTER 11

CONNOR

I HADN'T PLANNED on it. I hadn't planned on pulling her into my arms and holding her through her shakes and her tears and her sobs. But it felt like the right thing to do. I wasn't used to consoling people. There were very few instances where I'd ever had to console anyone. But having Charlie in my arms felt oddly natural.

"I'm sorry. Parents can be shitty people sometimes."

And wasn't that the truth? Didn't I know that more than anyone?

She sobbed into my shirt, which was already wet from the rain but now more so with her tears. I didn't know how long I held her, but I squeezed her tighter, and when I did, her sobs heightened.

I felt her pain. The pain caused by parents.

How many times had I cried myself to sleep in my younger years? How many times had my parents said they'd come home for my Christmas concert and then I'd wait and wait and they wouldn't be there in the audience?

But then there was always Nana. Nana always made everything okay. Making me her signature chocolate cookies that she seriously thought saved the world and made any situation better.

When Charlie's shakes stopped and her tears dried out, she took a step away from me and wiped at her eyes, not meeting my stare. I sensed she was embarrassed. It was in the way her shoulders cowered into her frame and how she held her stomach and mostly how she couldn't meet my gaze.

Only then did I survey the room. The paintings were everywhere, and they were absolutely stunning. Abstract paintings. Naked paintings of the human form. Splashes of paint against colors everywhere.

"This is what you're gonna showcase?" I walked around the room, picking up various canvases.

One of the paintings stood out. Darker shades of gray and black blended with whites. It was a solemn painting, an abstract one. I didn't know much about art. Just what was pleasing to the eye. But this signified something deeper.

But it was beautiful nonetheless, like you could get lost into the colors as though, looking at it long enough, you could feel the pain of the painter who had painted it.

"I painted that right after my father died."

My gaze moved back to hers. Her hair was matted to her face. And without thinking, I reached over and pushed her hair out of her eyes. She was freezing. No doubt from the rain. I took her hand and pulled her close, overstepping all boundaries and the little voice in my head saying that I shouldn't.

"Charlie ... you're freezing." I rubbed her shoulders.

"Chilled to the bone." Her teeth chattered against me. "The painting ... I was so mad when he died. At him mostly.

Didn't even make any sense. He died of cancer, and yet I blamed him for dying. How ridiculous is that?" Her hands were on my waist, and it seemed as though we were both using each other for warmth now.

"But he'd told me he'd never leave me. When he left, I felt so hopeless. No one supported me like he did. No one ever loved me like he did. His whole life was to ensure that I did whatever made me happy."

A shiver ran through her, and I pulled her closer against me.

"He said he would never leave. And he did." Her voice was filled with melancholy emotion.

"I'm sorry." That was all I could say.

Her losing her father would be like me losing Nana. They were the ones who had pushed us to greatness, the ones who had made us who we were today. I couldn't even fathom it.

"You're freezing too." She pushed herself up against me and met my gaze, rubbing my arms.

And shit, I wasn't that cold anymore.

"There is a dryer in here. And I'll go see if there is a robe somewhere." She moved across the room and into the bathroom at the far end of the hallway.

The pool house was huge, and they could rent out the space. A couch was in the main area, and the double doors made me believe there was a bedroom here.

"Is this your studio?" I walked around the area, taking everything in—the floral couch in the living room, the full kitchen, the flat screen TV against the wall, and paintings and canvases half-finished everywhere.

"Yep. My makeshift studio, but construction is being done to make the back room a bedroom, so I can move in here. It's just about finished, and the buildout should be completed next week or so."

She walked toward me, lifting up a white fluffy robe. "Ding, ding, ding. I think I have a winner here."

"Only one?" I quirked an eyebrow.

"Rock, paper, scissors?"

I smiled at her. "Real cute."

"No, you can have it. I'll just run to the house and get a change of clothes." She bit her bottom lip, and it was the sexiest thing.

I pushed aside all thoughts that she was wet and cute and talented in all things because I shouldn't—and wouldn't —get involved with her. Not when I was leaving soon. But damn ... damn, was she sexy right now.

"It's raining. And I left my umbrella by your garbage can. Is there an umbrella here somewhere?" I peered behind her at the front entrance.

"Let's go searching." She moved to the front closet right by the door. She opened the door, turned around, and frowned. "Nope."

"I'll just go home."

She shook her head. "That's ridiculous. The rain hasn't let up, and you're soaked. You'll catch pneumonia."

"Fine, you take the robe." I smiled at the look on her face. "Just throw me a towel."

She blinked at me, doe-eyed and beautiful.

"We are all adults here," I said.

Honestly, I should go home. I was wet and cold, and the proper thing to do would be to leave now. Get in my car and stop thinking about Charlie.

"Yes, we are all adults here ... but you own the company I work for, and this' seems highly inappropriate, don't you think? If it were to get out to Alyssa or Casey ... I'll just run to the house to get a change of clothes."

"You go out there in the rain, and you'll be the one to catch pneumonia. Then, you'll call in sick. Then, I won't meet my deadline. So, technically, I'm thinking about myself here." My voice was light, but I could not take my eyes off of her and how her T-shirt clung to her chest. I swallowed. Hard. "Go to the bathroom. Put on that robe and throw me a towel. The sooner we get our clothes in the dryer, the sooner I can get out of here."

The overhead clock by the kitchenette said it was three in the morning. I thought she was gonna argue with me because she pushed out her bottom lip. But then she turned, walked into the washroom, and shut the door, taking the robe with her.

Man ... I was in trouble. Because I was attracted to her. I had been attracted to her since that first day in front of the candy wall, and I was even more attracted to her now. It was as though the more time I spent with her, the more I liked her—liked her in a way I knew I shouldn't.

I shook my head. It didn't matter because nothing was going to happen between us. I could be attracted to her. Nothing was wrong with that. I just wasn't going to act on it. The end.

CHARLIE

Ten minutes later, I was seated on the couch. The robe smelled like it hadn't been worn in years. I bet this belonged to the former owners who used to live here. And to be honest, that was kind of gross.

Connor paced the room, only wearing a towel. My eyes

scoured his bare chest and the six-pack that had my mouth watering. Seriously, how much could one person work out? I purposely had to concentrate on his face because every time my eyes wandered, they would run further south down his abs to what lay underneath the towel, to what was visibly there. I swallowed.

"This is crazy. All of it." He motioned to the room around him. "Anyone who can't see that you have talent is obviously blind, no offense to your mother."

I smiled. Had been smiling ever since I sat on the couch. It was the way he made me feel ... like I was the absolute best artist out there—which I knew wasn't true, but still, it made me feel empowered.

"You have to draw something for me. I'll pay you."

"Draw something for you?" I perked up on my seat. Immediately, my mind went to the gutter, thinking of painting his perfect naked form. I forced my eyes to stay level with his face.

"I'll take it to New York with me. Hang it up. Kind of remind me of this fun adventure we had today."

Maybe it was wishful thinking, or maybe it was just me wanting to believe he had totally checked me out, but I swore his eyes had wandered over my neck, over my robe, down to my bare legs and feet. It wasn't a few times either. It was multiple times.

"Okay. Deal. I won't even charge you. I feel like we've upped our level of friendship somehow, given that we are both in this room, practically naked."

He laughed, and we shared an amused look.

"I want something that represents me. Something abstract. Nothing too serious. Unless you want to draw me naked? I'll take that too."

I coughed out a laugh and averted my stare. I wanted to tell him that had been the first thought that reined in my head.

I'd drawn male figures in the naked form before, but those people I didn't know. Those people had been strangers. This would be totally different, especially since I was attracted to him.

When I didn't respond, he said, "I'm kidding, Charlie. We've crossed all kinds of boundaries today. That would be a whole separate and new level of boundary crossed that I don't think HR would approve of. You know what? Draw one for Nana too. She has all these scenic paintings in her room, or actually ... I'll actually take that one of the guy with his penis hanging out. Nana has a funny sense of humor that way."

The way he talked about his nana made my heart full.

I loved how he cared about his nana's diet, cared about what she thought, cared about everything about her. How he was thoughtful even though she wasn't in the room. It was endearing. And sweet. And made me realize he was more of a family guy than he led himself or others to believe.

"And this ..." He made his way toward an abstract sculpture that was half the size of my body on top of a pedestal in the corner. To be honest, it was hideous.

"Yeah, I think I should stick to painting."

"Whatever it is, it's interesting."

The sculpture was made from plastilina clay, which was a sculpting clay. The figure was supposed to be a stick-figure model raising her hands to the ceiling. Her arms pointed to the sky.

I stood and followed him to the figure, remembering that day in class when I had been having the most difficult time getting the clay to move and form where I wanted it to. "I thought I was an artist, so that meant I could do it all. Nope. This sculpture obviously proves that."

"Shh. It's interesting. Is she pointing to the sky?" He touched the slender part of her arms. "Is she supposed to be holding something?"

"Nope. Those are her fingers." Which looked like she had Cheetos in her hands.

"Oh." He laughed.

"Yep. And this right here was supposed to be her elbow." My fingers touched at the place where her elbow should be if the clay had cooperated. She was supposed to be worshipping, and it just looked like she was standing weird, as though someone had punched her and she was screaming for help.

A chuckle escaped him. "And this?" He touched her midsection. "What is this?"

"That's supposed to be her stomach, but the clay dropped a little, so it looks like she has testicles." I giggled.

"And this?" He poked at her neck.

The statue teetered, and a series of events happened as though it were in slow motion.

As we both stepped forward to steady the statue, we bumped into each other, knocking the statue over. We both bent down to catch it but failed as the statue teetered over, fell to the floor, and cracked in two. In the process, my robe flew open, and somehow, his towel got undone. We tumbled to the floor in one heaping mess, his naked body on top of mine.

"Omigod! Omigod!" I pushed at his chest, and he stilled above me, eyes wide, as though he was in shock. His penis was on my thigh. "Connor!"

He stood, but the towel was gone. I watched his impressive wanger swing from side to side as he extended his hand to help me up, but too bad my robe was wide open, and he was blatantly staring.

I tore my stare away from his cock and wrapped my robe around myself. But when I turned to my side to get up, the back of my robe was bunched up, and it exposed my bare ass. I groaned, pulling it down.

What did Connor do?

He simply laughed.

"Ugh." I had no words.

"Don't tell HR about that one," he joked.

My eyes met his as he wrapped himself up again, and I scowled. "Not funny, Connor. I just felt your big ..." My eyes went to his package underneath the towel. "Against my thigh!" I groaned.

"You're really great for my ego, Charlie. My big ..." He let out a low laugh.

Gah! How did he think this was remotely funny?

Heat rushed to my cheeks, and I turned in the other direction. "I'm sure you know how to let yourself out."

"Charlie ..." I could feel him following me. "It was an accident. I'm just trying to make light of a very uncomfortable situation."

I walked straight into the bathroom and shut the door behind me. I locked it, mortified beyond belief, resting my back against the door.

Knock. Knock. Knock.

"Charlie ... I'd like to say I'm sorry, but I'm not."

He was laughing. Little bastard was laughing.

I shut my eyes tightly. "I quit." Because, how could our relationship go back to normal after we rubbed uglies? I scratched my temple.

"Don't say that." His tone turned serious now. "It was an accident. A horrible, embarrassing accident that will never, ever be mentioned again. Okay?"

I huffed.

"Charlie, I promise. It will be like it never happened."

His words were met by silence.

"Listen, I'm sorry that I tripped and fell naked upon your body."

"Connor ..."

"Okay. But you have to admit, it was kind of funny?"

"No."

A low tap hit the door. It seemed as though he was tapping his forehead against the door.

"You're not really quitting on me, are you?"

Another tap.

"Because I kinda need you."

Another tap.

"For this restructure."

After a silent minute, which seemed like forever, he audibly huffed.

"Charlie ... I'm going to leave. The rain seems to have died down a little. But I'm not leaving until you promise me that you'll be at work."

I kept silent, chewing on my bottom lip like it was my next meal.

"Please, Charlie. I'm not leaving until you promise."

Given what I already knew about him, I knew he was one stubborn man.

I opened the door and peered up at him through my lashes, frowning. "I promise. 'Kay?"

His eyes scoured my body, and it turned all my cheeks heated.

"See you then, Charlie."

I scowled. "Your clothes are in the dryer." I shut the door on him and let myself slip to the floor.

How is this even going to work now?

CHAPTER 12

CONNOR

I'D ALWAYS PRIDED myself on being headstrong, making a decision and sticking with it. I was the guy who had upped and left Chicago, determined never to come back. I was the guy who had wanted to rise to the director level at Financial State within a few years of starting. And so far, I'd never doubted my ability of sticking to my guns, but watching Charlie like I was a stalker straight up from a bad movie had me doubting myself.

I leaned against the wall, observing her interact with Nana. Part of me believed Nana broke her computer on a daily basis because she wanted to see Charlie. If I had to guess, I wasn't the only one charmed by the new girl.

Nana laughed at something Charlie had said and stuffed more cookies in her mouth. She was like the cookie monster on steroids.

But Charlie ... she was something else altogether. I couldn't stop thinking about her. All that bombarded my mind was her soft, naked body against mine, her perky breasts, the curvature of her hips, the little patch of hair ...

"What are you doing?"

I jumped back as Alyssa slid beside me.

"Shit, Alyssa," I hissed.

"What are you doing?" she repeated.

Her stare followed mine, and her smirk told me she knew what I had been doing—stalking.

"Watching Nana eat cookies. I'm going to stage an intervention soon." I cleared my throat and rubbed the back of my neck.

"Mmhmm. Sure."

Alyssa was one of the most perceptive women I'd ever met in my life. No one could bullshit this girl, so I wasn't even going to try.

"Anyway, did you want something?" I asked.

"Nope. I was going to grab Charlie for lunch ... unless you want to?" Alyssa lifted an eyebrow, smirking.

I shook my head, playing dumb. "Oh. We're not working on the rebranding again today."

"Oookay," she drawled out, this all-knowing look in her eye.

Great. She is onto me. Probably has been.

"All right, I think I'll talk to Nana later." I about-faced and got out of there like there was something very important waiting for me in my office.

I needed a cold shower. And stat.

———

About an hour before quitting time, I went to Charlie's desk because I wanted all this awkwardness cleared up. We had work to do, and sensibility had kicked in. We—more so me—

had to forget about everything that had happened between us. I had to forget about her hot body, the color in her cheeks when she was embarrassed, and the curiosity of making her turn pink in certain places after a night of rough—

Stop!

"Charlie."

She peered up at me from her desk, and her cheeks flushed all shades of pink. Unwanted thoughts filtered through my brain again.

I cleared my throat. "We need to talk."

She raised a hand. "Nope. If it has anything to do with what happened, I don't wanna talk about it. Forget it ever happened."

Believe me, I'd tried everything to forget, but nothing seemed to work.

"Okay, it never happened." I stepped into her, and my fingers itched at my sides. A strand of hair lay across her forehead, and I wanted to push it back so badly, but I held steady. "We have to work together and"—my eyes drifted to the curvature of her neck, and I swallowed—"I just don't want it to be weird between us."

She threw me a look, and I laughed.

"Okay, okay." I lifted both hands. "I just want it to be less weird between us."

She scratched at her forehead as though there were an intense mosquito bite there. "I just ..." She peered up at me and shut her eyes tightly. "Every time I see you, I just picture you naked. And we have to work together."

Me too. I don't just picture you naked. I picture a lot of other things.

"Charlie, open your eyes."

"No."

She pushed out her bottom lip, and all of me wanted to bite it.

"Come on."

She flipped her eyes open then, and at the span of green peering up at me, I could read all her emotions. She was nervous, scared, embarrassed.

"Hey." I angled closer. "It'll be fine, okay? It could have been worse."

"Worse?" She scoffed. "How?" She shook her head. "How could it have possibly been worse?"

True. She had me there.

I paused, thinking, and then added, "Wanker could have accidentally slipped in."

She blanched.

"See? Worse."

I tipped my chin because this conversation was going downhill by the second. "I bet you, by tomorrow night, when we're working on the campaign, me and my naked-ness will be the last thing on your mind."

I turned away before she had a chance to say anything.

If she is up to it slipping in ... that wouldn't be the worst thing in the world.

I blew out a breath.

Thoughts like that would only get me in trouble.

CHARLIE

The break room was empty, except for Alyssa, Casey and me. Although, notably, it was two in the afternoon, and we were having a late lunch.

"Can you believe him? I mean, why is he always here at the company and totally bothering me?" Casey flipped her brown hair over her shoulder. "I think he's stalking me. I'm going to get a restraining order soon."

Alyssa coughed out a laugh. "I think you like him stalking you."

Casey's eyes widened. "Absolutely not!"

And then went the bickering back and forth on Kyle and how Casey had invited him to stalk her.

I tuned out Alyssa and Casey, not on purpose, simply because all I kept thinking of was our meeting tonight ... alone in the conference room. The initial shock of embarrassment had died down, but hell, thinking of Connor and me alone, until the wee hours of the morning, with Chinese food, had my nerves shot.

My knees bounced as I stared blankly at my sandwich, all of a sudden not hungry, when I peered up to see Connor in an all-pink outfit. Pink bow tie, light-pink shirt, and even pink pants.

Alyssa busted out in laughter. "You look like a stick of pink gum. What the hell are you wearing?"

His eyes were strictly focused on me, and I laughed.

"Did you lose another bet?" Casey asked, girlie giggles escaping her. "What did I tell you about betting against Kyle? He'll never make a bet he's going to lose."

Connor turned around with an exaggerated effect and motioned to his shoes, which were also pink. "And for your information, I didn't lose a bet. We're revamping the factory uniforms with the rebranding. This is one of the options. Why not do it all?"

He sat right next to me, and all my body heated. Even in all pink, he was unbelievably masculine, this strength oozing out of his pores, in the strong set of his shoulders, his confident smile.

"What do you think?" he asked me.

"It's ... pink." I laughed.

"It's cheesy. That's what it is," Alyssa added. "Anyway, I have to get some work done today." She pushed her Tupperware and silverware into her designer lunch bag and stood.

When Casey stood Connor put his hand on my leg to still me.

Heat. Holy hecka, heat spread throughout me. My gaze dropped to the table, warmth spreading to my cheeks, no doubt flaming my face red.

"I need to talk to Charlie about our rebranding session tonight."

Casey waved a hand. "Okay, have fun."

"Okay. See you guys soon." Then, Alyssa smirked. After a slow nod, she winked.

What the hell was that?

When they were out of sight, Connor turned to face me. "So, we're still on for tonight?"

"Yep. I just need to go home and grab my sketchbook. Then I'll come back to the office."

"Chinese food sound good?"

"Yep." I crumpled up my sandwich bag, my gaze strictly focused on the bag in my hands, on the table, anywhere but meeting his eyes.

"Charlie, are you going to answer only to the table?"

My eyes flipped up to meet his. "I'm ready for tonight. Chinese is okay." And then I laughed because he did look ridiculous. "Right now, I have to go. A thing called work calls to me."

I walked to the garbage, and he followed.

"Do you like the outfit?"

"Honestly, it's over-the-top crazy. You're not going to

make everyone in the factory wear that, are you? 'Cause that's straight-up cruel." I laughed.

"No. I think people would quit. Plus, I really wore it for you."

The smile from my face slipped, and he answered my silent question.

"And now, you'll no longer picture me naked. Instead, you'll picture me in this pink outfit." He wiggled his eyebrows as though he were so sure. "See you tonight." After he tugged at the strands of my hair, he about-faced, and he was gone.

No longer picture him naked?

Yeah, right.

Highly unlikely.

CHAPTER 13

CHARLIE

"HEY," my mother called out.

My hand was on the door and I was on my way out of the house; going back to the office. I'd been purposely trying to avoid her, grabbing breakfast on my way to work this morning.

When I thought of my artwork in the trash, I wanted to cry all over again. I tried to dim this anger I had toward her, but it festered deep inside of me.

"Charlie," she called out again when I didn't answer.

Slowly I turned around.

She approached, bringing me my water bottle and the small gesture caused my heart to tighten. She handed it to me, and I tossed it in my oversized purse.

She tucked an escaping strand of hair behind my ear and smiled.

"I missed you this morning, Honey."

I swallowed down the hurt and pain and forced a smile to match hers. Missed me? *I miss you more, Mom.*

Maybe she didn't know what was being thrown out? Maybe someone else threw my paintings out?

That was a possibility. It could be.

I didn't want to start an argument or worry that I hurt her feelings, like so many times before—too many to count—so I bit my tongue.

"I just had to be at work extra early today and it'll be a late night tonight as well. I'll be having dinner at the office. I just came home to grab my sketchbook."

The smile slipped from her face and she stepped into me, reaching for my hand. "Okay, but we'll have to schedule dinner, just the two of us. I miss my girl."

I squeezed her fingers between mine. "I love that idea."

Part of the reason that I wanted to do this exhibit was to showcase all my artwork, all in one place so she could see it all at once. Then maybe seeing everything and witnessing everyone admire my work, she'd realize that this was not just a hobby for me, that it was built in my bones—to create.

"Remember that day that I told you I have something special planned?" I asked. "You blocked out that date, right?"

"Of course." She ran one hand down my cheek, pinching my chin. "It's already blocked."

Automatically I wrapped my arms around her and melted against her chest. The movement surprised her, but a nanosecond later, her arms wrapped fully and tightly around me. I sighed into her, needing this, needing this closeness from her.

⊏⊐

We were back at it, in the same room—the conference room —with the same Chinese food, brainstorming on concepts.

Concepts. Concepts. Concepts.

But things were different now, weren't they?

Luckily, we were so deep in thought that there was no room to think of him naked. Not when we were on a deadline.

I sat Indian-style on the chair, tapping the pen against my chin, my gaze flickering between the Chinese food down the long mahogany table, my sketchbook, and at Connor beside me.

He pushed his hands through his hair and stared at the blank paper in front of him.

When I laughed, his head peeked up, and he frowned. "What's so funny?"

"You."

He smiled then and straightened in his seat. "What do you think is so funny? That we have been at this forever, yet we have nothing? That my marketing team cannot think of a single thing to bring our ideas to fruition?"

"No. Just that you are too serious. Way too serious. I mean, this should be kind of fun, right? We need to display that in the product."

He overly sighed and leaned back in the chair, rubbing at his eyes as though we'd been at this for hours, though we were only thirty minutes in.

I shoved at his shoulder, and that same discouraged look crossed his features.

"We're so going to rock this. I feel it." But did I feel it? The thing was, maybe we were thinking about this too deeply, and ideas would flow if we eased up a little. "Can you pass me some fried rice?"

Connor stood, scooping fried rice onto a paper plate. After passing me my plate, he served himself one.

Then, it hit me like a wave of ideas and words in my

brain, the way creativity was sparked and a waterfall of ideas pushed through.

Food. Family. Chocolate.

Family eating.

But how did the family get to that place?

I dropped my plate on the table and began to sketch, emptying my ideas on the blank canvas.

It was crazy how my fingers could not keep up with the amount of ideas filtering through my mind.

"What are you drawing?"

When Connor peeked over my shoulder, I flipped it over and shot him a look.

"I'm not done, and you can't ruin my flow here."

"Just let me take a peek." There was a seriousness in his tone that was quite comical.

"No." I pointed to the Chinese food. "Keep eating. This might take a while."

I stood and moved to the opposite side of the twenty-person boardroom table and continued to draw.

And draw.

And draw some more.

Thirty minutes later, I was still at it, but I had the concept. I smiled big as I continued the last finishing touches.

"Charlie ..." Connor began again.

This man was impatient beyond words.

"I'm almost done."

He had finished all the fried rice, crab rangoons, and noodles and now was pacing the room.

I blocked everything out. Every. Single. Thing.

And I concentrated on the sketch.

When I flipped the page, he inched closer. "You done?"

"No." My head hadn't lifted from the paper in front of

me, and my pencil moved of its own accord. "Why can't you just let me work?"

"I'm not a very patient man. You should know this by now."

He inched closer like a stealth cat, but I ignored him because I was nearly done.

I felt him looming above me, trying to take a peek, and I laughed. "Get away, you stalker man, you." Then, I shut the sketchbook. "Done." I stood and lifted my chin. "But since you don't listen to directions very well, I'll show you it tomorrow."

"Charlie!" There was a little whine to his voice that was hella adorable.

When I hid the sketchbook behind my back, a small smile crept up his face.

"You are not being very nice."

My smile was bigger. "I never said I was nice at all."

"Charlie ..." His tone sounded like a parent scolding a child. "Do you know what I hated most when I was younger?"

There was a long pause after his sentence, and I shrugged as if to say, *What?*

"I hated Kyle teasing me. He'd tease and tease and take my toys and taunt me, and I'd stay utterly quiet until ... I'd had too much."

I laughed, which was the wrong move because he took a step forward, his face dead serious, devoid of any humor.

"I've eaten all the Chinese food, paced a short marathon on this floor, and been patiently waiting for you to finish."

"Patient? You?" I scoffed. "Well, that's your view on things. Let's test that patience, shall we? I'll let you see it tomorrow morning."

He reached for my sketchbook, and I squealed as I propelled myself toward the opposite end of the room.

"Connor!" I lifted the sketchbook above my head, taunting him.

He shook his head. "I'm a whole head taller than you. Just give up now."

"You'll see it tomorrow," I said, putting it behind my back again. "Just be patient." Seriously, I had just been kidding before, but now, I was considering keeping the plans from him, given his foul mood.

"My patience has just run out."

He dashed in my direction, but I swerved toward the other side of the room. Connor's stance changed, and he charged forward once again as I moved toward the center of the boardroom. He closed in with a slight smirk on his face, like he was going to win. Determined, I veered right, but I was too slow as he closed in on me.

I hopped on the table and lifted the sketchbook above my head as though I were the queen of the universe with a sword lifted high.

He reached for the hem of my long shirt. "Get down. You're going to hurt yourself."

"I have insurance."

"You're so annoying," he said, a smile surfacing.

He surprised me by getting on top of the table too. He was indeed a whole head taller than me, so I brought the sketchbook behind me. Thank God for tall ceilings.

"Charlie ..." There was his scolding tone again.

Stepping backward, I tripped on my own feet. Half my body was off the table, and when Connor tried to save me and pull me back from falling, he toppled on top of me.

Instead of relenting, I clutched the sketchbook to my chest. "No!"

I could feel his body on mine, his chest against my chest, his hips against my hips. Connor was a few inches from my face, and our breathing met in a slow tempo.

His hand gently brushed against my hip and I inhaled deeply. His eyes locked with mine, and the whole world stopped.

My breath caught in my throat, and everything around me turned vividly clear.

His scent filled my nose, and I felt an undeniable urge to close the gap between us to kiss him, to see how he tasted.

CONNOR

She was beautiful. The way her eyes squinted when she was laughing, the way her hair was splayed into tiny ringlets above her head. My stomach muscles tightened, and having her beneath me had me thinking dirty, dirty thoughts. My eyes flickered to her lips, and shit, I wanted to taste her, feel her lips against mine.

My cock hardened as I pictured us in the same position but with her naked beneath me.

Yep, not happening.

I cleared my throat and stood before she felt my hard length pressed against her.

I extended my hand to assist her, unable to meet her eyes.

All this sexual tension was about to make me combust.

Why was the universe throwing us together, naked first and now on top of each other the next?

I would have taken this as a sign, if only I believed in signs.

When her hand met mine, my cock pressed harder

against my jeans, as though she were the On button of his happiness.

I shifted and pulled her up.

Man, oh man. I needed to remind myself why I shouldn't date my employee.

1. *We worked together, which would complicate things. Our creative sessions would include brainstorming on the different positions I could make her come.*

2. *I couldn't get attached to anything here. This wasn't my home. New York was.*

3. *Lastly, I was leaving. I didn't want to start something with Charlie and not be able to go anywhere with it because that was where it would go—nowhere. Not when we were in different states.*

I simply stared at her, unable to speak. I shifted my weight to my other foot and scrubbed a hand through my hair.

After a beat, she lifted the sketchbook in the air and sported a victorious smile. "I won!"

Fuck. I am a goner. Because she was so damn cute.

I reached for the sketchbook, but she didn't relent. I tugged her forward, and her soft, delicious body slammed against mine.

I groaned.

After a sharp inhale, her eyes flickered downward. Yep. If she hadn't known that I had a boner before, well, now, it was pressing against her side.

Our eyes met, locked, and loaded.

I felt the compression of her chest, the rise and fall against mine.

I wondered if her nipples were hard, if she was aroused by being in my vicinity.

But the moment the thought registered, she pulled the

sketchbook, turned around, and dropped it on the table. "So ... yeah ... here it is." Her voice was shaky, and when I approached her from behind, I could feel the heat emanating from her body.

Charlie. Charlie. Charlie. Why are you so damn tempting?

"Well, show me." I tipped my chin toward the drawings, forcing myself to concentrate. "What do you have here?"

She turned to me, and her smile widened as a fire lit behind her eyes. "So, when you passed me the Chinese food earlier, I pictured us years from now at a kitchen table with kids, a family."

"Oh, did you now?" My voice was teasingly light.

"No." She shook her head, and a blush touched her cheeks, staring only at the sketches. "I didn't mean you and me. I meant, a family. Any family." She motioned to the sketchbook of a young man in front of a house, a house with a porch. With her pointer finger, she pointed to the young man with a box of chocolates behind his back. "It all starts with chocolate."

"The first date," I said.

"Yep. Always with chocolate and flowers," I added.

She flipped the page, and a couple was sitting at a table, seemingly on a date. "And chocolate with every anniversary going forward."

Another page flip.

"Until he gets down on one knee." She beamed.

The picture depicted the man on bended knee, behind his back the same box of chocolates and a ring box.

The pictures were endless.

My God, I could kiss this woman right now.

This is it.

This will work. This is the concept we needed.

"At their wedding ... on their dessert table."

"And when she's craving chocolate during pregnancy ..."

"Junior's Valentine's Day class party at school ..."

She stepped back and fiddled with the edge of the notebook. "What do you think?"

She wrinkled her nose as though she was unsure, but how could she be unsure when the idea was absolutely brilliant.

She let out a slow breath when I hadn't said a thing, and her next words came out lightning fast. "So, I thought it would be a way to hit on people's emotions and make it multigenerational, touching all ages. You can film the scenes in commercials to show the board and your father."

There was a long, pregnant pause, and she shifted. I liked making her uneasy. It was comical in a cute kind of way. She thought I hated it.

She scrunched her face. "Say something. I mean, if you don't like it, we can start ..."

I reached for her hand, so warm within mine. "It's fucking amazing. It's exactly what we need. It's perfect."

She was perfect.

Why did Charlie have to be beautiful and funny and smart and too damn attractive?

I let her hand fall between us, knowing I shouldn't hold her or touch her or think of her. I couldn't fall for her, and a one-night stand could not happen because, knowing me, I would want more.

"It's perfect. And I like the commercial idea. I don't want anybody knowing about this, just a select few. We'll film it ... together."

CHAPTER 14

CHARLIE

I KNEW it was gonna be a bad day. Because not only had I spilled my coffee on my suit this morning and I had to change, but my mother had also questioned my choice in clothing, so I'd changed again. If that wasn't an indication of a bad day, then I didn't know what was.

I could have ignored her, but my mother would and forever be my soft spot. After seeing my mother at her ultimate low with my father's death, I had an undying need to make her happy. And if all I had to do was change my clothes to make her happy, then that was a small sacrifice.

And if the coffee and double change in wardrobe hadn't been enough, I'd walked into the bathroom, sat on the toilet, and realized there was no toilet paper. I'd had to sit there and air-dry for at least five minutes to make sure a stream of piss wouldn't trickle down my leg.

I should've just stayed home and called in sick.

Should have. Could have. Would have.

When I stepped into the coffee room, Casey had two cups of coffee in her hand.

"Hey, hey, hey, Charlie. How are you today?"

She extended one in my direction, and I smiled big.

Her cheery demeanor lightened my day just a tad.

I inhaled deeply, taking the first whiff of coffee in. "I love you."

"I aim to please." She rested a hip against the counter.

After bringing the cup closer to my lips, I tipped back the cup and almost choked. This was not Starbucks, and this was not Dunkin' Donuts. This was some new concoction that tasted like old coffee grinds that had been sitting in the coffee machine for months.

"It's that organic place down the street," she said, smiling as though this coffee were a good thing.

I coughed and ran to the sink, spitting the coffee out.

Alyssa walked into the room with her venti Starbucks, and all of me wanted to jump her for it. "I told her not to try that shit."

Casey lifted her nose. "They're a small mom-and-pop shop. We should support small businesses."

"I don't disagree but not at the expense of your stomach." Alyssa sipped her coffee, and jealousy surged within me. I wanted to tell her about my day and maybe convince her to give me her cup of joe.

I stared at the brown recycled coffee cup and frowned. "I need some sugar." And a lot of it.

Casey scrunched her nose. "I tried to add that coffee creamer. The organic kind. But, yeah, it didn't really add any taste."

I walked to the counter and grabbed the sugar container, shaking it. I noted that it was empty, and my frown deepened. All I wanted was sugar—real sugar. With how this day had started out, didn't I deserve at least good coffee?

"It's okay. There has to be some sugar in here." I opened the cabinet, getting on my toes. "Or real creamer. Preferably a flavored one." I swore I had seen one in the cupboard the other day.

Casey assisted and opened the other cabinets that I hadn't checked. "Yeah, maybe I should try some real coffee creamer. A little bit won't send me over the edge. Anyway, I took my sugar test this morning, and it was fine."

Sometimes, I forgot that Casey was diabetic. I just always chalked up her eating habits to her being a healthy eater and being so slim.

"Casey, a good day always begins with coffee." Alyssa crossed her ankles and leaned back. "I know you're trying to be a good friend and buy Charlie some coffee, but just know that you're already a good friend to me. Don't go trying to buy me coffee."

Casey stuck her tongue out.

"Yes!" I lifted up the creamer and closed the overhead cabinet. It was just regular creamer, but I'd take it. After opening up my steaming cup of organic coffee, I scooped a couple teaspoons of creamer into the cup. "Did you find the sugar?"

"Nope, but I found peanuts!" Casey's face lit up as though peanuts were a staple food for breakfast. "I just can't get it open." She fiddled with the top. It was one of those containers where there was a silver ring you had to pull back.

"Why the hell are you going to eat peanuts at eight thirty in the morning?" Alyssa threw her a look. "Oh, forget it. Give it to me." Alyssa grabbed the container from Casey. "See here. It's not rocket science. Simply lift open and pull back." She struggled with the ring that she was supposed to pull back. The ring flew off, but then she pushed her finger in the slot and tried to manually pull the silver slit.

I gripped the counter as nausea hit me full force in the face. Because I saw it. Blood.

Not a ton, but enough.

It was as though the scene were happening to someone else. I saw the coffee slip from my hands. Casey screamed my name. Alyssa took a step forward and gripped my arm.

It was too late.

I hit the floor in a big, overwhelming, bone-crushing thud. And I blacked out.

CONNOR

Panic seized my chest when I walked into the coffee room. "What happened?"

"She fainted. Do you think she's dead?" Casey asked, her voice heightened with hysteria.

"She's definitely not dead. She's breathing, Casey. Chill out," Alyssa said.

My fingers automatically went to Charlie's neck, checking her heart rate. "Her pulse is elevated but nothing to be concerned about."

"Oh my God. Oh my God. What does elevated mean?" Casey screeched.

"Did you not hear him?" Alyssa yelled back. "He said that there is nothing to be concerned about."

"But she's not moving!"

"She fainted, you idiot." Alyssa tensed, her patience running thin. So was mine because now was not the time to freak out.

"I'm worried. Oh my God, what if she dies? We need to call 911."

"No, call the nurse," I shot out, needing Casey to do anything else but panic.

"Oh my God! Oh my God!"

"Will you shut the fuck up? You're making me nervous now." Alyssa stood and got into Casey's face.

"I can't. Oh my God. Charlie was a good person."

The faucet ran, and a second later, Casey yelped. "What the hell, Alyssa? Why did you throw water on me?"

"Because you're crazy. You're talking about Charlie like she's dead. Now, go call the nurse."

"There's no time. Maybe we should give her CPR?" Casey's voice shrieked on high alert. "Do you think it was the coffee I bought her? Maybe it wasn't the blood? Oh my God, I killed her with organic coffee."

"Shut up, Casey, or I'll tape your mouth shut."

The back-and-forth bickering between the girls was messing with my focus. "How long has she been out?" I touched her cheeks and her forehead and repeated the process.

Alyssa spoke up, "I mean, a minute or two. Not that long for sure."

Casey was still shocked and staring as though she were going to have a full-on panic attack.

I reached for my phone in my back pocket and dialed my secretary. "Hey, can you call Randy to the coffee room? Tell him it's an emergency."

Randy was the nurse on staff.

"This is all my fault. Why did I want peanuts this early in the morning?" Casey's face crumbled.

And Alyssa looked like she was going to beat someone with a bat. "Are you crying? Stop. Your. Damn. Crying."

"Oh my gosh, I think she's dead. She's dead. She's dead." Casey gasped. "No, I really think she's not breathing. She's not breathing. She's not breathing."

I felt under her nose and could see the rise and fall of her chest. "She's fine, Casey. Calm down. She's fine. She's breathing. She's just a little bit unconscious right now."

"No. No, she's not. You think she is, but she's not. The longer she's out, the more the brain damage will affect her." Her sobs turned hysterical. "Start CPR. Start CPR. Start CPR."

"She doesn't need CPR, you idiot!" Alyssa yelled back.

"Charlie, you'll be okay," I whispered, placing a large palm on her cheek and leaning in closer.

Where was Randy? I blew out a breath, anxiety seeping in.

"Please, Connor. Save her. CPR! Now! Now! Now!"

Without warning, Casey shoved me down, and my lips met Charlie's.

"What the fuck, Casey? You're batshit crazy!" Alyssa said.

I wasn't prepared for Casey to shove me down toward Charlie. But most of all, I wasn't prepared for Charlie's lips to be so soft, so warm, so damn sexy.

I shouldn't be aroused when she was on the floor and knocked out, but, shit, her lips were so damn delicious that I couldn't for the life of me figure out why I was still lip-locked with her.

It was only Alyssa's loud clearing of her throat that broke me from my thoughts.

"Ahem," she said.

I pushed to a kneeling position. "She's breathing." *Shit, but was I?*

My eyes flickered back to her lips. Plump. Pink.

I shook my head through the fog. "Where the hell is Randy, and why is he taking so long? And why did Casey do that? Where is she?" When I directed my question to Alyssa, I noticed she was smirking.

"I sent Casey to get him."

Oh, crap, I hadn't noticed.

For a hot second, I had blocked everything out, and the only ones who existed were me and Charlie—and her lips.

I reached for her palm and squeezed it. I didn't know if it was meant to comfort her or me so that I knew she was warm and fine and alive.

"Glad you checked she's all right." She leaned back against the counter and crossed her arms over her chest, a knowing look on her face.

I hated how Alyssa was always perceptive. All. The. Time.

I cleared my throat. "Casey pushed me toward her." My voice shook. It was almost as if I had to think of an excuse to give her because I had been kissing Charlie for more than a few seconds. And I wanted to do it again. Those lips were meant to be kissed, to be tasted, to be devoured.

"Yep. Saw that. Saw you down there for a while, being thorough." The side of her mouth quirked up.

I didn't have a chance to respond to her because Randy stepped into the room.

I reluctantly released Charlie's hand and made room for Randy, who knelt beside her with his medical bag.

"How long has she been out?"

"Five minutes or so," said Alyssa.

I gripped my own arms, forcing myself to stay still, because I wanted to hold her again, hold her so badly.

Randy took a small, clear vial out of his medical bag. He

twisted the top of the vial and placed it under Charlie's nostrils. "Did she hit her head?"

"She did." Casey sniffled.

"What is that?" I asked as he waved the vial in a circular motion under her nostrils.

"It's ammonia, an inhalant for those who suffer from syncope."

What the hell was syncope?

"Loss of consciousness," he replied, answering my internal question.

"Come on, Charlie," I caught myself saying.

I held my breath. I thought the whole room did.

After a few seconds, her eyes flickered open, then shut, and then opened again. Her eyebrows scrunched together.

"Yeah ..." Her voice was groggy. "I'm sorry. I fainted."

I took a step forward, but before I reached her, Casey basically pushed Randy aside and dropped onto Charlie, crushing herself against Charlie's body. "I'm so glad you're okay."

I released a long, heavy breath and lifted my stare to the ceiling. "Thank God."

With a tip of her chin, Alyssa nodded with a heavy smirk on her face. "Thank God indeed."

She knew.

She knew about my deep infatuation with Charlie.

There was no doubt.

CHARLIE

At five years old, when the nurse had taken my blood, I'd passed out at the doctor's office. That was how I knew I had an aversion to blood. And at every single appointment— yearly, I must add—I fainted. It was an automatic response.

It didn't matter if I closed my eyes or they laid me down. I always fainted.

Was it at the sight of blood? Was it the smell of blood? Was it all in my brain?

I didn't know.

All I knew was that I couldn't see it, smell it, or even imagine about it.

I had been known as Fainting Charlie in grade school. It was a widely known nickname throughout my childhood. All those science projects where we had to dissect frogs and worms in class, I had to opt out of those. I'd had a doctor's note.

It was the oddest thing, fainting in front of my coworker-friends and boss man. I usually fainted around doctors or my parents but never in front of other people. I could predict when an episode would happen because it was always during annual appointments, and I avoided any situation where I would possibly have an attack. Donating blood events? Nope. Never going to happen.

When I had gained consciousness, Casey had treated me like I was a little child, bringing me lunch the next day and buying me my favorite Starbucks coffee. Alyssa had simply nagged Casey for crowding me.

But what was weird was Connor. He couldn't stop looking at me. His nonstop staring had heightened since the pool house. I mean, I'd turn, and he'd just stare—not in a creepy way, but in a way that would make my cheeks warm and make me feel as though he was picturing me more than naked in the pool house.

Which was absurd because, this was me, and he was hot millionaire Connor.

I was fixing Mr. Nelson's computer. I was reaching to

the back of his monitor when Connor's voice almost had me tipping the whole screen over.

"Charlie."

I jerked to a standing position and steadied the screen. "Yep?"

His eyes flickered to my lips and then back to my eyes.

And, yes, he did that often as well. I wondered if my lips were dry or chapped or bleeding. When I licked them, his eyes would always flash.

I took my ChapStick out from my back pocket and reapplied it. Going by this rate, I'd have to buy the economy pack of ChapSticks by the end of the week.

"Can you stop by my office to talk about the marketing plans?"

I blinked up at him. "Yep. Sure. Let me just finish up here."

His eyes scoured my body, and I warmed everywhere his eyes touched.

Good gosh, were we ever going to get to the place of normalcy? I knew we had been close to making out on the boardroom conference room, but we were semi-normal after that. Maybe this was how it was always going to be.

If you could call this undeniable attraction to him as normal, but it was as though he felt it too.

I mean, I'd felt his hard length against my thigh. Unless I'd imagined it.

"I'll wait for you in my office."

"Okay."

He backed away backward, which was odd because, hello, walking backward. And his eyes were on me the whole time.

He knocked into a desk before laughing, turning around, and trekking back to his office.

I checked out his fine ass. If he was going to seemingly check me out, I wanted to enjoy the view as well.

CONNOR

I had an issue. A major damn issue.

I couldn't for the life of me get Charlie out of my system. When I closed my eyes, she was there, and I preferred to be in the office, so I could see her more. My infatuation for her had heightened to unhealthy proportions. Shit, I had to jack off multiple times to tame the ever-loving hard-on I got every time I thought of her. At this rate, there was no doubt I'd have carpal tunnel soon.

When she entered the room, I took her in.

Her hair was up in a flowy ponytail, and her pants hugged her hips and ass as though they were cold. And I was jealous of her damn pants. I wanted to keep her ass warm.

I swallowed.

"Sit down." She walked toward me.

In my head, it played out like a porno—her moving stealthily like a cat toward my chair. In my dreams, she'd hop on the table and strip for me.

"So ..." I adjusted my collar. *Is it hot in here?* "I was thinking"—*about your lips, about your body*—"about the commercial we are going to do."

She laughed as she took out her ChapStick and reapplied it to her lips again. The tint made her lips fuller.

I blew out a breath.

"I haven't even agreed to anything yet," she said.

She'd come up with the grand idea, and we were going to do a commercial to launch the concept to the board. I wanted us to film the commercial and present it together.

"I'm the face of the company, so it makes sense that I am involved, and it was your idea, so it only makes sense that you are involved."

"I'm not commercial material." She pulled her hair over her shoulder, twiddling with the ends.

"Whatever. You're beautiful ..." Our eyes locked again, and I cleared my throat. "It'll translate well on camera. And you know the emotion that we are trying to convey. Charlie ... please. I need you."

Weren't those the words of the century? How many times had I uttered those words to only this woman?

I needed her to help with the marketing efforts and rebranding of Colby Chocolates, and now, I needed her to film this commercial.

She chewed on her bottom lip like it was her favorite meal, and I wanted to help with the process and tell her I was hungry too.

"Okay. I'll do it."

Her agreement had my eyes flying up to meet hers.

I didn't think I could smile any bigger. "Perfect. We'll go shopping tonight."

"Shopping?" Her eyebrows flew to her hairline.

"I've secured the production company to film this commercial. I've talked to my friend Wyatt about booking the locations where we are going to film. He owns a small production company and is the director for short films. I've also hired hair and makeup, but we need to go shopping for what we have to wear."

She blinked again. "Can't I just wear what I have?" Then, her eyebrows furrowed. "Forget it. I have nothing to wear. Tonight?" She straightened in her seat. "Okay. Tonight works."

"Dinner first and then shopping?" Man, I was asking her on a date.

My question took her aback. "You mean, boardroom Chinese food?" There was a glimmer of amusement in her eyes.

I hadn't meant Chinese food in the boardroom. This woman deserved a nice dinner, and if I was being truthful to myself, I wanted to take her out.

"I was going to take you somewhere special." I cleared my throat again, suddenly nervous.

When a panicked look crossed her features, I added, "You've done so much for me ... for this company. The least I can do is take you to a nice dinner."

She looked down at what she was wearing. "Tonight?"

"Yes. And what you're wearing is fine. I'll take you somewhere nice but not anywhere that requires a certain dress code, okay?" *There will be time for that later.* As soon as my subconscious brain filtered that thought, I paused.

Charlie stood. "I still have work to do, but I'll see you after work. I can't do dinner tonight though. I have plans with my mom."

My stomach sank and kept on going.

"All right, I'll see you after work." With Charlie, I realized I'd take what I could get.

CHARLIE

We were seated at the lunch table. Casey slid a Potbelly's sandwich my way. My favorite—a meatball sub.

"Hey, girlie pie," she said, plopping besides me.

Alyssa followed her in, sitting in her regular spot.

In a matter of weeks, I'd fit snuggly into their friend group, and I couldn't be happier.

With Casey and Alyssa, the trying phase had ceased, and I was allowed to just be my true self. If it was silent, which it hardly ever was because we had Casey, it was fine.

I unwrapped my sandwich. "You don't have to buy me lunch every day. You need to stop feeling guilty for things that were out of your control. I've been fainting at the sight of blood since I was five."

"I want to feed you. Then, I'll know you're healthy and alive and here," Casey replied.

Alyssa rolled her eyes. "If you haven't noticed, Casey will forever be the motherly type and try to take care of you. If you're getting free lunch out of it, keep reaping the rewards."

Connor entered the break room, and we all peeked up. He walked toward the vending machines on the far end of the room but not before his eyes met mine. I waved, and he smiled.

He greeted a few more of his employees right by the vending machines, and when he made his way back, he stopped at our table.

"Hey." He waved again. "How are you feeling?"

His eyes flickered to my lips, to my hair, to my chest, and I held my breath.

There were boundaries, and I wouldn't cross those boundaries with the boss man. And I got that going shopping was needed to film the commercial, but an added dinner right before seemed like it was asking for trouble.

And it seemed as though he were only addressing me and no one else at the table.

Alyssa and Casey shared a glance, and I warmed from the inside out.

"Good." I averted my stare and bumped shoulders

against Casey. "This girl has been buying me lunch ever since the fainting incident."

"Meatball sub. Is that your favorite? I wouldn't peg you as a meatball girl. Maybe sausage. But not meatball." His smile widened.

"And what is that supposed to mean? Can you just look at a woman and guess if she is a meatball or sausage girl?" Alyssa laughed beside Casey. "What would you peg me as?"

Connor's cheeks reddened. I'd actually never seen him turn red in the face. That was my job in our relationship.

"You ..." He pointed to Alyssa. "You're a meatball girl." He shifted his stance and held up his bag of Fritos. "Lunch. And I'd better get to it." He about-faced and walked straight out of the break room.

Casey and Alyssa shared their knowing glance again, and it drove me insane.

"What is going on? What's up with the looks, and what is it with Connor acting all strange?"

I knew why he was acting weird. I didn't want to throw in there that the reason was because, oddly, we always found ourselves in compromising positions—first naked and then on top of the boardroom table.

"Maybe ... it's because of you." Alyssa unwrapped her own sandwich, undoubtedly some fancy steak sandwich from a high-end bistro that wasn't a chain.

"Me?" I croaked.

"Or not you per se. But maybe your lips."

Casey shoved Alyssa, and her sandwich slipped from her hands and fell to the table. "Hey!"

"Ugh, do you have to constantly embarrass me? I'm already buying her lunch to make up for—"

"For shoving Connor's face down to Charlie's face. Niii-ice," Alyssa drawled out.

I stilled, and the blood drained from my face. "Shoved Connor's ..."

Alyssa turned to face me fully. "Our smart and nervous Nellie Casey was convinced you weren't breathing and needed CPR, so she volunteered Connor to do it."

"What?" I couldn't breathe. Could. Not. Breathe.

No wonder why he had been acting bizarre and kept staring at my lips.

"And I bet you he wants to do it again," Alyssa added.

"No, he doesn't."

Alyssa took an overly big bite of her sandwich. "Please ..." She began to chew. "I know men. I know how to read them. I should know. I grew up with three brothers." She swallowed and gave me a pointed stare. "And I know what they want. And I also know Connor." She leaned in and gave me a wink. "And I know what Connor wants—and it's you."

CHAPTER 15

CONNOR

THE LIMO BROUGHT us to the stores down Michigan
Avenue. My mother had a personal shopper, so I had called
up Susan to tell her we were on our way.

Lunch had been awkward, and I could admit that. But
ever since lunch, Charlie would not meet my eyes.

When I addressed her, her eyes would look past my
shoulder, at someone passing by, at the ceiling, at the floor,
anywhere but at me.

It was frustrating as hell because ... I couldn't stop
staring at her.

It was like the more I stared, the more beautiful she
became.

"Where are we going exactly?" she asked, looking
outside the window.

"Macy's on Michigan. I contacted my mother's personal
shopper. She's meeting us."

"Okay." She nodded. "Does she have the concepts of
clothing?"

I angled closer, and when my knee touched hers, she jumped, but then her eyes locked with mine.

"She does have the concepts. First date. Proposal. Wedding."

"Okay."

Her eyes stared out the window again, and I'd had enough.

"Hey." I reached for her hand without thinking what I was doing. "Why are you acting so weird?"

She stared at our intertwined fingers, and her breathing turned rapid. "I don't know. Casey and Alyssa were saying some stuff about me fainting ..."

When her gaze made it out the window again, I leaned in closer.

"Can you look at me? Charlie ... please."

She nodded, but she was skittish. "They said we kissed. Or more so, our lips met. And now, you're acting strange, which in turn is making me act strange."

My eyes flickered toward her mouth. Bad idea because she flushed red.

"Sorry." I shook my head.

"Why are you acting so weird?"

I focused on her hand in mine. Her hand was so soft, so feminine, and I couldn't stop picturing her fingers wrapped around my cock, stroking it—

Stop!

And because I needed this torture to cease, I wanted to know if she was attracted to me too.

"Because I can't stop thinking of your lips and kissing you again."

Her mouth slipped ajar, and without thinking, I ran my finger along her bottom lip.

I heard her deep intake of breath, and I decided I

couldn't take it anymore, so I closed the gap between us and kissed her.

For real this time

When she was awake and fully conscious.

CHARLIE

Oh my God.

Connor's palm snaked behind my neck and brought me closer. He was kissing me. Me? And it was a mind-blowing, toe-tingling, amazing experience.

The kissing lasted forever, as though I were floating in an abyss of bliss, and I never wanted him to stop.

With his other hand, he reached for my waist and guided me to his lap until I was straddling him.

I breathed him in, his strong, masculine scent, and every part of me tingled with want, of more of this man.

Connor Colby was an excellent kisser, as though he'd studied the art of kissing in school, mastered it, and now taught classes on the form.

I crushed my breasts against him, and he moaned against me. When he flicked the seam of my lips open, I let him in.

Our tongues tangled in a mesh of fiery passion.

We were all lips and kisses and hands everywhere.

I pushed my core against his hardness underneath his slacks, needing some sort of friction to tame this ache deep down in my belly. But it wasn't enough. I wanted more. I wanted closer.

His lips nipped a path down my neck and back up to my ear. "I've wanted to kiss you forever."

Our make-out session went from zero to a hundred in a matter of seconds.

After his lips moved to mine in delicious torture, he cupped my breast and flicked his thumb against my hard nipple that he could feel against my silk shirt.

"Your breasts are so damn perfect."

With my free hand, I untucked my shirt and guided his hand to my breast where he fondled me through my bra.

When I went on my knees, he pulled up my shirt, and he took my breast in his mouth. He sucked and teased me through my bra, and I wriggled above him as his head disappeared under my shirt.

But then the door flew open.

"Sir. We are here." It was the limo driver.

I fell backward off his lap and took Connor with me. But too bad his head was still underneath my shirt.

The door shut as quickly as it'd opened.

When Connor tried to disentangle himself from my breasts and shirt, he jerked back so fast that the buttons on my shirt popped out and flew everywhere.

"Shit."

"Fuck," he uttered.

He pulled me back into his lap, and when our eyes met, we started to laugh and laugh until full-on embarrassment hit.

My cheeks reddened.

What is going on here? I needed to get my hormones in check and stat.

I stared down at my chest, pulling my shirt—sans the buttons—closed. "What are we going to do now?" Panic settled in my gut.

"You can go shirtless. I won't mind." His tone was full of humor, but this was nowhere near funny.

I frowned. "That's not going to work, and your limo guy

just saw his boss fondling his employee in the back seat of your limo."

Realization set in. He'd gotten to second base, and at the speed we had been going, there was no doubt he'd have been at third if his limo driver hadn't stopped us.

"Steven won't say a word." Connor pulled me against him and kissed me.

He wanted a second round, and it took all of my willpower to place a hand on his chest.

"Connor"—I met his eyes—"what are you doing?"

"Kissing you." A sexy, lusty smile was sported on his face.

But kissing would eventually lead to other things ... and he was leaving. And this shouldn't be happening. He was the boss man.

"Where is this going?"

My question seemed to sober him up. Quick.

"I'm attracted to you, Charlie. And based on a minute ago, I think you're attracted to me too."

I hopped off his lap and sighed. Connor was all man, thinking like a man and acting impulsively on his feelings.

"You're basically my boss."

"I know," he sighed. His eyes flew shut, and he rubbed at his brow. "I've never felt an attraction this strong. I knew I shouldn't have kissed you, but I couldn't control myself."

His revelation had me cheesing, big and corny style. It was a good thing he had his eyes shut.

"I know. I'm pretty much hot stuff," I scoffed sarcastically.

His eyes flew open then. "You have no idea just how much."

"Yeah, whatever." I waved it off like I did every time someone complimented me.

His hand went to my waist and squeezed. "Seriously, Charlie. When I'm around you, I'm like a teenage boy with his first girlfriend. Literally, I walk around with a hard-on all the time around you."

My gaze flickered toward the ground. My heartbeat was pounding so hard that it sounded off, like a gun going off in my ears.

"You absolutely have the right to know that I want you. But I'm also leaving. Chicago is not my home. Never was. Never will be."

And as high as my insides had soared like a blown-up balloon, his words popped and inflated that balloon.

"Okay." I appreciated his honesty. It hurt, but I appreciated it. But I also knew then ... that nothing could happen between Connor and me.

He was leaving.

Here.

Me.

Which meant he wanted a casual relationship, which I did not do.

CHAPTER 16

CONNOR

MY WORDS in the limo had created distance between Charlie and me. I could sense it. It was in the way she walked a whole foot away from me, or when I tried to reach for her, she'd jerk away or flinch.

And it killed me. Just getting a taste wasn't enough. And though every sane part of me needed to stay away, all I wanted to do was touch her, kiss her, and do other things that I shouldn't be thinking about.

I had lent her my suit jacket to cover herself up, and just knowing that she was almost bare beneath it had me salivating.

We entered Macy's and went straight to the eighth floor to meet Susan. I'd only met Susan a few times when I happened to be shopping with my mother for a tailored suit.

Susan wore a fitted black pantsuit, and her hair was slicked back into a low ponytail.

"Susan, this is Charlie. There was a mishap to her shirt .Can you help her get another one before we get started?"

Charlie's cheeks brightened, and she smiled awkwardly with all teeth. "Mishap in the limo ... I mean, my shirt, it got stuck ..." Her stare dropped to the floor. Rattled, she tried to think of a lie, an excuse as to why her shirt had suddenly lost its buttons.

Yes, my head had gotten stuck in her shirt, but I didn't want to add that.

Susan smiled and straightened, beckoning a flustered Charlie forward. "Not a problem. I have a few silk shirts down this aisle."

Susan didn't ask about Charlie's shirt mishap even though she noticed that Charlie sported my suit jacket. Susan wasn't dumb, but I was thankful for her professionalism.

Ten minutes later, we were seated on a plush couch at the wedding area. Mannequins wearing these elaborate white bridal gowns surrounded us.

Odd how we were here, but given that there weren't any desks anywhere in the shopping area, this was the only place we could discuss ideas on what we needed.

Charlie took out the sketchbook and portfolio. When she flipped open the page, my eyes widened.

"You drew everything out."

I mean, she'd redone the loose sketches from our meeting in the boardroom to a more detailed portrayal of what needed to be taped. Right next to each scene, she had drawn out the props needed and the dress that each character would wear.

"I have some samples of the material I want to use," Charlie added, getting swatches of cloth out.

I blinked at her. I didn't know why I was surprised. She was an artist through and through, and her attention to detail was unprecedented.

"For the female, I like the feel and texture of this material for the date scene." Smiling from ear to ear, Charlie extended a piece of blue fabric with tiny flowers on it to Susan. "I want her to wear a nice, flowy floral shirt and white skirt that accents the flowers on her shirt."

"I have something perfect for your vision," Susan said.

Charlie bounced on her seat, excited, and flipped to the next page. "For the male, I'd like him to wear a solid blue polo shirt and dark-washed jeans." She turned to face me and pointed to her sketches. "Sorry ... this is your gig too. How do these look?"

She looked great, and the way her silk shirt stretched over her full breasts had me shifting in my seat.

"Connor?" Charlie lifted a brow, and my eyes moved to meet hers.

I blew out a breath. I didn't remember the last time I'd wanted a woman this badly. It wasn't because the lack of sex I'd had. I'd had casual friends with benefits in New York, and it hadn't been that long, but shit ... it seemed as though it had been, given my nonstop thinking of being inside Charlie.

"Yeah. It's perfect. You're perfect ... I mean, your vision is perfect." *Screw me sideways. What is my issue?* I tipped my chin toward her sketchbook in her lap. "What else do you have?"

"Oh! So, here ..." She flipped the page and pointed to the picture where the male was down on bended knee. "I think we should have her in a flowy dress, and the proposal should be at the lake or some sort of beach." She pulled the fabric stuck between the pages and extended it to Susan. "I was thinking chiffon."

"Yes. And maybe a touch of organza?" Susan's face lit up as she rubbed the fabric between her fingertips.

"You ladies do what you need to do. I'm just here to pay for whatever decisions you make." Because what was the difference between organza and chiffon?

Susan laughed. "And paying is what you shall do." She addressed Charlie, "Is that all?"

"Oh ... the wedding scene. I don't have anything particular other than a beach-themed wedding, so maybe something not too big or ballgown-style but a fitted piece." She lifted her shoulder to her ear. "But I think that's it."

Susan clasped her hands together and then stood. "Okay, now, the fun part begins."

When I squeezed Charlie's knee, she stiffened, and her gaze dropped to my hand. The smile on her face slipped, so I jerked back my hand. There was a sadness in Charlie's eyes—something that hadn't been there.

I could see what mixing business and pleasure was doing to her, which wasn't good. But besides her over-the-top good looks and her charming personality, she had insane talent that made her beyond irresistible.

But ... boundaries. Personal space. *Isn't that what they'd taught us in grade school?*

"Let's get started, shall we?"

"Yeah," I muttered, knowing that it would take continuous effort to try and stay away from her.

CHARLIE

"I love it!" I stood on top of the circular stand where mirrors outlined the room and lifted my hair to a ponytail.

I could picture it—me opening the door, seeing my date standing there, a little nervous. His hands would be behind his back as he held the chocolates and flowers within his fingertips.

"Do you love it?" I liked the feel and look of the light-blue floral top with short sleeves capped with ruffles at the end. It was girlie and pretty and totally the look I was going for.

"It fits you perfectly," Susan added.

I turned to Connor to get his approval, and he had the same dang gaze in his eye. Every time I caught him looking at me, heat would rush to every part of me, and arousal would set deep in my belly.

He ran one shaky hand through his hair. "Yeah. Looks great."

We'd just started shopping, yet he wasn't really talking, only responding with one- to three-worded answers to my questions.

I knew we'd have to talk about the elephant in the room once this shopping session was over, but I just wanted to get the look right for the commercial and get the rebranding done because numerous families depended on it.

"I really need you to have an opinion, Connor. Like, a real one instead of, 'Fine. Looks good,' and, 'That works.' " I placed my hands on my hips. "I'm not doing this for me. I'm doing this for you, your company, the employees at Colby's."

He cricked his neck from side to side. That was a new thing too. It was like he couldn't sit in his own skin. He stood and shook out his legs, as though they were cramped. "This is the thing. You're smart and creative, and you've got these concepts spot-on." He walked toward me and stood right by the circular pedestal, staring in the mirror in front of me, brushing his hand on my waist, leading up to my shirt and tugging at the end. "It looks great, and I'm not only talking about the shirt."

Good God, if I'd any doubt that Connor was flirting, I knew he was most definitely flirting now.

And it only continued.

Susan had picked out a cute, delicate white linen skirt. The front stopped at my knee, and the back was longer and flowed out like a little train. His eyes scoured my body as though he hadn't eaten breakfast and I was his next meal of choice. I felt his presence everywhere. I took back my earlier command on him having an opinion because, now, he had a lot of opinions, and they all were coupled by him touching me.

"Susan ..." Connor's fingers brushed at the hem of the dress.

Goose bumps prickled up my legs, and I held my breath as his fingers inched higher. "I think we should take the hem up." He lifted the fabric to my thigh, and his fingers were light as a feather, but he might as well have gripped it in a tight vise because I felt his touch everywhere.

His eyes never left mine as he inched it higher. "It's the first date after all. He's determined to impress her, and she's determined to impress him."

His eyes were filled with lust, and it was as though I could imagine the thoughts running through his head.

My breaths turned shallow, shorter, and I swallowed. I ran my fingertips along my neckline back and forth and forth and back again, and his eyes flashed.

"Maybe she's not going to give it to him on the first date." My voice was husky soft. "Maybe shortening this dress will give him the wrong idea."

"It won't." His fingertips inched higher. "And he'll wait. As long as it takes, he'll wait until she's ready."

Heat flushed my cheeks, and I exhaled a heavy breath. The insane part of my brain wanted him to take me in this room, not caring that Susan was watching. But I knew that was crazy. There was no way I would ever have sex with him, knowing it would lead nowhere.

I bit the inside of my cheek, getting blood to rush there instead of the rush of blood deep in my belly.

"I think it's fine as is." I tugged the fabric away from him, frustrated with myself, mostly at wanting him so badly. "Susan, I think this is it."

But when I turned around, Susan was nowhere to be seen. She must have sensed all the sexual tension that filled every corner of the room.

Connor noticed she was gone too, because he stepped into me and reached for my hand. "Charlie ..."

The way he said my name was like heaven and a curse all at once.

When I tried to pull my hand away, he tightened his hold and pulled me closer.

"What?" I snapped, beyond annoyed, mostly sexually frustrated.

"I'm tired."

"Then, go home. We're practically done. All we need is a wedding dress. I can ..."

"I'm tired of fighting my attraction, my feelings toward you."

The muscles in my neck tightened, and I simply stared at him.

When I didn't say a word, he continued, "I know you're attracted to me too."

No comment. No words left my mouth because how the hell was I going to deny that?

I was in a zombie-like phase. When he tugged me forward, I moved on his command.

His palm squeezed my hip, and my chest pressed

against his. When his eyes flickered toward my lips, my nipples pebbled beneath this shirt that I didn't own.

"It's so hard, being near you and not kissing you." His nose grazed my chin and up my cheek, making it up to my ear. "I'm really trying to fight this ... fight this attraction for you. I need you to stop being so damn cute, crazy brilliant, and funny, so I can stop wanting to touch you ... everywhere."

I hadn't realized I was holding his arms so tightly. I wondered if he would bruise.

I closed my eyes as his lips made it to the crook of my neck. "We can't. You're ... my ... boss."

"I'm not technically your direct boss who does your reviews. What happens between us has nothing to do with how your reviews will go."

I exhaled when he pressed into me, making sure I knew very well how much he wanted me. "You're leaving ..."

He pulled back, searching my face. "I am." There was a finality in his tone as though he'd just said the sky was blue. "Can't we just have some fun and see where this goes?"

I blinked up at him and stepped back as a heavy sensation settled in my gut. It was like a slap directly in my face. "You mean, sex without attachment."

"Charlie ..."

I smiled, and it was a sinister smile because that was what it was—just sex unless he expected me to uproot my life here and leave my mom and move to New York to be with him when we hardly knew each other. *Yeah. Right.* And I was sure that wasn't what he was offering.

"You said I was smart, right?" I lifted my chin, staring at him straight. The arousal I'd felt for him a minute ago was all gone as though it'd never happened. "Well, then, stop talking. You know what? I'm tired too. I'm just going to let Susan pick the wedding dress based on my concepts."

I moved past him, toward the exit of the fitting room, but he caught my wrist again.

"Charlie, stop!"

I flipped to face him. "No. You stop. Stop touching me. Stop thinking of me in any way other than your employee. Stop it all." I shoved an angry finger into his chest. "You begged me to help you, help you save your parents' company, and I have and continue to do so. And what do I get for it?" I threw up my hands. "An offer to sex you up with no strings attached. Thanks, but no thanks. Even with you and your promise to introduce me to Nui Cavinchi and her colleagues, you can hold nothing over my head." I got in his face so close that I could feel his warmth radiating from his body. "I have way more self-esteem and self-worth than you give me credit for."

I swiveled toward the door, practically running out.

CHAPTER 17

CONNOR

I FELT like the biggest dick, only thinking with my dick. She'd had every right to call me out for being a jackass because I was. Hands down, I was.

She insisted that she call an Uber, and I had to practically beg to just let the limo drive her home so that she could make it to dinner with her mom. I told her that the limo would drop me off at the office and that she'd have the ride all to herself. We'd only be in the limo for a short period of time.

It took some convincing, and I didn't blame her.

I opened her door, and she slid in the limo. I was formulating my words because, *Sorry I'm a horny bastard and I want your body*, was a shitty apology, and I needed my next words to count. Not only so she'd continue to work on this project with me, but also because I wanted her to know that I didn't think of her as some side chick who could get me off and then I'd be done with her.

I respected her more than that.

Her head was turned toward the window, as though I weren't in the car.

"Charlie ..." My heart raced in my chest. Yes, I wanted her, but right now, I wanted forgiveness more.

"Hmm?" she said, not taking her gaze from the outside.

"I'm sorry," I rushed out. I had this grand speech on how I valued her and that I was sorry that I had come on to her like that, strong and over the top. But my words got stuck in the back of my throat at the need to have her forgiveness.

"Yep," she said.

I stared at her profile, the strong set in her jaw, her focus at nothing in general out the window.

"I'd never hold anything above your head. I will introduce you to Nui because you're talented, and everyone needs to see what you have to offer the world." I swallowed. "It's one of the reasons I like you ..." My voice trailed off. It was the truth. I was attracted to her, but I was also attracted to her crazy, beautiful mind and her creativity.

"I can't deny"—I cleared my throat—"that I want you." I shifted and wrung my hands in my lap. I swore I had never experienced such anxiety before. I'd stood, giving speeches, in front of boardrooms, in front of the whole Colby's factory, in front of companies in New York on the verge of failure and I was their only hope, but, shit, that felt like peanuts to this. "And I'm sorry." My eyes dropped to the floor of the limo. "I don't know what else to say."

Her shoulders began to shake. *Is she crying?*

Shit. Shit. Shit. I didn't want her to cry.

She swiped at her eyes, and panic seized me. *What a way to end the night.*

But she wasn't crying.

When she turned my way, I realized that she was

laughing—not a little laughing, but full-on stomach shaking, tears-running-down-her-cheeks laughter.

My lips turned up because she was so damn adorable.

"I can't deny"—broken huffs left her lips—"that I want you." She cowered into herself, and when she met my eyes, her laughter heightened. " 'And I'm sorry'?" She threw up both hands. "What kind of apology is that?"

I laughed then because she was right.

Man, I knew I had it bad because I inched closer even with everything that had happened to us earlier. "Well, it's your fault really ..."

Her eyes narrowed, but amusement was heavy on her face.

Our knees touched, and my smile widened to match hers. "I'm sorry that you're so damn creative and that I need you to save the company that I probably can't even save myself. I'm sorry that your artistic ability is out of this world and that I'm honestly jealous. I wish I had an ounce of creative juices in my genes."

"Well, you know"—she flipped her hair over her shoulder in an exaggerated effect—"not everyone can be like me with my big, fat creative brain."

I laughed. "But most of all, I'm sorry that I can't keep my hands to myself—or my eyes obviously. I'm sorry I'm just so attracted to you. I am not joking when I say I don't recall a time where I've felt an attraction this strong for anyone else before."

Her smile slipped, but I kept on going, trying to keep it light but be serious.

"And I promise you, I won't touch you or make you feel uncomfortable in my presence. I value our friendship, Charlie. Above all, I want to keep that intact."

All humor vanished from the limo, and I sucked in a breath, waiting for her response, any response.

"Forgive me?" I added when there was a long stretch of silence between us.

After a beat, her shoulders relaxed, and she bumped her shoulder against mine.

"All's forgiven." Her eyebrows scrunched together. "And just because we're in the oversharing mood, I've pictured you having me on your desk multiple times."

I coughed and choked on my own saliva.

She patted my back and grinned. "But we can't go there. I can count my sexual partners on one hand." She lifted two fingers.

I nearly choked again. I mean, seriously, how was this woman still single?

"And I don't want my third to be with someone who is leaving."

"Yeah, I get that." There was a strand of hair over her left brow, and I wanted to brush it away. My fingers itched at my side, so I fisted my hands instead. "And I'll promise to stop staring, only if you promise to wear baggy jeans all the time and not bounce when you walk. I can't stop staring at your, ahem ..." And now that I knew how they felt in my palms, I wanted—

Stop!

"I do not bounce."

My eyes flickered to her breasts, which were covered underneath her coat. "You do."

Her arms crossed over her chest. "Stop staring at my boobs."

My eyes moved to her face. "See, done."

"Can we really do this?" she sighed and bit her lip in a

nervous gesture. "Be platonic friends when my nipple was in your mouth only hours before?"

My eyes flashed, and I licked my lips. "We have to, right?"

She nodded. "Yes, we have to."

CHARLIE

My mother and I went to one of our favorite restaurants, Pasta Scolla. We were seated at a corner booth. I cherished times like this, just the two of us alone, spending quality time together. But my mind kept wandering to what had happened earlier with Connor, to what had transpired between us. There was no way I could go there, not when he was leaving and we had to work together.

"So, how was work today, honey?"

Wasn't that the loaded question of the day?

"It was interesting ..." I began because I couldn't exactly tell her the whole truth. So, I told her what I could. "So, I'm helping with the rebranding and packaging of Colby Chocolates. That's why I've been working weekends."

She leaned in, her elbows on the table, one eyebrow raised. "Rebranding? Is that related to your job or added work?"

I reached for a piece of bread in the center of the table, swirling it in my oil. "Added work, but it's okay. The CEO's son asked me to help with ideas. He saw a mock-up I had done and—"

"The CEO's son?" Her eyes narrowed. "Why would he ask you, the computer tech girl, to help him with that—with rebranding and stuff like that?"

"I told you, he saw some of my drawings and—"

"I'm just saying, honey ... he's a guy, and I'd be a little—"

"I'm not naive, Mom." My jaw tightened. I knew where she was going with this. Yes, Connor had hit on me, but that was way after our initial deal. And even though he wanted to take things further, I'd definitely put him in his spot.

My mother's face softened. "I'm just looking out for you, honey."

"There's no reason to." I wanted to tell her that after my father had passed and before Richard had come along, I'd been looking out for the both of us.

I placed my hand over my mother's on the table and squeezed. "I know. Thanks, Mom."

After the waitress placed our pasta dishes on the table, I reached for my fork and smiled. "This is nice. I feel like we never get alone time anymore."

The corner of my mother's mouth tipped up. "Yeah, this is nice. I'm glad your schedule worked out."

"Remember when you and Dad would take me out for school-ditch days?"

She shook her head, her gaze focusing on her plate. "That was all your dad. Gosh, I'd try to convince him out of that, the importance of school and all, but, yeah ... now that he's gone, those were the most memorable times." Her voice quieted to a hush.

There were times that I didn't want to bring him up at all because it just reminded my mother that he was no longer here. But there were so many memories that I wanted to reminisce about.

"Remember when he kidnapped me in the middle of the day? He walked into school and told the front desk that it was an emergency. I had so much anxiety until he drove to pick you up, and we went to the zoo." I laughed, reliving the memory. I must have been eleven or twelve.

My mother shook her head. "I'd always pretend to be

mad at him for doing such things, and he'd always try to make me laugh to break me out of my mood."

"It worked though, didn't it?"

Her eyes crinkled at the sides as she met my gaze. "Each and every time." She let out a sad sigh.

We were quiet for a long beat.

"I miss him," I said.

She nodded, her stare dropping back to the table as she twirled her fork in the tomato-sauced spaghetti.

Why could she never say it back? Was it a sin to miss him? I knew she did. She could still be happy yet miss my father.

I was always walking on eggshells when talking to her about my father, about my paintings, about everything. I hadn't even confronted her about the paintings that had been thrown out in the garbage, not wanting to get into an argument.

"I scheduled this dinner to also talk about a few things." My mother forked the first of her pasta into her mouth. "I know you've made some friends at work, and I'm really glad you're making a life here."

"You should meet Alyssa and Casey," I gushed. "Casey talks nonstop. Alyssa is crass but sweet. They are like yin and yang—opposites in every sense of the word, but they balance each other perfectly. I'd like to think I'm the even-keeled one."

My smile hurt my cheeks. Seriously, they were my silver lining in this world of new and crazy. I stuffed more pasta in my mouth, letting it fill my belly with all its goodness.

"That's great, baby. Really. But I'd like it if you spent some time with Sandy too."

I felt the color drain from my face, my fork stilled midair.

Sandy? This dinner is about Sandy?

"She's been having a hard time with the transition, and I'm trying to make it easier for her ..."

Easier for Sandy? My whole body tensed. "How about me?" I said, finally finding the strength in my voice. "Don't you think it's been hard for me, moving here, leaving my friends, my life, everything I'd ever known?"

"Honey"—she raised her hand—"you didn't even let me finish my sentence. I just want to make this easier for the both of you. It's been a transition for all of us. Me included. All I'm saying is that you try."

My fork pinged against my plate. "I have been trying. I've been trying since the very first day when we were introduced, and she said one word to me. It was as if I were talking to myself the whole time. She's the one who's evil."

"That's harsh."

"Harsh? What's harsh is purposely making my life hell. How about scheduling dinners with just you guys, purposely not including me?"

"It's not like that."

"How about stealing my shit? She stole my suit on my interview day. Or how about how she purposely ordered a zero for my bridesmaid dress when she knew I wouldn't fit in it? She consistently tries to undermine me. She doesn't want me to even be in the house—even if it's the pool house. She consistently reminds me that it's her father's house, not mine." My tone heightened with fury with each breath that left my mouth. I wasn't going to waste my words, even telling my mother she'd only gotten me the job because Richard had firmly asked her to.

"She's just having a hard time through this. You're more resilient."

"Why? Because my father died? Is that why you think

that? That I can handle more because of all that I've been through?"

She opened her mouth to speak, but I was done.

"No, Mom. Sorry, but I've tried numerous times. I'm done trying."

I had no more energy to give that woman. I was done with one-sided relationships.

My chest tightened as I forced my gaze back down to the plate of uneaten food. This—her plan for us time—was all about Sandy. I should've canceled with my mother and had dinner with Connor instead.

CHAPTER 18

CONNOR

MY FOOT TAPPED on the floor as I waited for the coffee to brew in the coffee room. Employees scattered around in typical, normal workday fashion.

Over the next few days after our limo event, I had been good. As good as I could be. I set everything in motion. Called up Wyatt, one of my friends from Chicago who owned his own production company, a subsidiary of Bill Hendrick's Corp., the biggest media conglomerate in the world.

I had to save money where I could, so using my contacts was my best bet in doing that.

The best way in keeping things platonic between me and Charlie was to avoid seeing her altogether, but shit, that was hard. I settled on just keeping our run-ins short and sweet, but it didn't stop me from walking to the break room, knowing all the girls would be there, and getting some chips from the vending machine even though I didn't really want chips.

It didn't stop me from walking the floor, just to get a glimpse of her.

I'd spend more time with her when we filmed this weekend.

I told myself time and time again that staying away from her was for the best. Given her minimal experience with men, any drawn-out sexual relationship would not be good, especially with me leaving. I didn't want her wanting more, and I didn't want to hurt her in any way.

Platonic.

Friends.

Yep.

Good.

"Connor."

I jumped when I heard Nana's voice behind me.

"You totally blanked out there."

I smiled because there was no way you couldn't when she was holding a dozen cookies before nine in the morning.

I lifted an eyebrow and tipped my chin toward the box in her hand.

"I'm going to die anyway. Might as well let me die happy."

I shook my head and laughed. "Nana, you will live to be over a hundred. I'm not having it any other way."

Besides arthritis, Nana was healthy as my parents. I noticed she'd gotten a little slower through the years, but that was it.

"Yes, gotta see my great-grandkids."

She was funny; I'd give her that.

"It'll be a while until that happens. I have to find a girl first. Then, I have to get married—"

"Then, hurry it up! Your nana is not getting any younger."

I laughed and then poured myself a cup of coffee, watching the steam rise to the top.

And Nana grabbed it from me and winked. "Thank you."

I groaned. "Nana, that's my favorite mug."

"Now, it's going to be my favorite mug." She patted my cheek. "My birthday is just around the corner. Did you get my list?"

This woman, I swore, she was a handful. Her list was endless and consisted of every beauty product from her favorite cosmetic line and her favorite foods. Every year, Kyle and I would clear her list.

"I did." I took a paper cup and poured myself a second cup of coffee. "Is the house ready for the company party?"

"Yes. And why haven't you stopped by? You've been here for weeks, and you haven't seen me after work."

"Nana, if you're complaining about spending more quality time with me, I've taken you to lunch almost every day."

"Your parents miss you, Connor," she deadpanned, her tone telling me that I should know exactly what she meant. "Do you love your Nana?"

"Is this a trick question?" I knew exactly where she was going with this.

She pinched my shoulder and twisted, just as she had when she scolded us when we were younger.

"Nana! Yes, I love you."

"Then, you're coming to dinner at the house."

When I opened my mouth, she threateningly pressed her thumb and forefinger together in a pinching motion.

I raised a hand. "Fine, fine, fine." I conceded because I'd suffer an evening with my parents just to make my favorite person in the whole wide world happy.

"Hey." Charlie walked in, stopping when she saw me.

"Hey." I swallowed.

It felt as though it'd been weeks, not just days, since I last saw her. She looked stunning today. Her hair was in a half-ponytail, and she wore this green shirt that brought out her eyes.

"Hey," I said again, shifting from one foot to another. I guessed that was the only word I had today.

"I didn't have time to grab some coffee this morning on the way in, so I ..."

She sidestepped me to get a cup, but I offered mine.

"You can have this one."

Her eyebrows rose. "Oh ..." She took the steaming cup from my hand. "Thanks." She tiptoed to look behind me. "Is there any powdered creamer left?"

I grabbed it from the counter and then extended it to her.

"Thanks." She tipped her chin toward the cup filled with silverware. "A spoon, please."

"Yeah ... sure." I plucked one from the cup of spoons and turned to face her but noticed that her hands were full. "How many scoops?"

"Three is fine." She wrinkled her nose in the cutest way. "Or four or five. I like creamer in my coffee."

I spooned it in her coffee, stirred it, and took the creamer from her hand.

I was awarded with a beautiful smile that lit up her face.

"Thanks, Connor." Then, she turned to someone beside me. "Cookies for breakfast, Nancy?"

Shit. I'd totally forgotten that my grandmother was in the room.

"Yes. Breakfast of champions. Cookies and coffee."

"Well, enjoy." With a single wave, Charlie was out of the room.

When I turned to my nana, she was sporting an all-knowing smile.

I laughed. "What?"

"Mmhmm."

"What's that look for?"

She walked out, and I followed.

"You didn't offer me any coffee, but you single-handedly gave her yours."

"Whatever, Nana. It's just coffee."

"Mmhmm," she said louder, throwing me that same *I know what you are up to* look.

"And where is your cup, Connor?"

I stopped mid-step, turning to look at the coffee room, now a few good feet away. *How did I end up giving up two cups of coffee and walking out with none?*

Before I had a chance to answer her, she said, "And you gave her your creamer too. I think great-grandkids might be sooner than you expect."

"Nana, no ... no dirty jokes from you. Please," I said, searching to see if anyone had heard her.

"Mmhmm." Then, she kept on walking—with my cup of coffee.

CHAPTER 19

CHARLIE

I UNWRAPPED my sandwich and took an overly large bite.

I tried to concentrate on what Casey and Alyssa were talking about, but it was hella hard to do so because ... Connor Colby.

Holy sexual tension.

It was like my body knew what it wanted, even when my brain was screaming that it was bad for me. Like that extra cookie when I'd already had five.

Ever since his hot, naked body had pressed against mine, then the boardroom incident, and then the limo make-out session, I couldn't shake him.

And after seeing him this morning, it was almost too much to take.

It was as if the universe were trying to tell me something, but it was too bad I didn't believe in signs.

"Did you see this?" Casey's head was nose deep into a rag mag she was reading. The headline on the magazine was about groupies. "Seriously, look at this. They've interviewed all these groupies who stalk all these rock stars and sleep with multiple of them. Like one big sex pool. Ugh ... nasty." Casey's finger followed the words on the paper. "This one slept with Hawke Calvin from Def Deception. Hmm." Then, she laughed. *"Best lover out of all of them,* she said."

Alyssa cut up her steak beside her. "Why be such a prude, Casey? Don't tell me if you had a chance with Hawke Calvin, you wouldn't sex him right here on the table in front of"—she raised her knife and circled the room —"everyone."

"Uh, no!" Casey's tone heightened.

"Please, Miss Thang. You need to broaden your horizons, live life to the fullest, yada, yada, yada, and all that jazz." She took a small bite of her steak. "And bang all the rock stars when you get a chance."

"Nope. I'm not that type of girl."

Alyssa raised an eyebrow. "What kind of girl are you saying I am then?"

"I don't judge your choices in life. But mine are different."

"Listen, you've only had one dick all your life. Multiple times, but the same dick nonetheless—*ouch!*"

Casey flicked her finger at Alyssa's shoulder, like moms would do to their kids when they were in trouble.

"Hello? Just blab my whole entire drama to the whole entire world," Casey snapped.

Alyssa rubbed at her shoulder and then leaned into Casey with a seriousness in her tone. "If you ever"—she leaned in closer—"ever do that again, I will tell the whole world who that one dick belonged to."

Casey blanched. "You wouldn't."

Now, I was curious. "Who is it? Someone you dated in college?"

"No," Alyssa answered for her. "High school."

"Shut up," Casey said.

"It's okay, Casey. I've only had two dicks in my life. One in high school and one in college. I'm not that far behind you."

Alyssa turned to me, dropping her fork from midair. "How are we even friends? Life is short. Seize the day. Monogamy is overrated."

Casey tipped her chin toward Alyssa. "She's only like this because her brothers have shielded her all her life and she wants to rebel."

Right. Three brothers. Only girl. I couldn't imagine.

"Please," Alyssa scoffed. "My brothers are the reason *man-whore* is defined in the dictionary."

"Anyway, who was it?" I turned to Casey. "Who was the special man?"

"Kyle," Alyssa said without hesitation, not missing a beat.

Well, shit.

Casey flicked her again.

Alyssa's eyes widened before Casey threw one arm around her and covered her mouth.

Casey smiled toward the people around us and announced, "Carry on. Alyssa almost choked on something." She patted her back. Hard.

Then, she plopped down on her seat with a full-on pout on her face. "You were sworn to secrecy," she whined.

"This is Charlie, and she is part of our circle of trust now." Alyssa 's eyes narrowed. "She won't say anything. Right, Charlie?"

I shook my head. Lost for words. *Seriously ... Kyle?*

"I won't say a thing. But I thought you hated the guy."

Alyssa spoke up again, "She hates him because she loves him."

"Oh my god, Alyssa. Listen to yourself right now. How does that make any sense?"

Alyssa raised a finger. "See ... years ago, Kyle liked Casey, and Casey liked Kyle. Kyle popped her cherry and wanted more."

"No, he didn't," Casey interjected.

Alyssa's stare turned incredulous. "He did want more, relationship-wise. You assumed he didn't. And because you wouldn't talk to him, he moved on. Now, you hate him."

"I don't hate him. And he's not the settling-down type."

Alyssa shook her head. "See, you never had a conversation about it. You, and you alone, assumed he wasn't the settling type."

"You don't know how it was," Casey argued.

Alyssa nearly rolled her eyes. "I know how you are, Casey. You told me what went down." Then, she turned to me. "This is why you should always set expectations at the beginning of the relationship." She threw Casey a look. "Don't assume what he wants or what it's going to be. If you have an adult conversation on what it is, no one will get hurt."

"I'm not hurting," Casey said.

"You might not be hurting, but you're not over it."

"I am so over him." Casey crossed her arms over her chest. "And I don't hate him."

Alyssa overly huffed. "You are not over him, and I know he's not over you."

Casey's cheeks turned all shades of pink. "What do you mean, he's not over me?"

"He's not over you." Alyssa lifted her eyes to the ceiling.

"Why can't people see the obvious? Am I the only one who can see what's blatantly happening in front of me?" Then, she turned to me as though that comment was meant for me even though we had been talking about Casey seconds before. "In every relationship, set expectations. Then, you'll know for sure you will not get hurt. Know what you want. Know what it is. Don't assume. That's my many-dicks advice for you." Then, she winked.

CONNOR

Dinner with the parents. *Could anything be more painful?*

As Nana spooned more Mexican rice onto my plate, I smiled at her. Nana would forever want her grandkids fat. Period. In her mind, a well-fed grandkid was a happy grandkid. When Kyle and I had been younger, she'd follow us with broccoli and apples. She and Papa would have snacks ready after our games. So, when Nana placed a heaping pile of refried beans on my plate, I didn't even flinch. But when she added double the amount of food to Kyle's plate, I smirked. He stayed utterly silent, knowing he couldn't win with the woman who could beat her opponent down with words.

My mother scrunched her face. "Ma, look at Kyle. He's already too big as it is. Quit feeding him."

Kyle lifted a muscle and flexed. "That's right. Mom just called me swole." He threw me a look. "Jealous?"

"Yeah, you got me," I said.

Nana's gaze flickered between me and Kyle. "I think you need more food, Connor."

She spooned another heaping serving of beans on my plate, and the whole table laughed.

"You need to be benching more, not eating more food."

I picked up a chip and threw it at his head.

"Hey. Mom, did you see that?" Kyle said, almost pouting.

Her eyes filled with an inner glow. "It's good to see all of us together."

I didn't know when my mother had loosened up, when she'd stopped caring about the business as much.

A few years ago, care packages had made it to my doorstep in Manhattan, and random *just because* phone calls had begun. I had known that was her way of trying, of reaching out. But I hadn't forgiven her then, but more and more now, seeing her in this element, lighter, laughing, I knew I just had to let some things go.

"So, how's the rebranding going?" my father asked above the mariachi band playing at the far end of the room.

But with my father, nothing had changed.

I knew my mother kicked him under the table because he jumped.

"Not now. Not during dinner."

My father quirked his head, unaffected. "Why not now? We don't see him enough as it is. I just want to make sure that we're not wasting all of our time."

This was my father—only caring about the end result. If I had gotten good grades and made the honor roll, if I had won that football game or the state championship.

He didn't care about the details, only the end product.

"Tom!" my mom scolded. "I told you ... not now."

"No, Mom, it's fine." I turned to my father, spooning some steak into my tortillas, unfazed. "You'll have to wait till the board meeting, but what we have planned is phenomenal. I'm working with our marketing team and Charlie, who is an artist. Her vision is nothing short of spectacular. It's exactly what we need to jump-start our sales."

He nodded, satisfied. "I sure hope so." His tone was terse, sharp, short—nothing that I wasn't used to.

"It is."

There was no guarantee, but damn it, Charlie's ideas and vision were on target. I wasn't a gambling man, but I'd bet all my money on Charlie—any day.

CHAPTER 20

CHARLIE

THE WORKWEEK WAS INTENSE. It was nine in the evening. Everyone was gone for the day, but I was working on refiguring the whole floor and installing the updates to our software. It was either do this all in one day or stay overtime multiple days when I had to get home and get to painting and preparing for my exhibit.

I walked into the office closet to look for more extension cords. The light flickered above me like it was going to go out real soon.

"Where the hell are the extension cords?"

It was a typical tiny office closet with cabinets lining both sides and boxes of random stuff. I dug to the bottom of one box in search of an extension cord. I swore, if there was a creepy-crawly in this box, I'd scream like a hyena.

The door opening caused me to look up. It was Connor.

"Oh." He closed the door behind him. "Hey."

"Hey," I said.

His body was bigger than life in this small room. His

eyes took me in from the little baby hairs by my forehead to my pointy heels, and my body reacted immediately. Warmth flushed every part of me, and it was difficult to get my next breath in.

"I was getting some staples." He ran one hand through his sexy hair.

"I was looking for extension cords," I whispered, dropping my gaze because, shit, he was too fine to look at.

Against the soft cascade light that flickered, he looked like Adonis in the flesh, an untouchable god who should be admired from afar.

Goodness, I needed to get a grip on my hormones, on reality, on life, on this situation.

"They're right over there." He walked right beside me and pointed to somewhere over my shoulder, but I looked and couldn't figure out where "there" was. "Right over there." He cleared his throat. "Excuse me."

He brushed past me but not before I felt every inch of him pressed up against me because this closet had not been built large enough for two people.

He reached over, grabbed the extension cords, and turned to face me. "Here." His voice was low and guttural.

A part of me was glad he was feeling all the same things I was feeling at the moment—pure, unadulterated lust.

"Thank you," I said, grabbing it right where he'd laid it —against my chest.

There was nowhere to move and nowhere to look but at him, so I closed my eyes.

He laughed then. "Why are your eyes closed?"

"Because you're too beautiful to look at."

Seriously, did I just say that?

Well, after the limo episode, there was no way to hide what I thought of him.

After a beat, when silence had spanned a few seconds between us, I opened my eyes and noted his eyes were closed.

"What are you doing?"

"Closing my eyes."

Now, it was my turn to laugh. "Why?"

"Because you're too beautiful to look at too."

His eyes flipped open then, locking on to mine. The air was sucked out of the room, and I couldn't breathe. I could not get my next breath in.

His eyes flickered to my mouth, and when my tongue darted out to lick my lips, his eyes flashed.

I could feel every inch of his hard body against mine. His thigh by my thigh, his chest by my chest.

"You can't use my line," I whispered, inching closer, not able to help it.

"Not even if it's the truth?"

Please, someone, help me.

I needed to resist.

Then, he shut his eyes again.

"I think I'll keep my eyes closed the whole time you're around." He let out a slow, shallow breath. "Maybe it'll help stop me from wanting you."

My heartbeat raced at his words, at his proximity.

It was taking every ounce of my self-control to stay away from him. To give in to my wants, knowing that this could end only one way.

But why did it have to end in my heartbreak? I'd never had a sex-only relationship with no strings attached. But just because I'd never entered into that type of relationship, that didn't necessarily mean I couldn't handle it, right? We were all adults here.

If I knew the stakes in the beginning and if the rules

were all laid out on the table, I'd know what to expect—or in this situation, what not to expect—and not to expect more.

And in that moment, I made a decision. I did exactly what Alyssa had told me to do because from what I knew about Connor, this would be on my terms.

"Maybe I don't want you to stop."

When he opened his eyes again, his irises were a liquid, molten chocolate, blazing and full of lust that heat pooled in between my thighs.

I inched forward, feeling more of his body against mine. "You're leaving."

"I know."

"And I think ..." I angled up and forward, where our lips were barely touching, and I gained enough courage to simply take what I wanted. "I think I might be okay with that." Closer. "Because ... how can I deny this?" Moving even closer, I could feel how much he wanted me.

"Yes ..." he breathed out.

It was this connection between us.

I felt it. It engulfed me—this undeniable force between us. Whenever he was near, I needed to be closer as though it were unnatural for us not to be together, even though I used all my energy to stay far away from him. But this ... this felt easy, natural. When he was not by me, I still craved being near him, like it was difficult to breathe when he was not in my vicinity, and once we're in close proximity again, my whole body would relax as though that was where I was meant to be.

The light above us flickered off, and it startled me. I gripped his biceps.

The heat and sexual tension between us was heightened to immeasurable temperatures.

Even in the pitch-black darkness, I knew his look. I'd

recognized it through the weeks we spent together. His eyes hooded, his jaw clenched. As though he was using all his restraint to keep his distance from me too.

All my senses were heightened—his masculine scent that engulfed me, my hands squeezing his biceps, his lips by my lips, his soft breaths escaping him.

I knew that we shouldn't step out of bounds. He knew it too. But it was hard to avoid each other.

We'd accidentally found ourselves in the office closet, as though fate had locked us in together once again, but we were the only two people pushing against what was meant to be.

Heat radiated from his body, and he angled where his cheek was by my cheek. I heard the thud of the extension cords, and his arms wrapped across my lower back.

"I'm trying my best here." His nose grazed my ear, inching back to my chin and up again.

Every nerve ending of mine was awake and tingling.

"What exactly are you trying?" My voice came out horny and embarrassingly low and lustful, revealing exactly what I was thinking.

"I'm really trying to keep this professional. I'm really trying to keep my distance." His hot breath against my neck sent shivers to run down my spine. "But it's so hard. It's so hard to stay away from you because ... because I like you."

"You do?"

"I do." His fingers made slow, tantalizing circles at the base of my spine. "And staying away and keeping this thing platonic have been hard."

"I know." I kissed the corner of his mouth, and I heard the sharp intake of his breath.

For once, I wanted to take control, take what I wanted,

live in the moment, and not think too deeply about the future.

My tongue darted out to outline his bottom lip, and when he leaned into me, I pulled back just a tad.

"What if we pretend?" My heart raced, and my mouth turned dry as I anticipated the things to come. "That I'm just a girl in like with a guy. And you're just a guy in like with that ordinary girl."

I kissed the other corner of his mouth, and he shuddered.

His hands moved lower—to my ass. "Let's just pretend ..." He kissed my nose. "Pretend I'm not leaving. Pretend my family doesn't own this company." He kissed both my eyelids, lightly cherishing me, and I felt his kiss everywhere. My body was on fire. "And I can't pretend you're ordinary ... because you're far from it."

As soon as he finished that sentence, his lips crashed against mine. And it was beyond exquisite. A thousand fires were unleashed within me. He lifted me up, and my legs wrapped around his waist as he kissed the path down my neck, unbuttoning two of my first buttons before tipping kisses lower and lower. I turned to the side, giving him better access, holding his arms and gripping them for support.

"Not only do I like you, but I also want you. Charlie, I want you so bad." His lips made it back to mine, where he teased and sucked me.

My thoughts were mush because his hands were everywhere. In my hair. Skimming my back. Grabbing my ass and pushing at my center. And I loved it.

He turned around and anchored me against the file cabinet. In the darkness, I felt like a queen, and all my insecurities flew out the door.

"You smell amazing. You feel amazing." He cupped my breast, and I thanked the heavens that I'd picked the right bra today. He bent down and took my breast in his mouth, biting down hard and sucking until I nearly screamed.

He captured my lips with his. "Baby, you have to be quiet." The way he called me baby sent a shock straight to my heart this time.

And I decided, in that moment, I wanted him too.

"Do you have a condom?" My words were muffled against his lips. But I knew he'd heard me because he went utterly still.

"Charlie ..."

"I want you."

"Are you sure? Like this?"

His breathing was labored, and I answered him by untangling myself, planting my feet on the floor, and unzipping him.

I took him in my hand and stroked his velvet softness, up and down and down and up and again. His breath caught.

"Charlie ..."

"I thought we were role-playing. Billionaire CEO, ordinary girl. Just this one time." My voice was a breathless, horny promise against his skin.

In the darkness, it was easier to imagine that we'd work out, that he wasn't moving away.

His lips were back on mine again, searching, needing, and as if he couldn't take it anymore, he reached into his back pocket. I heard the rip of a condom and helped him slip it on his length.

"I've wanted you ever since I laid eyes on you. In front of that candy wall." He lifted me up in his arms again and kissed me like I was the last woman on earth, leaving me unable to form words. "It's so hard to stay away from you, Charlie. You just don't understand."

"Then, don't."

He lifted my skirt, and in one swift movement, my underwear was ripped off and tossed to the side.

"Make sure you put the panties in an envelope and have it delivered to my office."

Registering his words, I pulled back just a tad. "That's from my book."

His lips skated across the base of my neck. *"Sexy Filthy Boss."*

"You've read it?" My voice was horny, breathy, hot.

"I had to know if the boss got the girl. Glad to know he did."

He anchored me against the file cabinet, and with one push, he was inside me.

Oh, God.

Pleasure rushed throughout my whole body.

"Charlie ... you feel ... amazing," he grunted out, moving in and out of me in slow, languid movements.

I couldn't speak. I couldn't move. I couldn't do anything but feel ... every single push and pull. Every single nerve of mine tingled with sensation. It'd been a long time since I had sex. And I'd never had sex outside of a bedroom before. It felt forbidden in a way that excited parts of me that I never knew existed.

It didn't take long for my heart to pound louder, faster, and stronger against my ribs and for exploding currents to race through me. My body shivered, and I bit down on Connor's shoulder to prevent me from screaming his name as I let go, crescendoing in an orgasm that never seemed to end.

With one final push, he gripped my hip so tightly that I

knew for sure I'd bruise in the morning. In the next beat, his whole body went lax against mine. "Charlie ..."

"Hmm?" I murmured, trying to catch my breath, trying to find my bearings, trying not to move from the oversensitivity my body was feeling.

"Can we do that again?"

I laughed.

"Is that a yes?"

I ruffled one hand through his hair. "Yes."

"Because I want to make the most of my time here ... with you."

<hr>

It was really, really late by the time we exited the closet. We wanted to make sure that it was late enough that no one would see us both walk out. By this time, it was way past dinnertime, and I was so hungry from our workout that my stomach was eating its lining.

We'd had sex twice in the closet while we waited for time to pass. The only people in the office now were security, which was what Connor had wanted to ensure.

I adjusted my skirt and buttoned up my shirt. It was pitch-dark, so who the hell knew if all my buttons were on in the right places?

"My underwear?"

"Oh, shit. Yeah," he whispered.

He'd ripped it off in the heat of passion.

We couldn't see a dang thing. This was a problem.

"We need to find it."

"Okay." He kissed my hand before opening the door and peeking out to see if anyone was there. "All clear."

Light peered in the closet, and my eyes scanned the area. "Where did you toss them?"

He smirked. "I don't even remember. I just needed them off."

I playfully slapped his shoulder. "Not funny."

I looked behind the cabinet and on every spot of the floor. Nothing.

"Connor, where are they?" Panic seized my chest. This was the worst possible thing that could happen. Seriously.

Connor's smile slipped as he stared out in the hallway. "Someone is here."

"What?" My stomach turned with a queasiness that I swore would knock me out.

He motioned for me to get out of the room. "Let's go. I'll look for them later."

"What? No!"

"Charlie"—he tipped his chin toward the hallway —"there's no time. I promise I'll find them. Let's go."

I rushed out of the closet and down the hall, and he followed behind me. We raced away as though we were teenagers about to get caught in one of our parents' bedrooms.

When we rounded the corner, I flipped to face him. "Promise me that you'll go find them."

He stepped into me, grabbing me by my elbows. "I promise. Cross my heart. Hope to fly."

His arms wrapped around my lower back, bringing me in. His hair was a disheveled mess, but his eyes were light, and he wore this smile that seemed to be permanent on his face.

"How about we take advantage of this no-underwear situation?"

"Um, you did that. Twice." And right now, I wasn't thinking about sex. "And I'm hungry."

He grabbed my backside and pulled me in closer for a kiss. "I'm hungry again too. Round three?"

I shoved his shoulder. "You're insatiable. I'm hungry for food, not more sex. I think we've burned enough calories in there that we're allowed to binge."

He dipped me back and playfully bit my neck. "How about you eat food ... and I eat you?"

I leaned back until we were eye to eye. "Hey, our pretend space is only in that closet."

Connor squeezed my bare ass and walked us back. "Let's find another place. I'm not done pretending yet."

I painfully pressed a hand to his chest because we were not thinking clearly now. He was kissing me out in the open. "I'm serious, Connor. We don't want anyone seeing us. Right?"

He visibly frowned as though I'd popped his balloon. "It's only our cleaning service, but you're right."

He released me, and his fingers intertwined with mine. Even though we shouldn't be holding hands, I let him.

"I know this great Italian restaurant I want to take you to," he said, pulling me down the hall.

"Italian. Yum. I'm starving." I went on my toes and kissed him one last time before we were out in the open outdoors. "Only in the pretend closet."

"Only in the pretend closet."

It was a solemn oath, but after dinner, it was broken—in his car, at his apartment. And the next weekend later, the closet, his car, and his apartment all over again.

CHAPTER 21

CHARLIE

WE WERE in the break room, and Casey was complaining about Kyle again because he'd happened to stop by her gym this morning.

"He's so annoying." Her eyes flittered throughout the room. It was as though a light had flipped on her head. "Are those free chips for everyone? The vending machines were empty."

Her change on topics gave me whiplash.

"What I don't need is another bag of chips." Alyssa frowned. "Seriously, I've been stress-eating a ton."

I nodded, but my thoughts were on Connor.

Connor had invited me to lunch, but I'd declined. If we had lunch, I knew that we wouldn't be discussing the branding and remarketing plans; we'd be discussing which position he wanted me in and our next exciting place to have sex.

It'd been a few weeks since we crossed that boundary,

and somehow, it'd turned him into a sex fiend. But holy moly cannoli, life was grand.

"You've been working late hours, haven't you?" Alyssa said above her chicken salad sandwich croissant.

I shook my head from my Connor-filled thoughts. "Yeah. A little. Trying to tighten things up before the filming."

She smiled, and I got a strange gut feeling that Alyssa knew what was up.

"When are you presenting to Mr. Colby?" Casey asked, pushing around her salad.

I blew out a breath. "Next week. After we film and the videos are edited."

Alyssa's voice lowered. "What kind of video?"

My eyes widened because she was insinuating things. My mind played back the events of the week, trying to recollect if she had seen Connor and me together anywhere.

Where I was careful, Connor was touchy-feely and kissy, not careful.

I cleared my throat. "We're filming a commercial to show his dad. It'll give him the whole feel about the brand. Connor will be in it." I left out the part that he wanted me to be in it.

Casey basically jumped in her seat. "When can we see it?"

I shrugged. "That's up to Connor, but I'm assuming after we present it to his father and they present it to the board, the whole company will see it at the relaunch."

I stuffed the rest of my sandwich in my mouth because I didn't want to be grilled any further.

"I'm excited!" Casey clasped her hands together. "It's going to be epic; I know it. Because you've worked on it together."

My smile slipped. *Did Casey know too?*

I straightened. No, I was for sure just being paranoid.

I didn't want the gossip mill starting, especially since Connor was leaving and I'd be left here.

The thought sent an ache straight to my chest, and I let out a slow exhale.

Casey's eyes moved to the other side of the room. She leaned in and whispered so only Alyssa and I could hear, "There they are."

I looked over to find Jared and Nina from production just taking their seats at a lunch table.

I leaned in to hear what Casey had to say.

"So"—her eyes teetered from me and Alyssa to Jared and Nina on the other side of the room—"I was getting staples the other day when I found dirty underwear between two file cabinets."

My face paled, and my heartbeat picked up speed in my chest. There was no way. We'd always been careful. He'd looked for those panties, and they were gone. We'd figured the janitor had thrown them out.

"Did you throw them in the garbage?" I practically squealed.

"Ewww. Nope. I thought someone would find them and toss them, and it wasn't going to be me."

"How do you know it was theirs?" Alyssa asked, but her stare was solely on me.

My heart beat raced and I kept my eyes strictly on Casey. "Yeah, how do you know?"

"Well, that's the thing ... I was here late yesterday, and I heard noises in the closet." Her cheeks flushed pink as she leaned in and lowered her voice even further. "People were having sex."

"Oh my God." I purposefully widened my eyes and

covered my mouth with one hand because, shit ... goodness, we had been so sure no one was in the office.

"I know, right?"

Alyssa said nothing but smiled, not taking her eyes off of me.

"So, I waited and waited, and then they went for another round."

"How disgusting!" The heat from my face spread all over my body, and I wanted to crawl under the lunch table and die.

"So, I went to my office, grabbed my belongings, and waited by the elevator bank. Well, guess who showed up, hand in hand, waiting for the same elevator?"

"How do you know it was them in the closet?" Alyssa asked.

"Duh! It was, like, nine in the evening. No one was at work or should be at work. I'd only gone back in because I'd forgotten my laptop." Casey threw the other table a dirty look. "I mean, seriously? Go home and have sex. Why in the office?"

"Because it's exciting." Alyssa smirked and tipped her chin my way. "Don't you think? Sex in the office is more exciting than missionary-style sex in the bedroom."

I shrugged. "I guess so. I mean, I wouldn't ... know."

Her eyes narrowed, and she leaned in, both elbows on the table. "Don't tell me you've never had sex in the office."

She knew! She had to.

Lie like your life depends on it. "No."

"No?" Her voice turned incredulous. Then, she leaned back in her chair and examined her nails. "Everyone should try it at least once."

"Maybe, one day," I said, laughing, "I can be that spontaneous." I crumpled up my napkin and stuffed it in my lunch bag. "Toodles, ladies. I've got computers to fix." *And underwear to look for.*

CONNOR

I lifted my head to Charlie slamming my office door behind her. She bit her lip, rushed to my desk, and planted both palms down, leaning toward me. Her neckline dipped, and immediately, my cock stiffened. Insatiable little bastard.

Her face was filled with concern, and all I was filled with was horny thoughts.

Someone, save my soul.

"Hey, what's the matter?" I stood and cupped her face, the desk a barrier between us.

Her cheek pressed into my palm, and I loved it.

She let out one long, shallow breath. "Someone found my underwear from over a week ago." She leaned back and ran both hands through her hair, her eyes going wide. "I mean, we looked for that thing everywhere. She said she found it between two file cabinets. We looked there. We tore that room apart." Her voice heightened with hysteria.

"Who found them?"

"Casey!"

Well, now, didn't this complicate things?

I made my way around my desk and pulled her in by her forearms. "It'll be fine," I said because Casey knowing I was having sex with Charlie wasn't the worst thing in the world.

"It won't be fine. People will know. You will leave, and I want to stay here. I kinda like the people here."

To her, this had just been a job, a means to an end, and now, she was going to stay permanently. That filled me up with all kinds of happiness.

"Hey ..." I pulled her closer, wrapping my arms around her lower back. "You're shaking." I rubbed her back as she nestled into me. "Casey doesn't have any proof that they're yours, and she's not one to gossip."

"You don't know Casey very well, do you?" Her words were muffled against my chest.

I bent down to kiss her hair and got a whiff of her intoxicating shampoo, and then I was a goner.

"It's fine," I said again, but this time, my voice was guttural.

"My underwear is still in the office closet."

I took a fistful of hair and gently pulled her head back, so she was looking directly in my eyes. God, she was beautiful. The green in her eyes were mesmerizing. "I'll go get them."

My eyes flickered to her lips, and her eyes locked with mine. There was this shift in the air. I felt it every time I was around her. Her tongue darted out to wet her bottom lip, and my stomach tightened.

Someone, help me because around this woman, I can't think clearly.

I pulled on her hair with a little more force, and she yelped.

My lips found the crook of her neck, kissing a path from her neck to her ear. "We won't be having sex in the office closet anymore." I moved her to my desk. "I've found us a new location."

"Connor ..." My name was a breathless whisper, a plea, and I was more than happy to oblige.

My tongue flicked over the seam of her mouth, and I devoured her because she was mine.

All mine. Mine. Mine.

"People might walk in." Her hands gripped my biceps tighter against her.

I was too hungry for her to even lock the door. "No one will come in."

The only person who would possibly come in unannounced was my brother, but I'd just talked to him, and he was on the other side of town. It would take him at least thirty minutes to get here. This had to be quick. I'd savor her for hours later tonight.

CHARLIE

I shifted in my desk, not wearing any underwear. Why? Because, once again, Connor had ripped them off in the throes of passion. And now, I was sure I needed to buy some more after work.

My messenger pinged on my computer.

I got the goods.

A picture of him with my underwear in his mouth appeared.

I laughed back and typed.

Nice.

What's nice is you and me. Tonight, my place. I'm cooking dinner.

We need to finish our plans for this commercial.

Yes. My place. After dinner.

What exactly will we be doing after dinner?

Things ... and then fine-tuning the final rebranding specs.

I laughed again.

Mr. Colby, dinner, final rebranding specs, and other things—in that order. Or else I'm not coming over.

There was no more direction in my life. I still needed to finalize a few more paintings for my collection.

"Charlie."

I slammed my laptop shut and turned around to find Casey with an overly cheesy smile.

"I can't believe you. You've been keeping things from me."

I straightened in my seat and let out a nervous laugh. "What?"

"Connor?"

My smile slipped, and I gripped my armrests like I was going to fall out of my chair.

"What about Connor?"

"That he's banging ..."

"Let me explain—"

"Sienna."

I blinked up at her.

"Sienna from accounting?"

She was in her fifties.

"Yes. So, today, I passed the office closet, and then lo and behold ... Sienna walked out, following none other than Connor himself." She placed her hands on her hips. "I would never have guessed that one. She's twice his age and a divorcée."

I should end this charade now and not have Sienna take the fall for the underwear and sex-in-the-closet incident. But I couldn't. "I guess you really don't know people's types." I was pure evil.

"Yep. Anyway, I thought you'd like to know. Alyssa didn't believe me. She said she knew Connor was having an affair but wouldn't tell me with who. She thinks my conclusion is preposterous. As if." She shrugged. "I knew you'd believe me. Anywhooo, back to the world of no candy-tasting but testing." With a wave of her hand, she was off.

My shoulders relaxed, and I let out a long, audible sigh when she was out of my vicinity.

Wait till Connor heard this one.

━━━

Connor had cooked chicken potpie, and I was impressed.

I pushed my fork through the pastry, picking up bits of chicken and peas along the way, and stuffed it in my mouth. It was delicious. "There's a rumor going around," I said mid-chew.

"What would that be?"

"That you and Sienna are having an affair."

He choked, coughing, and hit his chest with his fist before full-blown laughter escaped him. "She was in the closet first when I walked in. She was looking for folder tabs, and I helped her find some. When she walked out, I followed, and a few seconds later, Casey greeted me at the exit." He shook his head, smiling. "I should have known she would jump to that conclusion. Now that I think about it, you should have seen her face. Anyway, Sienna is dating someone."

I laughed. "Well, now, Casey thinks that someone is you."

I finished off the rest of my fantabulous meal, stuffing my last bite in my mouth. The flakiness of the crust was divine.

The corner of his mouth tipped upward. "Did you not like it?"

I laughed because he was being sarcastic. "It was delicious-mondo. Is there anything you can't do?"

His smile fell. "Ask me in a few months."

He was nervous about the rebranding.

"We've got this in the bag. No doubt." I stood and placed his plate on top of mine before making my way to the sink.

He followed right behind me "Charlie, just leave it."

"Nope. You cooked. I'm cleaning. This is how domestic relationships work."

I placed the plates on the counter and turned on the sink, but he flipped it off and turned me to face him.

"Is that what we're in now? A domestic relationship?"

I should have caught my words earlier, but it'd slipped out so naturally. I swallowed. "I mean ... I mean, temporary domestic relationship." I smiled, but it didn't seem genuine because there was a direct disconnect between what was happening in my head and heart.

He was leaving, and that left an intense ache in my chest.

I pushed his hands off of me and turned the sink back on, sudsing up the sponge and cleaning the dishes. "I mean, that's all this can be, right?"

There was silence between us—an awkward silence. It was so silent that I wondered if he could hear my heartbeat thrashing in my chest.

Why couldn't I just accept what this was and not want more? There had been an agreement before we started this arrangement, and I was breaking all my rules now by feeling.

His arms wrapped around my waist, and he rested his chin on my shoulder. "Did you get my present today in the break room?"

I turned to face him, and there was this sly, secretive smirk on his face.

"Present?"

"The chips and cookies on the table. We're going to start offering them to our employees too."

I scrunched my face, confused.

"I told our café managers that I'm getting rid of our vending machines."

I blinked, still beyond confused. "Thank you?"

"I remembered what you said before ..." His voice trailed off. "About not liking chocolate because it reminds you of when your dad was sick. Getting chocolate from the vending machines."

My heart seized as he brought back the memories.

"And I know I can't help the chocolate part because that's what this company is made of ... but I don't want anything else bringing up unhappy memories ... even when I'm not around anymore."

My voice was as soft as a whisper. "So, you got rid of the vending machines?"

He nodded, and tears welled up behind my eyes. Full-blown emotions hit me in the chest.

And in that moment, that tiny moment, staring into his liquid chocolate-brown eyes, I knew in my heart that I could fall for this man, if I wasn't there already.

"When we're together, we're happy, okay? Because we don't have an endless amount of time left."

I nodded and let out a long sigh, and when I did, he turned off the sink, flipped me around, dried off my hands, and threaded both of his hands through my hair, bringing me closer.

"If we keep dwelling on the fact that I'm leaving, we'll both feel miserable and waste time, feeling miserable. When I'm here, I'm dead set on making the most of our time together, making you happy."

Our eyes locked, and in the first time in forever ... I felt an utter desolation of the future because I was going to miss him terribly. Though we hadn't known each other long, I knew I'd never—before Connor—felt like this toward another human being. This intense connection. I'd had love before but not passion like this.

I peered up at him, and the only consolation I got was the hope that he was feeling the same. "You said *we*."

His eyebrows wrinkled.

"You said, 'We'll both feel miserable.' "

He smiled then, but it was a sad smile. "It's not just you, Charlie. I wish I could slow down time. I wish things were different, but my life"—he exhaled—"it's in New York. My apartment. My job. My friends."

A little voice in my head said, *But I'm here.*

"And, yes, *we*. I'm going to be miserable leaving ... because I'm going to be leaving Nana and Kyle but, most of all ... you." He rested his forehead on mine. "That's why"—he nipped at my lips—"we need to make every second count." Another nip at my lips. "And the marketing stuff can wait because we're doing things in order of importance. Food." Another nip. "And now, it's time for dessert."

He lifted me in his arms, and my legs automatically wrapped around his waist. As he took us back to his room, I wondered if we would even get to finalizing the marketing plans tonight.

Probably not.

CHAPTER 22

CONNOR

IT WAS the beginning of the longest day of my life. Filming day. We'd prepped and practiced and dressed, and now, filming was a go.

We were at Ellie's house, one of Wyatt's friends. All we needed was a suburban home with a nice porch because this was where I would be picking up Charlie on our first date.

I'd changed into a suit, and I had flowers and Colby Chocolates with the new packaging in my hand behind my back.

For the third time tonight, I rang the doorbell to do the scene yet again.

Charlie opened the door in a white skirt and light-blue flowery silk shirt that Susan had helped her pick out. Her hair was no longer down but swept up in a ponytail.

And even though it was the third time we'd done it, each and every time she opened the door, she took my breath away.

Her makeup was light, the pink in her cheeks and on her lips only highlighting her beauty.

"Smile bigger, Charlie. More natural!" Wyatt yelled out.

They wouldn't hear the outtakes on the commercial, as it would be set to music that evoked emotion.

I stepped into the house and swung the flowers to the front and then the chocolates.

Charlie fake beamed, which had me smiling in response.

"Tip your chin to the side, Charlie. Bigger. Smile!" Wyatt yelled out as two cameras were focused on her face. "He's picking you up for a date for the first time, and he's just given you flowers and chocolate. Show that excitement, that nervousness."

"Tanner, focus on the chocolate, get a closer shot. Yeah. There. Ah, fuck. Charlie, you can't look directly at the camera. Cut."

My whole body tensed. "Wyatt, chill out," I snapped, not liking how he was talking to her.

He raised both hands, strolled toward Charlie, and reached for her arm. "Sorry. I was just really in the moment. You're doing great, Charlie, really." He addressed his production crew, "Everyone, let's take ten."

After he stepped away, she rubbed at her brow, visibly frustrated.

I pulled the bouquet of flowers in her hand toward me, essentially crushing the dozen between us. Tipping up her chin, I noticed her frown. "Hey ..." I whispered. "You're doing an amazing job. We have one more scene after this, and we should be done for the night."

"I suck. Remind me to never, ever go into acting."

I pinched her chin and leaned in. "Stop. You're doing

amazing. Wyatt even said so. I think everyone's just tired right now." I placed the chocolate and roses on the side table by the door, wrapped my arms around her, and pulled her into me. "Plus, the most important thing about being on camera is being cute. And you have that down. You've mastered the cuteness. More than any other woman I've ever met."

"Nice," she drawled out.

"Let's just get this over with. We'll get the next scene done and go home."

Home. That last word had fallen out naturally, effortlessly.

I pushed any deep thoughts about it to the side as she groaned and fell into me.

"Charlie, it's just like how we discussed, how you pictured it. A young male—let's call him Connor—he's nervous. He's picking up this girl and taking her out on their date for the very first time. He wants everything to be perfect because this girl—let's call her Charlie—he wants to impress her, wine and dine her, treat her like the queen she is.

"So, he's staring at the house, anxious. He turns off the ignition of his car, wipes his hands on his jeans, and grabs the chocolate and flowers he bought for her." I pulled back, and she met my smile. "And then ... he's walking toward the front door. His mouth goes dry, and he swears he's never felt like throwing up before, but he's this close because he's so worried about impressing her. All he wants is to see her, take her out."

Charlie wrinkled her nose, and I continued, "He rings the doorbell, and everything around him heightens—the pounding of his heart, the loud breaths from his mouth. But when she opens the door ..." I paused, waiting for her to finish my thought because these were her ideas, not mine.

"Everything quiets to a hush, and all of his worry and anxiety disappears because when he hands her the chocolate and flowers, she smiles. It's a smile that tells him that everything is going to be okay, that their night is going to be okay, that they are going to be okay."

Wyatt storms to the front and circles around, motioning to the crew and telling them what to do, interrupting us. "Let's go, go, go. I'm picking up some doughnuts, on me, if we get this in one shot."

He clapped his hands together, and I gave Charlie a wink before grabbing the chocolates and flowers, turning toward the door again.

Lights shone on me, and a camera was fixed on my face as I positioned myself and rang the doorbell.

A moment later, the door opened, and I stepped into the house. When Charlie smiled, it was genuine this time, and just like she'd said, everything disappeared, and it was just the two of us in the room.

The overhead light caught the green in her eyes, and my stomach tightened. I had an urge to kiss her, right here, right now, but then I remembered where I was.

Shit.

"Connor? What the hell, dude? You missed your cue."

Well, damn.

Charlie laughed, crossed her eyes, and touched her nose with her tongue.

And just then, she smiled, and I knew everything would turn out all right.

CHARLIE

This evening was humid, but now, a light breeze brushed against my bare arms. My flowy green dress that Connor had purchased hugged my waist, billowing out to right above my knees. I wrapped my arms around myself to get warmth inside of me.

What I should have done was stayed in the car.

This was what living in the Midwest entailed—a drop in forty degrees in one day. At times, it felt as though we experienced all four seasons within a span of a week.

Warm hands wrapped around my arms, rubbing up and down, the friction making me feel better.

"He said we're starting in five. Do you want to wait in the car till then?" Connor said, turning me to face him and wrapping his arms fully around me, running his hands up and down my back.

I cowered into him and inhaled deeply, taking in the masculine scent of him. The cotton from his polo was soft against my cheek. It was short-sleeved, so I knew he must be freezing too.

"Five minutes?" I lifted my head to take in the trees surrounding us, the small lake to our right, and the string of lights that the crew was hanging from tree to tree. "This will take way more than five minutes. Let's go." I linked my fingers through his and practically dragged him to our destination—his car.

"Wyatt!" Connor called out. "Call me when you guys are set."

Once in the car, Connor turned on the engine, and the heat blasted in the background. "This weather is ridiculous."

"You can say that again." I leaned back against the seat and let all my muscles relax.

We'd started prepping for filming this morning, and yet we weren't done. The director wanted to catch the perfect scene for the proposal, so here we were, almost late into the evening. We would have to film the wedding scene on a different day. No one had accounted for the time it would take to retake each scene and set up.

"If this is what acting entails, I don't want anything to do with it."

"Me too," Connor said.

My eyes moved toward him—his chiseled jaw, his full bottom lip, his face of an angel, his body of a god. "You'd get paid millions. If you don't want to be an actor, you should definitely take up modeling."

His deep chuckle filled the small space between us. "I smile weird. No one would ever hire me. Plus, I love my job."

"Not true. And for your information, I love your smile."

He tipped my chin with the lightness of his fingertips. "No. I love your smile. It's one of my favorite parts of you."

His thumb brushed against my lips, and heat spread throughout me so fast that I wondered how I had ever been cold before.

If we started this, my makeup would be ruined. I already had to redo my lipstick.

"Are we back to smiles?" I asked, pulling his hand down and intertwining our fingers.

"I guess so."

"Well, I think we need to think about how we're going to reenact this first scene. Prep ourselves, so it'll be faster. If we can do it in less than ten takes, we'll be all set to do the next scene and then go home."

He nodded. "Good idea. I'm all about going home." He tipped his chin my way.

I thought back to our very first brainstorming session and the idea of the commercial. I thought about the feels we wanted to give our target audience—family, love, celebration. "So, today is the big day. The couple has been dating for two years."

"Two years?" Connor scoffed. "Six months. A year is already too long to know."

I reeled back. "You think it only takes six months for a couple to know that they can spend the rest of their lives together?"

"Yeah."

"But they hardly know each other."

"True. But I'm a firm believer in the saying, *When you know, you know.*" He shrugged with this amused smirk on his face. "And they have the rest of their lives to get to know each other. I learn more about myself each and every day—what I want, what I can do, my limits."

"Still ..."

He leaned in, giving me that look again, the lusty *I want to kiss you* look.

"It's not about the time and how long a couple has been together; it's the feeling they get when they are around each other."

"But sometimes, those feelings are just in the beginning, and once the honeymoon is over, then it's real fights, real life."

"Yeah, and all the *real fights, real life* stuff is worth it in the end because you've found your person." He wiggled his eyebrows.

I laughed. "You are a hopeless romantic. I never knew." I waved a hand, getting back on track with things. "So, they've been dating for six months. He's madly in love with her, and he can't live without her, so he decides"—I lifted my ring finger and wiggled it—"this is it. He's going to put a ring on it, so no one will beat him to it."

"So, he plans this extravagant event," Connor continued. "He plans this awesome way on how he's going to do it." He tapped his temple in an *I'm so smart* way. "And he strings lights from tree to tree, illuminating the area. That, and the stars make the date have this romantic feel. Then, he takes her to the lake, to their very first date."

"So, she's going to know he's going to propose then if she sees this." I laughed.

"No." He shook his head. "Because"—he lowered his chin and tapped my nose with his forefinger—"she thinks he's planned this extravagant event for their six-month anniversary. He's so romantic that he plans month celebrations."

I smiled bigger. "With chocolate."

"That's right."

Our eyes locked, and we high-fived.

CHAPTER 23

CHARLIE

MY FAMILY WAS all seated at the table, eating dinner. I could have spent the night at Connor's house, like I had been, but I'd promised my mother I'd be home for the family dinner. It seemed like weeks since I'd sat and eaten dinner with her since I had been with Connor recently.

My mother never asked me where I had been spending the night at when I hadn't come home.

On one normal Wednesday night, I'd thrown out that I was meeting Alyssa and Casey out for drinks, which was true. I hadn't told her that Connor and Kyle were there, nor had I told her that I went home with Connor.

Sandy's voice grated on my nerves, like nails on a chalk-board. Luckily with her, I had trained my ear to have selective hearing. I cut up my chicken Parmesan, which Elsa had prepared. It was over-the-top delicious, and I enjoyed each savory bit as I tried to concentrate on the positive—my satisfied stomach.

"Yeah, two Saturdays from now," Sandy piped up, which had me peering up, with my fork midair.

I counted the days to my exhibit.

"My company is being honored in the Under Thirty Entrepreneur Awards ceremony, so save the date."

Wait. What? No.

My mother practically jumped out of her seat. "How amazing, Sandy. Congrats." She placed a hand on Richard's hand on the table as he beamed at his daughter.

"Is it a black-tie event?"

"Yes, Daddy. Your tux will do fine. Me? I'll need to find something to wear." She smiled, flipping her hair over her shoulder, and stared at me. "You're invited too, Charlie. I actually hope you can come."

"Of course she can come," my mother answered.

My heartbeat sped up in my ears, anxiety threatening to cripple me.

That was the night of my exhibit.

"I actually can't. Mom, remember ... I told you to keep that day open."

All the time spent on my pieces and all the money saved for the space led to that one day. All to that one day.

I hadn't exactly told her that I was showcasing my work on that day. I'd just informed her that it was very important that she left that day open for me.

"Oh, honey"—she visibly frowned—"what's going on again?"

I gritted my teeth. "I told you, I have a surprise for you."

"Oh. Can you just reschedule?" Her eyes teetered to everyone in the room—from Richard to Sandy and finally resting on me.

I blinked at her. "No, I can't," I snapped.

I had told her that this was a very special date and that I

needed her to come. I'd had her physically check her phone calendar in front of me before I secured the space to ensure that she would be available.

"Honey, I'm sure whatever you have going on ..." She paused and assessed my features before continuing, "Did you book tickets somewhere? Could we reschedule? I mean, this is a black-tie event for your sister."

There was no sympathy shown in the crowd of three. None. There would be no arguing, no winning in this situation. But I was only mad at one of them—my mother. Because she'd promised. She'd promised me that she would be there.

"Honey ..."

I shot up so fast that the chair knocked over. "It's fine. What I do, what's important to me, has never mattered to you anyway."

"Charlie—"

"No, Mom. And if you want to know what's so important on that day, it's my exhibit to showcase my artwork. But since you think my work is utter shit, you shouldn't go anyway."

My mother stood, her hand outstretched, but I was too far mad to even listen or turn around. I stormed out of the house and into my haven—the pool house—where I admired all my work by myself.

I thought my mother would come check on me, but I knew her. She was giving me "space." But what I needed was for her to apologize, to tell me that she would pull through on her promises for once, to pick me and choose me over her new family.

That night was the first time since my father had died that I cried myself to sleep. I wished he were still here. I wished that he could see me showcase this exhibit. I wished my mother loved me unconditionally, just how my father had loved me. But all my wishes would never come because my father was dead.

CONNOR

Charlie was in a sullen mood today, and I was determined to make her feel better. Whatever had gotten her down, I would cheer her up. It was my mission of the day.

But I couldn't get her alone. Every time I turned, there was Casey and Alyssa, chatting it up by her desk, like they didn't have their normal jobs to do.

"Hey." I walked on over, knowing it was the end of the day and I wouldn't see Charlie tonight because she had plans to get ready for her exhibit. "Can I talk to you in my office? It's about the rebranding."

"It's fine. We have work to do anyway," Casey said, turning to walk away, her tone kind of annoyed, as though I'd interrupted some very important conversation.

Alyssa stood from the edge of Charlie's desk. "Hmm. Rebranding sounds kind of fun." She winked, following Casey out.

When they were out of sight, I crooked my finger at Charlie, raising an eyebrow. When she leaned in closer, I stole a kiss, and she widened her eyes.

"In my office," I said.

"No, Connor." Her eyebrows scrunched. "Not now. I just don't have the energy."

She thought I was talking about sex, but I wasn't. I mean, come on ... I cared for her. That wasn't the only thing on my mind. It was mostly on my mind, but not the only thing on my mind.

"Just come to my office, Charlie." I turned around, not giving her a second to deny me.

A few moments later, Charlie walked into my office, dragging her feet, her eyes downturned.

She crossed her arms over her chest, not moving far from the door.

"Charlie, sit." I tipped my chin to the empty chair in front of my desk.

"Like a dog?" She shot me a look. "Connor, I'm in a foul mood. You just don't want to be around me right now. Promise, I'm no joy to be around."

"Which is exactly why I want to talk to you. I want to know what's wrong."

Her frown deepened.

I walked toward her, toward the door, and grabbed her elbows, pulling her in. "We're not just sex buddies, okay? I like you. I care about you. I want you to tell me what's bothering you, and I want to be here to cheer you up. And I'm not talking about the kinky stuff."

I brushed her hair from her forehead.

Her lips trembled, and in the next second, she was in my arms, a broken, shaky breath escaping her. "I'm s-sorry."

When she tried to pull away, I tightened my hold around her. "Stop. It's me."

Hell, my heart broke as she pushed her face into my shirt. *Shit ... is she crying?* She was. My stomach dropped and kept on going.

"Charlie ..." I kissed the top of her head and pulled her tighter against me.

I would do anything in my power to make her feel better. Practically anything. Slay dragons. Defeat her demons myself.

She pulled back, ducking her head and blinking up

against the lights, swiping at her eyes. "I planned this great exhibit. Planned it for months and months. Put a down payment on the place, got this job to secure payment to fulfill it. Worked on my paintings nonstop and then ..." She shook her head and dropped her head into her hands. "She's not going to my exhibit."

"Who?"

She lifted her gaze to mine, and the look in her eyes was like having a truck ramming against my chest.

"My mother." A tiny sob escaped her.

What in the living hell is wrong with that woman?

I didn't know her mother, but I didn't like her already, just for the fact that she always made Charlie feel like shit.

"Why the hell not?" I snapped a little too loudly.

"Because my wench of a stepsister ... is having ... an awards ceremony then. Like, she sprang it up. Like she did it on purpose, which I know is stupid 'cause how could she possibly know that?"

Full-on tears fell down my cheeks.

It was all too much for me to take.

"Come here."

"Connor ... no."

I pulled her into me, unable to handle her crying, needing to console her, needing her tears to stop.

Her elbows were by my chest, her arms tight, but I wrapped my arms around her fully.

"Stop fighting me, Charlie. Why don't you let me comfort you?"

She pushed at my chest, but I wouldn't relent.

"Because I can't rely on you like that. Because you're leaving."

She was right.

I released a heavy sigh and closed my eyes tightly.

I got where she was coming from. She didn't want to rely on me, especially when I was going. She didn't want me to be that person, her person, given our circumstance.

I held her in silence, letting her get her all emotions out, knowing I couldn't be anything else to her even though she was my person. Wasn't she? She knew everything about my own family issues, had consoled me and tried to lighten the bitterness that I had toward my parents. She was even helping me save this company when it wasn't her job to do.

I kissed the top of her head.

Yes.

My person.

CHARLIE

I didn't want to lean on Connor, didn't want to have him here to comfort me now, knowing that he wasn't here permanently. I could confide in Alyssa and Casey because I knew ... I knew they would be here for me months from now, maybe even years from now. I'd formed a bond with them in a short period of time, and I knew we would be friends forever. Plus, when I complained, they always made me feel better, but there was nothing ... nothing that made me feel better than being in Connor's arms.

Like his arms were meant to be around me, like he was born to keep me there.

And I couldn't take it anymore. I couldn't hold the words in and not depend on him like I wanted to.

"I wish ... I wish I were good enough. Gosh, I don't understand why I need this affirmation from her, why I still seek it. It's just ..." I hiccuped. "There's this void now that my dad is no longer here. I want her to fill that void. I want her to believe and know I'm talented. That this passion I have is in me. I want her to see what my father saw, what everyone tells me about my art." As soon as the words came out, sadness was replaced with a bitterness I felt in my gut. "I just hate her sometimes." There, I'd said it. But it was true. *Did she realize how much she was hurting me?*

Connor lifted my chin. "Why do you need it? Her approval."

He cupped my cheek so tenderly that tears nearly formed again. I tried to push them down, welcoming the anger, but it wouldn't come.

"I just want to know ... that I'm enough."

"Oh, baby, you're more than enough." His forehead leaned against mine. "Old people are too stuck in their ways to see anything else ... to see what's right in front of them. Their minds are fixed, unchangeable. But know this: you're brilliant. Your crazy, gorgeous mind is what's going to save this multimillion-dollar company. Seriously, your art, your creativity blow me away." He framed my cheeks with the lightness of his fingertips, and I drowned in the sea of brown looking down at me. "Believe it. Your father saw it. I see it. Your friends see it. Damn, Charlie ... you'd have to be blind to not see how insanely talented you are."

This man. He was amazing, and a different type of emotion stirred within me—this undeniable urge to be closer to him, to feel him everywhere.

So, I closed the gap between us and kissed him with a fervent passion, shocking him. He pulled back, stunned. I leaned in closer and kissed him again.

"Charlie," he rushed out as my lips went to the crook of his neck. "That's not why I called you into my office."

"I know. But I want you, Connor. I want you to make me feel better this way."

I anchored myself against his hip, rubbing him and

myself in all the right places, needing a release, needing to forget, even for just a moment.

I went on my toes and nipped on his ear. "Don't make me beg for it."

He shuddered against me, and then it was game over. I was going to win this cat-and-mouse chasing game.

He groaned and lifted me by the ass. He kissed me, matching the same hunger that I had for him. Lips against lips. Hands over my body. Papers flew off his desk, and he slowly guided me to my back.

"Not the underwear. Don't rip my underwear," I moaned.

He laughed against my lips and took off my heels one at a time. Then, he slipped his fingers through the edge of my panties and slipped them off.

My body tingled from anticipation, and I wiggled beneath him.

"Just never wear underwear again." He released me, only long enough so he could unzip and slip on a condom.

Then, we were all wet, sloppy kisses again and hands everywhere.

My need for him, to touch him, to feel him was undeniable, and when I reached for him and positioned him at my entrance, beads of sweat lined his brow. When he entered me, I moaned loudly at the fullness of him filling me. My head flew back at the ecstasy of him moving in and out of me.

His half-hooded eyes watched where we were connected, his stare filling with a lust so strong.

It didn't take long for tingles to travel up my spine. "Connor ... I'm ... I'm—"

"Connor? I didn't see Claire in the front."

Casey?

My eyes widened as I slapped at Connor's hands and pushed him off of me.

"Casey! Get out!" Connor yelled.

Panic tore through me.

"Oh my God! Oh my God!" Casey yelped.

A second later, I stood.

I hadn't had time to straighten or for Connor to put his dick back in his pants before Casey stormed in.

Immediately, I dropped to my knees, crawled under Connor's desk, and hid, hugging my knees, shrinking into myself.

"Wait," she said, her voice firm.

"Casey, get out!"

"No. No. No. I know I've caught you in a compromising position, but that's not Sienna ..."

Her feet were in my view, but Connor was blocking the desk.

Then, she ducked.

Her eyes went wide, and then she blinked. "Charlie?" Her voice was unbelieving.

I tried to hide my face, but it was no use because she'd dropped to her knees too.

"Charlie! Shit, Charlie. You're banging the boss? That's crazy."

I groaned.

"Casey, get out." Connor lifted her elbow, and Casey stood, shell-shocked into silence.

"I just don't understand. I mean ... are you a thing?" Then, she ducked again and looked at me. "Do you like this guy?" A second later, she stood, and her voice turned hard. "Tell me you're not banging Sienna too."

"No! Get out, Casey. Out."

"Fine, but you'd better be a good guy, Connor. You'd just better be a damn good guy."

He walked her out, and when I heard the door slam shut, I stood ... mortified.

My shaky hand flew to my forehead. *Omigod. I can't believe that just happened.*

"I hate my life."

"Don't say that." He pulled at my hand, bringing me into a full-on hug. "They're on your side for this one. They won't tell a soul. Did you hear Casey?"

I had. I'd heard her loud and clear.

And I knew there would be nonstop questions, and I would have to answer them soon.

━━

Talk about an odd conversation I so didn't want to be having.

"You little wench. You were holding out on us all this time?" Casey said, her PB and J untouched.

I kept stuffing my mouth with food because I wasn't in the mood to divulge information. I swore I was about to choke.

"How big is his dick?" Alyssa said. "Never mind. That's kinda gross. I don't want to know about Connor's dick."

"I saw it. It was"—Casey blushed—"pretty impressive."

"Casey ..." I didn't want anyone talking about Connor's impressive package.

After I swallowed the last of my sandwich, I chugged my water and stood. "Tons of work to do."

Casey reached for my arm and pulled me to sit.

Her face was menacing, lips pursed, eyebrows scrunched.

It actually scared me, her out-of-character demeanor.

"We've been a good friend to you, Charlie. You know things about me ... about my past that only"—she lifted three fingers, and then she pointed to Alyssa, herself, and then me—"a few people know about and about a person who should not be named. And so, I'm a little offended over here. Do you not trust us or something? If not, why the hell not?"

I sighed overly loud.

Alyssa's face was expectant. Casey ... well, if I didn't give up the goods, then I was sure we would no longer be buddies.

This was what girlfriends did, right? They overshared.

"It's not that I don't trust you guys. It's just that this ..." My gaze dropped to the table, and the inside of my chest stirred with uncertainty. "What's going on with me and Connor ... it was so unexpected. And it's also very temporary, and we both know this."

"And ..." Alyssa leaned in, getting in my line of sight.

"And what? He's leaving."

"So?" Alyssa prodded. As though him leaving shouldn't change anything. "You're in love with him," Alyssa stated as a fact, as though she was so sure.

I reeled back as though I'd been doused with a cup of water. "I'm not." But there was no gusto behind my tone.

"You are or else you wouldn't be so heartbroken over it."

"I'm not heartbroken," I said, knowing I was lying because if I were being honest with myself, I was. I didn't want what we had to end, but it would.

I rubbed at my temple, feeling an ongoing migraine coming on, and then I let it all out. I needed to get it out because it felt so much better to get it all out.

"I am in love with him. I mean, there's no way I couldn't be." My voice was so soft that I barely heard myself.

I stared at my hands, wringing them together on the table, as my chest tightened.

Moments later, warm hands wrapped around me. It was Casey.

I peered up, and thankfully, no one else was in the break room.

Her arms wrapped around me tighter. "He'll stay for you. He has to."

I peered up at her, and my voice cracked, full of emotion. "He won't."

I knew that much. So many times, Connor had indicated that his life, his job, his friends were in New York.

"He's a jackass," Alyssa snapped. "Nice guy but always been a coward."

Casey piped up, "How so?"

"All Connor's ever done is run away from this place when this is where he needs to be. He's a coward if he goes." Her warm hand patted my back. "And you don't deserve to be with a coward. No matter how big his dick is."

I laughed but then frowned the next second later. "We have one more film before we present to Mr. Colby. I just need to get through this, and I'll be fine."

Because as long as Connor was still here, I knew there was impending heartbreak to follow. I couldn't do it ... I couldn't move on with my life, and I needed to.

Casey tipped up my chin. "Right now, no thinking of Connor. You have a big event that you need to think about. Your exhibit."

Yeah, but too bad filming had to happen before that.

"And who cares about your mom or your stepdad? Because your favorite people will be there to support you."

Casey's gaze flipped to Alyssa, grabbing her hand. "We'll be there. Now, group hug."

Alyssa groaned. "Casey ..."

"Come on! I'm not taking no for an answer."

Both girls—ones who I'd only known for a short period of time—hugged me fiercely, and in that moment, I wanted to cry because I'd never had this before, this camaraderie.

CHAPTER 24

CONNOR

WE WERE FILMING the wedding scene today around the city of Chicago. The air was humid, but the sky was clear, and I couldn't have asked for a more perfect day to film.

I was sitting in my car, watching the film crew set up on Monroe Harbor, in front of Lake Michigan.

Many weeks ago, when Charlie and I had discussed a family feel to Colby Chocolates, she'd mentioned that in every occasion from dating to anniversaries, people celebrated with chocolate or candies. Students gave their teachers candies for Valentine's Day or boyfriends brought flowers and chocolates on their first date and also on their anniversaries. Chocolates and candies were universal gifts. It was Charlie's idea to go with that theme, and she couldn't have been more spot-on.

According to her, the beginning of a couple's life together into forever began with marriage. This would be the ending scene in our commercial, capturing the feel of the whole campaign and hopefully winning my father over.

I turned to the knock on my window. It was Charlie.

She slipped into the passenger seat, and my breath caught. She was in a form-fitting, elegant white dress that hugged her in all the right places. Her hair was pulled up with curls flowing endlessly down her back.

I took her in and was caught speechless because she was breathtakingly beautiful.

I swallowed. Hard.

"It's hot out there." She pulled down the visor and fluffed out a few of her curls.

"It's hot in here," I said, taking her in.

She had makeup on—not a lot, but enough to make the green in her eyes pop. Her lips were a pinkish color that made me want to bite them to see if they could get any pinker.

"You're beautiful," I said without a second thought.

Her eyes met mine, and her cheeks reddened, making the color she'd put on even more prominent. She focused her attention to the mirror on the visor. "You think?" With her ring finger, she fixed some of her eye shadow.

"I know."

"Do you think I look okay?"

I pulled down her hand, forcing her to face me. "Stop. You're perfect."

And she was, wasn't she. Beautiful, smart, creative, caring, and the list went on forever.

"I want to kiss you so bad right now." My gaze flickered to her lips and back to meet her eyes. "But I'll be good. We're filming in ten minutes."

She lightly patted my cheek and smiled. "Thanks for being good."

I wiggled my eyebrows. "I'm not that good. I showed you how naughty I could be last night."

She attempted to slap my shoulder, but I caught her hand midair. I kissed her open palm and intertwined our fingers.

"What are you doing this weekend?" I'd been thinking about this for a long time. I'd had this unsettling feeling in the pit of my stomach until I came up with the most brilliant idea.

"This weekend, meaning two days from now?" She blinked. "Finishing my paintings for my exhibit?" she answered my question with a question. "Given that this is the last portion of the presentation to your dad, I figured I really needed to prep and finish a few more paintings before next week's exhibit."

"Can you finish that during the week because I want to take you somewhere?"

She smiled. "Where?"

"To New York."

And that gorgeous smile slipped. "Why?" She blinked up at me, doe-eyed and stunning.

"To show you around. To show you New York because you've never been. Show you my place. Take you to a Broadway play. To thank you for all you've done for me and my family."

She chewed on her bottom lip, and her eyebrows scrunched together. "I ... I'm not sure."

"You don't think you can get away?"

"That's not it. But I just don't know."

There was a long, pregnant pause after that.

"But?" I prompted.

"What's the point? We agreed that we'll both be miserable after you leave. What's the point of me going to New York, seeing your life there, knowing you're leaving your life here?" There was a tinge of bitterness in her tone.

I got where she was coming from. I just wished she understood where I was coming from. "I just want to show you a good time, an all-expenses-paid trip to New York to show my gratitude for you helping me out."

She focused on the view of the Chicago skyline, the skyscrapers in the vicinity, the lake in front of us. Finally, after a long beat, she spoke, "I don't want to see your life in New York and think about your life there, when you're gone. I want to remember you with your life here, in Chicago, with me."

"Charlie ..." I paused, thinking of how I could say this without scaring her away. Because the only way I knew I could survive this was if she came with me. I'd been dreading the time ticking away until the drop date of when I had to leave. Before her, I couldn't wait to get back to my life in Manhattan, but after being with her, time had been going by so fast, and I needed it to stop. There was only one solution to my situation. "I want you to come with me, to move with me to New York."

Her eyes flipped to mine and then widened, but any hope of her coming with me got crushed at the look on her face. She huffed out a long breath, released me, and pushed the passenger door open. "You know I can't do that. I don't understand why you are making this more heartbreakingly difficult."

She stepped out the door and into the humid air, hugging her center.

Immediately, I exited the car. I walked toward her and held her at her elbows to face me. "Why not?"

"Because my life is here, with my mom, with my new friends."

"So?"

"So!" she scoffed, her voice high-pitched. "You might not love your family. But I love mine, okay?" she snapped.

"The family who won't even go to your exhibit." The instant those words left my mouth, I regretted it.

She reeled back as though I'd slapped her.

"I'm sorry. I didn't mean that." I reached for her, but she crossed her arms over her chest. I tugged at the fabric by her waist, feeling the silk between my fingertips. "Charlie, I'm sorry. Really."

Her gaze lowered to the ground, her chin to her chest.

"I shouldn't have said that. I'm sorry, okay?" I hated how our interaction had turned sour in the matter of minutes.

She nodded, but I knew she was lying. I pulled her into my arms, but she stiffened, distant and disconnected.

I wrapped my arms fully around her so she couldn't escape. "I'll come visit. Nana is here. Kyle is here. You're here."

Long distance. Could I do that? I'd tried that before, and that hadn't ended well, but this was different. This was with Charlie. I knew I'd do everything in my power to make us work.

"Yeah, maybe I'll be with my new boyfriend by then."

My whole body went rigid, and I knew she felt the shift in tension because she added, "And you'll be with your new girlfriend by then too. Then, we can all double date."

The thought of her with someone else, someone touching her, kissing her, made all of my muscles tense and had me wanting to punch something badly. I didn't want to be with anyone else but her.

"You're just being mean now." A weight settled in my gut, making me feel nauseous. "I don't want you to be with anyone but me, but I know that's not how the circumstances go." I pulled back and cupped her face. "Just think about it, okay? Think about New York. If anything, it'll be our last big hurrah before I'm scheduled to go back to my bank job."

She turned toward the lake, to the crew of people set up to film us. After she pulled away from me, her gaze dropped to the ground. "We should get started. You pay them by the hour. I'm sorry ... I'm just not in the best mood."

She turned to leave, but I gripped her hand and locked eyes with her. I wouldn't be able to handle her being with anyone else, so I had to try again.

"Charlie ... promise me you'll think about it."

She smiled and nodded but didn't say a word as she walked to the crew.

CHARLIE

The air brushed against my skin, my neck, my arms, and my bare back. The dress was beautiful with its alluring halter top, the way the neck scooped and revealed just the right amount of cleavage, and how the fabric hugged my hips and cascaded into a pool of fabric like ripples in a lake at my feet.

"Charlie," Wyatt, the director, called out. "Okay, run to Connor."

Why did I feel like I was on some sort of romantic cheesy film? This was the fifth time I ran through the sand, barefoot, my dress flowing around me, my curls bouncing against the wind, before I jumped into his arms. Our backdrop was the Chicago skyline.

It didn't feel natural because it wasn't. I was still uneasy about our conversation earlier, and there was this tension between us that was palpable.

I couldn't help it. I was bitter that he was leaving, but it didn't make a lick of sense because I had known this. I had known this was going to happen. But what I could have never predicted was falling so deeply in love with him.

Wyatt yelled to the crew of cameramen in front of him, "Okay ... again." Then he turned toward us. "Please. Let's make this believable. Do we need a break?"

Connor waved a hand. "Yeah, let's take five." He walked toward me, gripping my elbow, and pulled me to the side.

For the life of me, I couldn't look him in the eye. I needed to get over this and stat.

He lifted my chin with the lightness of his fingertips. "I'm sorry, Charlie. For what I said earlier about your mom."

I gently pulled his hand down, and my focus landed at the lake, at the beautiful skyline of Michigan Avenue. "We're okay, Connor. Promise."

"Then, why won't you look at me?"

When my stare made it back to his face, he closed his eyes, squeezing them tightly.

"What are you doing?"

"Closing my eyes."

The corner of my mouth ticked up for the first time in this whole session.

"Because it hurts to look at you. You're so damn beautiful," he repeated my words from many weeks ago, in the closet, our first time together.

My heart beat loudly in my chest—not just one beat, but two and three and four beats where there was a whole marching band in my chest.

"You're crazy ..." I said, full of emotion.

He opened his eyes, took my one hand in his, and went on bended knee. "I'm sorry, Charlie. Forgive me for wanting to spend every waking moment with you. Forgive me for wanting you to move with me."

My breath caught as I stared deeply into the sea of brown gazing back up at me.

"But most of all, forgive me for falling in love with you when I wasn't supposed to."

"Connor ..."

He stood, taking my other hand too, rubbing the top of my fists. "Listen, I don't want to fight with you, not when we don't have that long together. I know we both couldn't have predicted this, but can we just do what we promised each other in that closet, in the dark ... and make the most of the time that we have together?"

I swallowed back the lump in the back of my throat and nodded, falling into his arms. Because that had been the deal, that had been the plan—to live in the moment.

He squeezed me tightly against him, his arms wrapping along my lower back, and I nestled into his chest, a spot I swore that was meant for me.

"Let's never fight again, okay?" His warm breath brushed against my temple.

"Okay," I said, pulling back and giving him a sweet kiss.

"Hey!" Wyatt called over. "Lovebirds, are you guys ready? I'd like to get this done in the next hour."

"Hold your panties. We're ready," Connor snapped back. He cupped my cheek, leaning so close that I could smell the mint on his lips. "Hey, read back the script for me."

My hands fell on his wrists. "So, they're past their first date, past the dating period ..."

"Of six months," he added.

I smiled. "And past the engagement ... to the now. They're here, just the two of them, professing their love to each other, on the beach, because this is how they always pictured it." I went on my toes, our lips a millimeter apart. "This is the ending of their dating period. The finale. The end of their single life. But this ... this marriage is the beginning of their lives together, as a family, as one."

My heart fluttered, and my stomach dipped when he closed the gap between us and kissed me. He kissed me like I was the first woman he'd ever dated and the only woman that he wanted to spend the rest of his life with. He kissed me like this was real, like we weren't playing a part, but this was our own happy ending.

And I reveled in it, pretended that just for a moment, he wasn't leaving, and this was us—our own happily ever after.

CHAPTER 25

CHARLIE

FILMING WAS OVER, and a rush of butterflies filled my stomach as it had on the beach. I carried the bag of greasy fries while Connor held our burgers.

We entered his apartment, and I took his bag and placed it on his glass kitchen table.

"I'm so hungry." I rubbed my belly, needing to fill it with all the greasy goodness. I made my way to his cupboard as though this were my own house and grabbed some plates and napkins. After the weeks we'd been together, I knew this apartment inside and out.

He had been quiet the whole way home, and though I'd wondered what he was thinking, I had also known not to ask because I was thinking the very same thing.

There was a ticking bomb on our relationship, and the bomb would explode on the day he moved back to Manhattan. And every time I thought about it, I wanted to cry, but I had known this. Right? I'd made an adult decision to enter into this relationship with Connor, knowing he was going to leave. But the stakes were different now, weren't they? Because he'd asked me to move with him, and I hadn't predicted that I would fall in love with him.

I bit the inside of my cheek and focused on unpacking our burgers and fries and placing them on the plates on the table.

Connor's eyes burned through me. I knew he was watching my every move even though I wasn't looking at him.

I moved back to the cupboards to get some glasses. After pouring water, I sat down but still didn't meet his eyes.

Why does this have to be so hard?

I stood. "I should change before I get grease on this beautiful dress."

When I stood, he reached for my wrist and tugged me until I fell into his lap.

"Don't. Leave it on." His voice was quiet, almost sad.

"Okay ..." I fisted the edges of the silk that clung to my body. "What are we going to do with this dress? It's thousands of dollars, and we can't return it. I'll have to look up where we can donate it."

His fingers gripped me tighter, and he rested his forehead against my shoulder and sighed.

"Go to New York with me ..." His words were uttered in a dying plea. When I didn't answer, he lifted his head and guided my chin to face him. "Charlie ..."

I held his face within my palms. "Why such the sad face?" I squeezed his cheeks together until he formed a fish face. Then, I pecked his lips.

Didn't we decide we'd take it a day at a time?

His eyebrows scrunched, and then he sighed. "I want you to move in with me. I need you with me, Charlie. I love you."

I stared deeply in his eyes, saw his sincerity behind his words. "And I love you."

I clenched my teeth together in a tight smile. I wouldn't cry, not when he was here. When he left, I knew I'd cry a million tears, but until then … I'd be happy and enjoy his presence, just like I'd promised myself in the office closet, just like I'd promised him earlier.

I extracted myself from his hold and sat on my own chair, lifting the bun from the hamburger and taking out the tomatoes. "You can't say things like that and expect everything to be okay between us. You know I can't go with you."

"We'll come back here to visit every weekend."

He knew I still had my mom here, but that wasn't the reason that I didn't want to go. I had just upped and left my life in Wisconsin to move to Illinois, and now, I had a job I didn't mind and friends who I loved. I wasn't even considering moving to Manhattan. Simply, he might be the right guy, but now was not the right time.

I picked up my burger and then placed it down on the plate, my appetite now gone when, a minute ago, I could have sworn my stomach was eating its own lining.

"Why does this have to be so hard?" The words slipped out before I could stop them.

In the next second, Connor was beside me. He pulled me to stand and held my palm in the tenderness of his fingertips. "It doesn't have to be. All you have to do is say yes."

"Yes to the dress?" I scrunched my nose, but he didn't get the reference because he had probably never watched the show.

"Yes to me." He nipped my lips and then bent forward. "Yes to moving in." Another kiss. "Yes to New York."

The last kiss lingered and ticked up in tempo. He

flicked his tongue over the seam of my lips, intertwining his tongue with mine.

My whole body tingled with arousal when he slipped his hands behind my knees. I wrapped my arms around his neck, never breaking contact.

He led us to his bedroom, and I couldn't help but think he was carrying me over the threshold. Me in this form-fitting silk designer wedding gown. Him in his tux that fit him perfectly. And us together, lip-locked in this soul-wrenching kiss.

Gently, he laid me down in the bed, and I stared up at this Adonis of a man. This man. For a hot, brief second, over the past few weeks, he'd become my man.

He undid his bow tie and chucked it to the side before untucking his shirt.

With the flick of his fingers, he unbuttoned his shirt, and with each one that came undone, my body wriggled beneath him in anticipation.

When his shirt was off, my mouth went dry. I went on my elbows, licking every line of his six-pack. Without a second thought, I sat up and traced my tongue against every curve of his abs.

"Charlie," he rushed out, threading his fingers through my hair.

I licked a path higher and higher until I made it to his nipple, where I locked eyes with his and flicked my tongue, circling the sensitive area over and over again, watching his breathing labor.

Patience was not his strong suit, and he pulled me up to kiss him. We were all tongues and wet, sloppy kisses. He slipped the dress off my shoulder and nipped at my neck, pushing me onto the bed.

My head flew back as he pushed the dress further

down, exposing pasties on my breasts, tearing them off with his teeth.

His fingers made a sensual path on my leg, brushing against my thigh and to the apex between my legs. I gripped his hair, moaning his name as his fingers pierced me, ripples of pleasure tingling all over.

"Connor ..." His name was a harsh, broken puff falling from my lips. I lifted my head and tugged at his hair to meet his eyes. "I need you in me."

The devilish smirk was heavily displayed as his fingers pushed and teased inside me. "I want to see you come."

What was it with his dying need to see me undone each and every time? As though he hadn't watched me the dozens of times before.

"I want you, baby," I moaned out. "Please. I need you."

With my plea, he pulled at the dress and my panties until they were a puddle of mess on the floor. "You're keeping the dress."

I laughed, and as he pushed down his pants, I reached for him before positioning him at my opening. "Why? So we can reenact this scene? I hear married people have more sex than single people."

I pushed my pelvis up to meet him, and once we were connected, I sighed.

He groaned.

But in the next second, our eyes flew open and locked.

He wasn't wearing a condom.

He pushed himself up on his hands but didn't extract himself. A sheen of sweat was heavy at his brow.

"Do you want me to put a condom on?" he breathed out, touching his forehead against mine. "I'm clean, baby. I've never had sex without one."

"Never?"

His stare locked with mine. "Never." His voice was ragged, his body still, as if he was waiting for my answer for his next move.

I locked my legs around him. "I'm on the pill," I said. It was reckless and dangerous, but I hadn't been with anyone for years, and I wanted him to make love to me with nothing between us.

He swallowed and then lowered himself on me. He kissed me with a fervent passion I felt everywhere.

I anchored my pelvis back and forth and forth and back again until his breathing turned ragged.

"Charlie ..."

CONNOR

I'd never had sex without a condom. Ever. And I'd had a lot of sex in my lifetime.

Even in my long-term relationship in high school, I'd always capped my shit. There was prestige and power and money behind my name, and I had goals and direction and plans ahead of me. I didn't want a woman using me for that. One wrong move on my part, and I'd be stuck in Illinois for good, so it'd never happened.

But this was different. This was Charlie.

She felt amazing. Skin to skin. Being this close to her wasn't enough though. I needed closer.

I took the lead, pulling her hands to the top of her head, driving into her faster, deeper, and harder until low moans escaped her lips.

Her eyes were at half-mast, her lips parted slightly. As I went down and kissed her, really kissed her, a shudder ran through me.

My movements slowed until everything around me

heightened—her short, quick breaths that left her mouth, her legs wrapped tightly around me, her one hand that made its way to my back while the other threaded through my hair.

And it hit me.

I'd never loved another woman like her. I couldn't imagine getting close to feeling what I felt for Charlie for anyone else, and that scared me.

Sweat beaded on my temple, and I gripped her waist tighter because the realization punched me straight in my chest. I rested my forehead against hers, moving above her, inside her. If there was any woman out there meant for me, it was this woman—and I let her know with every movement of my body inside of hers and with my words.

"I love you," I said, locking my eyes with hers.

She touched my face, searching my eyes for something, anything. Then, she lifted her head and kissed me.

I knew she was close, so close to coming. I felt her tighten around me, and I released my lips as her head fell to the side.

When the first of her orgasm took her over, she tightened around me, which sent me over as well.

I fisted the blanket right next to her head and lost myself to everything that was my girlfriend, who I loved.

An hour later, she lay where she was meant to be—her head on my chest and my arms wrapped tightly around her.

In the silent of the night, her warm breaths brushed against my chest. I held her against me, wondering how lucky I was to have her in my life. Her beauty astounded me. It wasn't just her physical beauty, but also her beauty from within. And how, when she loved, she wanted to nurture and take care of everyone around her. She loved so deeply, and I wanted to be a recipient of that love.

All I knew in that moment was that I wasn't letting her go. If I had to move her mom, stepdad, and family to New York, I'd do it. Whatever it would take to get her to come with me. I'd come here to save a company. I didn't care about how much more it would take to fight for and win the woman I loved.

I'd fight till the end, until I won.

CHARLIE

The days seemed to blend together. Spending the weekend with Connor and not wanting to leave. I'd never wanted to slow time down so badly.

In a few days, it would be my exhibit and then the presentation of our new rebranding campaign, and then Connor would leave.

I focused on the task at hand or else I'd get all sappy and emotional again, and I didn't want to do that.

I blew out my hair from my face and stacked my paintings horizontally in the moving box. The pool house looked bare without my paintings against the chairs and off the counter, almost dead, like an abandoned warehouse.

Connor would be here tomorrow night to help me set up my paintings at the exhibit, so I needed everything to be in moving condition.

The door opening had me glancing up from the boxes I had been trying to rearrange.

"Mom." I had kept my distance from her the whole weekend, not wanting her to see how badly she hurt me.

"Hey, honey." Her voice was low, and she fiddled with the edge of her shirt. "Can I ... can I come in?"

"Sure." My back straightened, and my heartbeat picked up in speed as I remembered our last conversation, the hurt hitting me directly in the chest. My focus was back at packing the canvases.

She walked in and surveyed the area, her hand grazing the couch and the table. "Getting ready?" Her voice was soft, almost fragile.

"Yep." My gaze dropped to the box again, staring at nothing in general, and everything stopped because, for the life of me, I couldn't stop replaying that awful scene in my head—on how she'd picked Sandy over me.

"Honey, you've been avoiding me. Last time we spoke, it didn't end well." Her voice trailed off.

I didn't peek up to look at her, moving the canvases around as though they weren't straight enough, which was stupid because they were already in the box.

There was a silence in the room that sucked up all the air, and I couldn't breathe, anger threatening to choke me.

I needed to stay calm. I needed to just do this for myself. This was no longer about pleasing my mother and getting her approval. Connor was right. Nui would be there, and she was the professional after all. The weight of an artist wasn't measured by her mother's approval, was it?

"Mom, let's just not talk about it."

"No, honey. We have to." She walked toward me, and I stared at her sandals, the ones that Daddy had purchased for her when we were on vacation.

We had gone to Destin, Florida, driving there from Wisconsin. We were window-shopping down a row of local shops, and my mom stared at the shoes forever, wanting to buy them but knowing she shouldn't splurge. My father, being the man that he was, had gone back to the shop to get them and surprised my mother with them the next day.

"I ..." She bent down and knelt beside me. "I don't know how to act in front of them."

Her words forced me to look up at her, her honesty revealing a vulnerability that she hardly ever showed. She fiddled with her fingernails, her chin downturned, and all of me wanted to hug her in that very moment.

"I ... I love Richard. I do. But I don't know where I quite fit in yet, and I want everyone to just get along. I want Sandy to like me. I want Sandy to like you. I want you to like Sandy. I want you to love Richard like he already loves you." She peered up at me and offered a sad smile.

I hadn't realized this, that she was having a hard time with the transition. I'd assumed that she was happy.

"Mom ..." I reached for her hand and squeezed it.

The first of her tears began to fall. "No. Listen, Charlie." She swiped at her eyes. "Your dad will and always be the love of my life." Her tears caused my own tears to well up. "He always took care of us in the best way he knew how. But we struggled, and you know that. I didn't want that to happen to you. Parents want their kids to have a better life."

She met my eyes then, cupping my face as she used to do when I was younger, when I was still her little girl. "And I know you're talented. God and everyone knows you have talent, Charlie. Maybe I was afraid of that talent, that it wouldn't pay the bills, that it would ruin your life, and for that, I'm sorry. I just didn't want you to ever struggle like I did, so that's why I pushed you in college. But not once did I think you hadn't been born with a gift, a gift of creativity, a gift of art."

Did she really believe that? The one burning question in the back of my throat filtered out. "Did you throw away my paintings?"

Her eyebrows furrowed, and she reeled back, confused at my change in subject. "What?"

I swallowed, my gaze dropping to the floor. "My paintings were ruined, put out in the rain, thrown out in the garbage." I remembered that day vividly, the pain slicing my chest like a dagger to my heart. I held my breath, meeting her eyes, waiting for an answer.

She vehemently shook her head. "I swear to you, I didn't. Why would I do that? Honey, do you think I hate your art?"

I released a breath because that had been weighing heavily on me for the longest time. It had to be Sandy because who else hated me that much?

She bent down, lifting my chin with the lightness of her fingertips. "I love you and everything about you, and my biggest mistake, my biggest downfall, is not making you believe that. For you to even consider that I'd do such a thing ... because I would never ..." She sighed. "I just wanted to make sure that you were taken care of, that you'd have a stable future."

I placed my hand over hers on my cheek. "I know, Mom. I understand."

After a beat, she kissed my forehead before motioning around the room. "We have everything now though, right? Life should be perfect, but it's not, is it?" Her smile was sad. "You're unhappy. I can see it. I see the tension between you and Sandy. I just ... I want everything to be okay. For everything to pan out for us. When your dad was alive, he made sure everything was okay, and I only want to do the same, baby girl. I want to make sure you're okay."

"And I want to make sure you're okay too, Mom. That you're happy."

Her eyes crinkled, showing her years of wisdom. "I am happy. How can I not be ... when I have you?"

The first of many tears fell, both of us a crying mess now.

She bent down again, and we held each other's hands, letting all the emotions spill onto the table.

"I'll do better. I promise." Then, she pulled me into a hug and tenderly kissed the top of my head. "I'll be there."

My throat was choked full of emotion that I couldn't speak, and I buried my head into her shoulder, my tears soaking her shirt.

She ran one light hand through my hair. "There is nothing that will make me miss it. Nothing, okay?"

I nodded. "Okay."

CHAPTER 26

CHARLIE

TODAY WAS THE DAY. The day that I'd been saving for, the day where I'd show the world that I had talent, just like my dad had told me I did.

The doors opened at seven, and I would show up at eight. That was the deal.

But every second felt like hours as I paced the hallway of Connor's living room, gnawing at my bottom lip.

Connor had helped me in the wee hours in the evening to move and hang everything up at the place. The exhibit was perfection personified. Still, I couldn't shake my nerves.

"Gray tie or blue?" In a sharp gray suit and blue button-down shirt, Connor strolled in, holding up two ties.

I scrunched my face and shook both of my hands out. "I-I don't know." I peered up at the ceiling and blew out a breath. "It doesn't matter. Everything looks fine."

Taking a few short, shallow breaths, I paced the room again, retracing my steps.

"Charlie."

When I turned to face him, he approached and reached for my elbows, pulling me in. He leaned in, his head so close to mine, and smiled. "Breathe."

But I couldn't. Instead of breathing, I inhaled and held it there for a long time, most likely turning all shades of unhealthy.

He gave me a little shake. "Baby, you're turning blue. Breathe."

I exhaled but didn't let all the air out. "I can't."

"You'll die if you can't."

"I don't know if I can do this. I mean, even if Nui doesn't show up, other people will be there. Alyssa and Casey invited their family members." I closed my eyes, the heightened anxiety making me want to throw up.

He pulled me into him, his lips brushing against my temple. "I wish you had the same level of faith in yourself that I have in you."

And right then and there, he was my father, pushing me to be the best, to share my art with the world.

I lifted my chin and rested it against his chest. "You remind me so much of my dad."

He chuckled and raised both brows. "And that is just weird. Please don't say that."

"But you do." I kissed his chin. "You make me feel so much better about myself. Like I'm meant to do this."

He angled closer until his eyes were intently locked on mine. "Charlie, you're the most talented person I know. And I'm not just saying that. Alyssa and Casey and everyone in the office knows you are. Your father knew you were. All you need is to believe in yourself. It will be amazing, I promise."

He leaned in, sweetly kissing me on the lips. "You're going to kill it tonight. Now, tell me ... since I'm meeting the

Ps, gray tie or blue? I'm a little nervous. You know I haven't been introduced to parents in a long-ass time."

I sighed. "Gray."

But what I really wanted to say was ... why did it matter? What was meeting my mom and stepdad going to do for us? He'd be gone and out of my life before the end of this month.

"I hope they like me." He smiled all teeth, and it was boyish and cute and all kinds of handsome.

It was all too much to take, so I patted his lapel down. "They'll love you. Just like I do."

CONNOR

The exhibit was packed with art buffs and spectators, all perusing and enjoying my girlfriend's creations. As Charlie fidgeted by my side, I fiercely held her hand as people congratulated her, and asked her about specific pieces.

The walls were painted a faint, light gray, and all around, her paintings were hung up. Mostly abstract, but some of people, men, and random photos.

No doubt she was nervous. It was in the way her shoulders cowered inward and the way she nodded with this forced smile, but what she needed to do was push out her chest and own it, own her talent and not be shy.

Part of me wanted to scoop her up and take her somewhere, away from all this anxiety, and the other part of me knew this was good for her.

I stepped back and watched as two people approached her.

They pointed to a painting where the blues and greens and yellows splattered into a ball that exploded like fire. After a beat, she dropped her hands and gestured to the work of art. The more time that passed, the more animated she became, to where her shoulders shook from laughter as she pointed to the painting.

I had to ask her what that was about, where she had gotten her inspiration.

When someone shoved at my shoulder, I flipped around to find my brother sporting a sly grin.

"Look at you, all suited up, and it's not even your show."

My focus went back to Charlie. "Meeting the parents."

Kyle let out a low, hoarse whistle. "That's pretty serious stuff, dude."

"Yeah." But we were pretty serious stuff.

"So ... you've convinced her to move to New York with you?"

"Not yet."

He laughed, and it irked me. "What does that mean?"

"I'm still trying to convince her, and I'm not giving up." When was there ever a time where I didn't get what I wanted? "She just upped and left her life in Wisconsin to move here, and I get that, but that doesn't mean she can't adjust to New York. I just have to persuade her that there are better opportunities in Manhattan. Plus, if I talk to her mom and—"

"Don't go there."

I flipped to face him, my muscles tightening.

He grimaced. "I'm telling you right now, you go there, and it will be bad."

I huffed, frustrated, knowing I didn't have that much time left to convince her. "And of course, I'm going to feel her mom out first before I tell her about New York."

He paused, opened his mouth, and shut it again. "Okay, your funeral." After a shake of his head, he patted me on the shoulder. "Please, do not use *feel her mom out* in the same sentence."

Normally, I would have laughed, but his earlier comment had put me in a foul mood.

Thirty minutes later, I was still watching Charlie from afar. She had a dozen people lined up to meet her, the artist, and I stood, taking it in like it was my very own exhibit.

When my phone buzzed in my pocket, I reached in and put it to my ear.

"Connor, honey? Where are you?"

It was Nui, and my eyes searched for Charlie at the far end of the room. "It's in the Theatre District—232 Madison. Are you here?"

"I landed at O'Hare an hour ago, and it was a pain in my ass to get an Uber. When I finally did, he looked like a creeper, so I hopped out of the car and got into another Uber. Then ... it was just bad. Anyway, I'm here."

"You're here? Okay, come in. I'll get Charlie."

I started walking toward Charlie, but there were a few people talking to her. When I waved at her, her eyes met mine. She placed a hand on the older woman's forearm and excused herself.

"Hey, baby."

Charlie's smile was so relaxed and at ease until I ducked my head and whispered in her ear, "Nui is here."

"What?" Her eyes went wide.

"She's walking in."

Charlie gripped my hand with such force that it cut off the blood flow. "Where?"

I tipped her chin up. "She's in the front."

She gritted her teeth together, and before she had the time to muster words of nervousness, Nui appeared in her four-inch stiletto heels and her Louis Vuitton purse, which I was sure was the latest version.

"Connor ..." she cooed as though we were the best of friends. She pressed her cheek against mine and then to the other cheek like the Europeans we weren't.

When she stepped back, she smiled and gave my girlfriend a once-over. "And you must be charming Charlie ..."

She extended her hand, and Charlie shook it graciously.

"Yes. And I love your work. I follow you on social media, and I love the artists you feature." Charlie's voice heightened with excitement.

"And you are one of the talented artists that I want to feature on my blog." Nui spread her arms and turned in an exaggerated circle. "Look at this. I mean, the depth of these abstracts and the paintings ... you've caught great detail on some of them." She pointed to the other end of the room. "There's one there that's breathtaking. It's of a daughter and father."

Charlie's smile widened. "That's me and my dad."

"There is so much emotion there, just from his stare. It's pouring out of him in waves. Endless waves."

Charlie sucked on her bottom lip, teetering back on her heels. "Yeah ... it was one of the last pictures we took together before he died."

Nui's smile slipped and she leaned into Charlie. "He'd be so proud of you. Your artwork is ..." She paused for dramatic effect, which was signature to Nui. "One word: remarkable."

Charlie let out one long breath, and her shoulders relaxed.

"Charlie."

My head turned to the woman who had called her name. It was Charlie's mother, I had no doubt. Because twenty-five years from now, I could see Charlie standing in front of me, stunning as ever, her eyes a vibrant emerald green.

Charlie's mother's face was exuberant, smile wide, eyes bright. "Look at this, honey. It's amazing."

Charlie bit her bottom lip, nervous, but as soon as her mother took her in and wrapped her arms around her in a hug, Charlie's whole body relaxed.

"Look at all of this."

Automatically, I smiled. 'Cause, shit, this was all Charlie had wanted from her mother—acknowledgment of her work.

Her mother pulled back and cupped her face with a lightness of her fingertips. "I'm so, so proud of you, honey." She motioned to the spectators around the room. "Look at all the people who have come to see your work. It's a full house."

Charlie laughed. "Yeah, I'm pretty shocked. I wasn't expecting this type of turnout."

"Kid, I wish your dad were here to see this. I've been walking around for ten minutes, looking for you, just listening to random people admiring your pieces." She leaned in, squeezing Charlie's hand. "Good job, baby girl."

They shared an emotional-filled glance.

After a beat, Charlie turned to us. "Mom, this is Connor, and this is Nui."

I had my spiel ready—how stunning she looked and there was no wonder where Charlie had gotten her good looks from. I was about to tell her that I'd been waiting to meet her, but I faltered a bit because Charlie had lumped me in with Nui, as though I were a friend.

I took a step forward, extending a strong hand to Charlie's mother. "Nice to finally meet you."

She eyed me for a moment. "Nice to meet you, Connor. I'm Olivia." Then, she turned to Nui. "What did you say your name was?"

"Nui. I have to tell you, Olivia, I'm an artist myself, and your daughter's work is beyond this world."

They began talking about Charlie and individual pieces and which were Nui's favorites.

As their conversation continued, my jaw tightened. I'd wanted a better introduction. I didn't know what I had expected. I hadn't expected for her to treat me like one of the people who had just shown up to her daughter's exhibit. When I stepped into Charlie and placed a hand on the small of her back, she took a step forward.

What the hell?

Then, the next series of events happened so rapid fast that it took a while for me to take in what was going on.

CHARLIE

"Connor!" From my far left, walking toward us was Sandy, holding a champagne glass.

I had known Richard would be here, but why the hell was Sandy here? She didn't even like me. Plus, she had an event at work today. And how the hell did she know Connor?

"Sandy?" Connor's eyes flew wide open when Sandy wrapped her arms around him in a tight vise.

I gritted my teeth together in a smile, the type of smile that hurt because I was grinding my molars.

Richard strolled in right behind him. "Connor, I haven't seen you in forever."

It was as though I were in the twilight zone, watching

Richard hug Connor as though he knew him ... really knew him.

"Did you move back?"

"No, I didn't, sir," Connor said. "Just helping with the business for a bit. I'll head back to Manhattan soon."

Sandy adjusted her hair, pulling it all to one side.

"Nice pictures, Charlie. They're ... pretty," Sandy cooed as though she were telling me I had a pretty dress on.

Richard pointed a finger toward me and then Connor. "So, you guys know each other from work. Connor, did you know that Sandy got Charlie the job at Colby's?"

Connor coughed, almost as if he'd choked on his own saliva. "I didn't know that."

Connor's eyebrows scrunched together, as though he were working something in his head, but I was slow on the uptake.

"How do you guys know each other?" my mother asked, motioning between Sandy and Connor.

"We dated in high school," Sandy responded.

A dizzying current overtook my body, and for a moment, I couldn't breathe. *Only long-term relationship. In high school. Loved her, but it hadn't worked out.*

The dizzying current amplified until I swayed, and when Connor threw an arm around my shoulders, bringing me in, I fell into him simply because I thought I might faint.

"I should thank you then for bringing us together like this because ... we're dating."

There were very few times I could recall where my life played like a movie on slow motion. It was an out-of-body experience, seeing it as though it was not happening to me but to someone else, unbelieving that it was my reality. When they'd pulled the plug on my father on his deathbed —my reality. My father's funeral—my reality. My mother crying her eyes out for months after—my reality. And now, this moment—this exact moment—my new reality.

The moment Connor revealed that we were dating.

The moment that I realized that the person I despised the most had dated the person I loved.

Sandy's glass slipped from her hand, shattering over the floor. "Wait, what?" Her voice was high-pitched and screechy.

The glass was everywhere.

Alyssa and Casey called out my name from a far corner.

When my mother bent down to clean up the glass, Richard told her to stop, but it was for nothing because she sliced her finger.

And I saw it.

The little drops of blood.

So, I fainted.

On the floor.

In front of everyone.

At my first exhibit.

"Good gosh, not again."

It was Casey.

And that was the last thing I remembered.

CHAPTER 27

CHARLIE

SOMETHING COLD and damp hit my cheeks ... my fore-head ... my eyelids.

One of my eyes opened and then the other. I squinted against the white light, my eyes not fully open, adjusting to the sensitivity.

"Hey ... beautiful."

It was Connor.

My eyes flew shut again because the overhead lights above me had blinded me.

Where am I?

Am I at a hospital?

Then, it hit me.

Exhibit.

I shook myself from my dazed stupor and pushed myself off whatever I was lying on.

"Hey. Easy." Connor placed his hand on my shoulder, guiding me back to lay on the couch, but I didn't want to lie back down.

"Wait ... no." I was fully awake now, eyes open, noting the empty exhibit.

The patrons were gone. Nui was gone. My mother was gone.

"Where is everyone?" Panic threatened to choke me.

"They left. You've been out for the last two hours."

Wait, what?

I stood, feeling unsteady but using the couch against the far wall, right below one of my paintings, for support. I gripped the top of my hair.

"Two hours?" My breathing accelerated, and I shook my head over and over again. "I missed it." My voice trembled, and a lump formed in the back of my throat.

Months and months of work and money and effort and energy into this one day, and I ... I had missed it. I'd missed it all.

My arms wrapped around my stomach, queasiness coming at me full force.

"Baby, it was a success." Connor pulled me in, his hands on my forearms, but I was looking past him, toward my wall of paintings, toward the vast room with no one standing in it.

He lifted my chin to meet his eyes. "You sold over six thousand dollars' worth of paintings tonight."

I'd missed it.

Then, without warning, I started to cry.

"Where's my mom?" I extracted myself from Connor's arms and walked around in circles.

"What?"

"Where did she go?"

"She just left. She insisted that she stay, but I told her I drove you here and that you'd stay with me tonight."

"Why would you do that?" I snapped.

He took a step back and blinked. One hand was on his hip, and he rubbed at his jawline with the other hand. "Charlie, what is this?"

"What is what?" I paced the room, walking back to the couch, looking for my purse. *Where the hell is my purse?*

He reached for my arm and jerked me to face him. "Charlie, what is this—us?" His voice was hard this time.

But I pulled my arm from his grasp, searching for my purse. "Where is my purse?" Full-blown emotions rushed through me like a volcano ready to explode.

"Charlie!" he yelled, causing me to pause. The muscle in his jaw twitched. "What is this—us? Where is this"—he motioned between me and him—"going?"

"You're going to do this here ... now? Really?" My expression pinched. "How selfish can you be right now? I've worked for months leading up to this one day, and I basically missed it all." I was too far gone and over-the-top frustrated to stop now. "You dated Sandy?" My voice didn't even sound like my own.

How could someone like him date someone like her and then date me?

He reeled back, his facial features falling. "That was forever ago. It was a time in my life I don't even remember."

I tore my eyes from his and went on my knees, looking under the couch for my purse. I couldn't think clearly in his vicinity, and I needed to leave. "What are the chances, right? Yep, this is my life."

"I couldn't care less about Sandy. This is about me and you. Charlie ... I'm trying to talk to you here. Answer my question."

I stood then.

"What's going on between us?"

I straightened to my full height, that volcano of emotion

spilling over in a gigantic eruption. "Nothing. How can this"—I motioned between us—"be anything when you're leaving?" I snapped.

He took a healthy step back as though I'd slapped him. "I asked you to move in with me. To come with me to New York."

"And I said I'm not going to." I needed my purse. I needed to get away from him. All this news was too much for me to take—the bombshell news of Sandy and Connor, my wasted exhibit, his freaking-out moment.

"You're a grown-ass woman who can function on her own and without your mother, whom you didn't even introduce me as your—"

"As what? As my boyfriend?" I threw up both hands, screaming at this point. "Because you're not. Why the hell would I introduce her to someone who was not going to be here in a month anyway?"

"I asked ..."

He was like a never-ending broken record on repeat.

"I know, and I said no." I shoved a finger into his chest. "I know I'm a grown-ass woman, but contrary to your belief, it's my choice to stay here because I want to. Because I love my life here and my friends and my mom. Because being in the same state as my mom is important to me. Because I want to be with her and have her watch my kids and watch her grow old and happy with Richard. Just because you don't want to be by your family and you're not close doesn't mean that I'm the same way because I'm not. You're not winning this one, Connor. And I'm not choosing my mom or my life here over you. I'm choosing me. This is my decision."

Between the corner of the couch and the wall, I saw a sliver of silver—my purse.

I rushed toward it, chucked the strap over my shoulder, and headed toward the door. "I'm calling an Uber." It was probably too late to call my mom.

"Charlie ..." He followed me outside.

Shit. I had to lock up.

I walked back in toward the light panel, shut off all the lights, and walked outside again to lock up.

When he reached for my arm because I wouldn't respond to him, I jerked back. "Stop. I want to go home."

Both of his hands were up. "Fine. Please, just let me drive you."

"I'll catch an Uber." I pulled out my phone, but then he grabbed it from me. "Connor! You're such an ass. Give it back!"

His whole demeanor flipped like a coin, and he bent down, his facial features softening. "I'm sorry. Okay?" He reached for my hand, but I pulled back, stubborn. "I'm sorry for saying such shitty things in there. I didn't mean it. I just want more. I get it ... I get that you're not willing to give me what I want. And I respect that. I have to. Just please ... Charlie, let me drive you home."

We held each other's stare for a few good solid seconds before I nodded and crossed my arms over my chest.

CONNOR

The ride home was silent. I wanted her to come over. I wanted us to stop fighting and maybe talk things through at my apartment because, right now, talking was not happening, just a lot of narrowed glares and blank stares into the highway in front of us. I was afraid that anything I said, I'd regret. I didn't want to let emotions lead our conversations. I was usually composed. It was one of my qualities that I valued the most.

But with Charlie, that all flew out the door.

Normally, I would have pushed it but not tonight.

We didn't even discuss the subject of Sandy, which, in my opinion, was a nonissue because it felt like years and years ago when we had been together.

What I wanted to concentrate on was the here and now and the future, but right now, our future looked bleak.

Maybe I could ask her if we could try long distance—but how would that work? She would never move, and neither would I. So, we were at a stalemate.

I parked in front of her house, a house that Richard had bought—my ex-girlfriend's father. *How was this even a possibility? How could I have predicted this?*

When she reached for the door handle, I grabbed her other hand.

"Hey."

Her eyes were tired, sad even, and shit, it hit me directly in the chest.

"Charlie, you did an amazing job today. Your exhibit was a great success. Nui said she'd be reaching out to you within the next few days to feature you on her blog."

She nodded, but there was a blank expression in her eyes. "Thanks for driving me home."

She pushed the door open, but I wasn't ready to let her go ... not yet.

"Charlie."

She turned toward me, one foot already on the pavement.

"I love you." Wasn't that the truth though?

After today, I knew that everything would change between us, and she had to know that above all things. That was one thing I wanted her to remember. The one thing that I wanted to highlight was that I loved her.

She leaned back in the car and pressed her lips to mine.

It was a long, lingering kiss, but my stomach dropped, and it kept on going.

Because it wasn't a kiss good night. It felt like a kiss good-bye.

CHARLIE

I thought things couldn't get any worse, but as I stomped back to the pool house, I saw Sandy sitting on a bench by the pool.

I raised a hand and walked past her. "I don't want to hear it. Not fucking today, okay?"

I couldn't take anymore, not without breaking down any further.

Just as I inserted the key into the door, she said, "He'll never stay for you. As much as he loves you or says he does, he won't stay. I should know. Years ago, I was where you are."

I gritted my teeth, having enough of her bullying bullshit.

"What happens between me and Connor is none of your business. None of it." I lifted my chin to the sky and placed my hands on my hips. A full moon shone brightly above us. "Of all the luck in the world, you're the ex." I closed my eyes and took a deep breath, trying to calm this anger within me that wouldn't let up.

"I'm not in love with him or anything like that. I don't want him back. I'm just here because I feel sorry for you."

Her words hit me so hard that it was as though she had physically struck me.

I flipped to face her, eyes narrowed, jaw clenched. "Why do you hate me so fucking much? What have I ever done to you?" I was practically screaming at this point, and I wouldn't doubt it if my mother could hear me in the main house. "I mean, to even throw away my paintings in the garbage like they were trash is the ultimate low, even for you."

She reeled back, and her eyebrows rose to her hairline. "What are you even talking about?"

My hands fisted at my sides. "My paintings. I found them ruined in the rain, thrown out like trash."

She threw up both hands. "For the love of God, really? Why the hell would I do that? Maybe it was the construction workers who had renovated the pool house for you. They threw out a ton of stuff. I don't have the time or the energy to do such a thing." Her eyes widened just a tad, and she stood, the arrogance back. "You know what? I'm leaving. I came here to do you a favor. I don't need to listen to you berate me for it." She slipped her designer purse over her shoulder.

"Me? A favor? When have you ever done anything nice for me? Ever!"

Maybe she hadn't thrown out my paintings. Fine. But God only knew that she'd hated me from the very first time we met.

She shook her head and rolled her eyes. "Well, this is the first time and last time I do you any favors. That's for sure." She turned to leave but paused for a bit before facing me fully again. "You walk around like you have it so hard when your life is practically perfect."

Wait, what? I scrunched my face, struck into silence.

"With your perfect mom and your perfect life and your perfect friends and your perfect talent."

For a moment, vulnerability shone heavily in her eyes as her tone softened. "I don't have any of that. My mom left us when I was thirteen for another man and never looked back. Nannies and my grandma raised me, not my own father." Her jaw clenched, and she tore her gaze away from mine. "Shit, my father even sold my childhood home to give everything up for you and your mom. He would never offer to renovate the pool house for me." She waved a hand in the air. "I have my own place, so whatever ... I don't even care, but he'd never do for me what he's doing for you guys." Her jaw clenched, and she shook her head to erase the vulnerability that had been in her eyes moments ago. "So, don't go moping like you have a sucky life because you don't, okay? I hate people like you who have everything, yet you think you got dealt the wrong cards. Do you think I want to be around that all the time? Subconsciously comparing myself to you."

"Perfect life?" I spread my arms out wide. "My whole life was upended from Wisconsin to move here. My father is dead. At least yours is alive. And I just missed my whole exhibit because I fainted."

My laugh was cynical, but hers was worse.

"Who the fuck cares, Charlie? Who cares! You left your life in Wisconsin but then adjusted here like it never fazed you—new job, new friends, new boyfriend. My girlfriends only call me if they need something, and I've known them forever." She took a step toward me, getting into my line of sight. "And I'm sorry about your dad, okay? That's shitty that he's not here anymore. But let me tell you a secret." Her voice was strong and firm, which matched her gaze. "Your father was more of a father to you in the short time that he was alive than my father will ever be to me in his lifetime. So, you think about that, okay? You just think about that."

I blinked, realization slapping me in the face through the fog of anger, sobering me up real quick.

She was right.

Lately, I'd been looking at my glass as half-empty when, in reality, it was half-full. I'd adjusted to my move, making new friends who were true friends, friends to last forever. And, yes, she was absolutely right about my father. The amount of love and support I'd felt from him could last me a lifetime. I was lucky to have such a father, a father who loved me unconditionally, whose support was unwavering, all until the very end.

As I stared at Sandy, I realized her looks, her job, her overall demeanor were a facade, and I'd judged her for it. I had known about her real mother, that she'd left, but I hadn't gotten the full story. Although Richard seemed like an okay father, I'd never known he was never around for Sandy.

"I came here to check on you 'cause I know firsthand about how Connor feels about here and his parents. Ironically, we're more similar in that our parents were never around, growing up." She waved a hand. "But whatever. Check mark my good deed for the year." The sass was heavy and back in her tone.

As she turned her back toward me, walking out toward the exit, I called out to her, "Sandy ..."

Our eyes locked, and I realized, in some ways, we were similar, where we were still both a little lost in our lives, still trying to find our way.

"Thanks."

After a beat, she tipped her chin, and in Sandy-like fashion, she said, "We're not best friends after this. Just so you know."

I nodded. I doubted we'd ever be that. "I know. It's worse than that ... we're sisters."

Her face softened at my words, and a smirk emerged. It was small but visibly there. "I don't know if that's better or worse."

"Me either. All I know is that it's for life now."

Because judging by how much Richard and my mother loved each other, they would be together for the long run.

"Do me a favor, Charlie? I know how it is. I've been where you are right now. Just don't have hope, okay? That's what killed me before."

She walked away before I even had a chance to respond.

I'd heard her but not really because even if I didn't want to have hope that Connor would decide to stay here, I did.

CHAPTER 28

CHARLIE

TO SAY that tensions were high between Connor and me was an understatement. Luckily, we were overwhelmingly busy with preparations for the presentation for the board that we hadn't had much time to talk about us. But I knew that the conversation would happen—and happen soon—and the inevitable would come. I wanted to come out of this semi-intact. I knew that I couldn't come out of this fully unscathed, but I'd try to minimize any damage to my fragile heart to protect myself.

We sat in the boardroom. Funny enough, it was where everything had started what seemed like forever ago—brainstorming over Chinese food. My chest tightened because I was already cataloging the good times, the times we'd shared, as though I was thinking about us as a breakup.

But wasn't that how this would end?

Mr. Colby's tone was serious. No emotion showed on his face as he watched the commercials play in front of us.

But the rest of the board, enthusiasm showed on their features.

Music sounded in the background as the first clip played of Connor, placing the chocolates and the flowers on the porch before wiping his palms down his slacks, picking them up again, and ringing the doorbell.

Someone in the room said, "Aw."

I couldn't help but smile because Connor was such a good actor. My cheeks reddened when the door opened, and there I was. Sweating occurred as I shifted in my seat, seeing myself on the overhead screen.

No one's eyes made it my way because everyone was so fixated on the screen.

The commercial played, and so many emotions poured out of me. It felt so real, so heartfelt. Living through the motions on-screen brought so many feelings bubbling up to the surface.

The first date.

The slow dance.

Him on bended knee.

Me in the silk white dress on the wedding day.

And a slew of scenes danced in my head—the scenes not seen.

Endless laughter.

Connor making love to me.

Connor telling me he loved me.

Connor asking me to move in with him.

A lump formed in the back of my throat.

Why couldn't he stay? Why did it have to be like this between us, just when I felt like I'd found the man of my dreams?

Why wasn't I good enough?

In a hot two seconds, full-on tears would flow down my face, in front of everyone.

The room was dark, and I didn't look to see if Connor was looking at me, but I knew he was watching me when I stood, quietly opened the door, and stepped out.

And I speed-walked to the restroom before the first tear fell.

CONNOR

A big part of me wanted to go after Charlie, just to see if she was okay, but the commercial hadn't finished yet.

The wedding scene brought so much emotion to the surface, seeing her in that wedding dress—a dress I still had at my apartment. She'd left it there after the day of filming, and I'd placed it in a garment bag in my closet, unsure of what to do with it but knowing I wasn't going to throw it away or sell it.

I still remembered the way she'd looked that day, her hair up and flowing with endless curls, her light-pink makeup as though she had been kissed by the sun.

Seeing her on the big screen brought back the day where I'd gotten down on one knee and told her I loved her for the first time.

My feet tapped on the floor, as I was impatient, needing to check on her.

Finally, when the commercial was done, which included me dipping Charlie and kissing her, the board started clapping.

My mother's smile was big and wide as she clapped along with the others in the boardroom. "I love it, Connor. It's exactly what we need."

The corners of my mouth turned up in response, and I

stood, flipped the lights on, and walked to the whiteboard in the front of the room.

"The vision that we want to portray going forward is *family*, and when people think of Colby Chocolates and Candies, we want them to have our product as their go-to for every event. From first dates to weddings to kids' parties to school parties to baby showers." My smile widened as I went in for the killer selling point. "We want Colby's to be at the forefront of their minds when it comes to bringing families together."

My shoulders relaxed when there were a few enthusiastic murmurs of agreement. My father's face was stoic, but that wasn't a surprise because he rarely showed any enthusiasm—ever.

It was not until he knocked on the table twice and said, "I don't think it'll work," did I stagger.

I held my breath for two long seconds and stared at everyone else sitting at the table, who were equally shell-shocked. He was the minority in this situation; I was sure of it.

Every muscle in my body tightened, and my hands fisted by my sides.

Keep calm, I repeated the mantra in my head, but I already knew it wouldn't work.

"What don't you like about the concept exactly?" My voice was steady.

Breathe, Connor. I swallowed, waiting for his response, clenching my jaw tight.

"I just don't think that it's the concept I want to portray for Colby's. The branding is off. I want older people to reminisce and remember what it was like to be a kid, eating a Colby's Chocolate Bar. There is something about the original packaging that I want to keep. Maybe if we can change up the commercials to be a kid growing up."

"That won't work," I said, knowing in my gut that we had to show the series of events as they happened to evoke emotion.

"Well, I don't like it how it is."

Without warning, I slammed my fist against the table. "This is bullshit."

"Connor," my mother scolded.

But I was too far gone. There was no saving me now.

All hope of keeping my anger at bay was out the door.

We'd worked on this for months, and judging by everyone else's reaction, I knew I was exactly right with this concept. My father was dead wrong.

"Your original branding is dated, and the fact is, your profit margins are dwindling because you are trying to cater to an audience that's most likely dead. You're not getting any new customers."

"Connor!" my mother yelled above the noise, standing.

"Calm down," my father said, his face devoid of emotion while I was raging.

"We have worked so hard on this, and I know this is a winning direction. What?" I threw up both hands. "You don't want to take the family approach because you don't know what family is about, is that it? Well then, we can lie, just like how we lie to pretend that we are one big, happy family when it's all bullshit."

"Connor, that's not what this is," my father said, standing. "Calm down."

My eyes went around the room to the people that I'd seen most of my life, growing up in the factory—the boardroom members.

My face heated. They didn't deserve my wrath. My father did.

My mother grabbed my arm to try to still me, but I shrugged her off.

"No. I'm done, Mom. I'm fucking done." I flipped to face my father full-on. "Save your own company."

I charged out the door and went to Charlie's desk, but she wasn't available, so I pulled out my phone and called her, but her phone went to voice mail. Casey would know where she was.

I walked directly to Casey's office, and when I knocked twice, she opened the door. Both her eyebrows rose.

"What's going on?"

"Have you seen Charlie?"

"No. Why?"

I shook my head, not giving her a chance to ask me more questions, and stormed directly to see Alyssa. Financial statements were spread across her desk. *Should I tell her there was no point in trying to figure out projections for next quarter, that layoffs would be happening soon?*

"Hey."

She lifted an eyebrow. "She left. She's taking a sick day."

"What? She looked fine this morning," I stated because she had been.

She had almost been giddy about the presentation, knowing that the board and my father would love it. *Wait till I broke the bad news to her.*

She shrugged and tore her gaze from mine, focusing back on the financials.

"Aren't you curious about how it went?"

With nonchalance in her tone, she said, "Not really." Then, her eyes met mine again. "I'm assuming it didn't go well or else you wouldn't be huffing and puffing and there wouldn't be smoke blowing from your ears."

I placed my fists on my hips, totally not getting why her sharp tone was directed at me. "He's such an idiot. My father ..."

Alyssa gave me a pointed glance. "You're the idiot."

"He won't even listen to me. I came here to turn the company around, but he won't even listen to what I have to say."

"Then, change it."

"Change what? It's not my company."

"It's not your company because you don't want anything to do with it."

I huffed, beyond aggravated, not needing this lecture from her too.

"Yep. This is the thing. Maybe instead of suggesting the changes, for once, you act like a man and institute the changes and push them through."

"What? I told you, it's not my company."

"It's your company if you want it to be. Listen ..." She stood, getting into my face. "You won't want to hear this, but because you know me as a no-bullshitter, I'm going to tell you anyway." She pushed her finger into my chest. "You have everything you'll ever need, right here at this company, right here in this town, but all you've ever done is run because shit's not going your way, because it's hard. Yeah, it's hard to live with family. Yeah, it's hard to run a multimillion-dollar company, but tough shit. It's called life."

"You don't—"

She snapped her fingers in my face to shut me up. "Shh. Not done. Real talk now." She leaned in, narrowing her eyes, her tone serious. "Quit crying like a baby and man the fuck up. Quit complaining and get the job done. Stay for the company. Stay for your family. Stay for the girl."

"It's not that easy."

She turned to her financials then, already done with a conversation I wasn't finished with. And as though she hadn't heard a word I said, she uttered, "And leave Charlie alone. Don't be cruel. Give the girl a break."

"You know nothing," I said.

But of course, Alyssa always had to have the last word in. "I know everything."

I stormed away, out the door and making it toward the suburbs. *She would've gone home, right?*

But she wasn't there.

CHARLIE

I turned off my phone. I wanted to be alone, to wallow in my sorrows, just for once.

I had so much to look forward to. Nui and I had been communicating via email, and early next month, I'd be featured on her blog. She wanted to do a whole spread and interview. Her blog was so popular that she had tons of sponsorships on just her page alone. Who knew what opportunities would open up for me then?

My relationship with my mother was better—on its way there at least.

I had everything I'd ever wanted finally falling into place.

I picked up a stone and tossed it in the lake. "Daddy, I wish you were here. I wish you would tell me what to do about this man."

I laughed because I so knew what he would say. He'd tell me to move in with Connor, to pick the man. Because

Dad would want me to live my own life. But that was the thing. I wasn't going to be that girl—the girl who moved for a guy and left her whole life behind.

His place would be my place. His friends would be my friends. That wasn't the kind of life I wanted to live.

I pulled out my phone and turned it on, knowing I'd have to face the world sooner than later.

Twenty-two texts—all from Connor.

Five voice mails from him.

All of me was curious about the decision of the board, so instead of going through the texts and voice mails, I decided to call him instead.

"Hey."

"Charlie, where are you? I've been going crazy, trying to find you. I even rang your doorbell at home when you weren't at the pool house."

"I'm sorry."

"I don't care. Where are you right now?"

"I'm at the lake."

"Where? What lake?" There was urgency in his tone.

"The same spot we filmed at."

Before I uttered another word, he said, "Don't leave. I'll be there." And then he hung up.

Thirty minutes later, Connor showed up.

He plopped down and sat beside me, staring out at the lake. Taking in multiple boats whooshing past us, the skyscrapers in the horizon, the sun setting in front of us.

"Hey, are you okay?" he asked.

I nodded, smiling. Having him this near me did things to me, and I couldn't ignore the way my heart flipped and then flopped at the sight of him.

"Why did you leave?" His voice was soft, tender, coaxing.

"I think the commercials worked. They got me so super emotional that I had to leave." A small laugh escaped my lips. "How did it go?" I switched the subject so fast, probably giving him whiplash. It was either that or ... tell him the truth, which I wasn't about to do.

"He hated it." There was heavy disdain in Connor's eyes.

"Wait, what? Why?"

We had such a solid campaign.

He shook his head, staring back at the lake. "I don't know. Maybe he hates me. He's doing this to spite me."

"Oh, Connor ..." I took one of his hands in mine. "I'm sure that's not it. Maybe the case for him is not wanting change. It's difficult for older people to change." I squeezed his hand, and his eyes flickered to where we were connected. "I can imagine that he set up the original branding, and it's hard for a stubborn man to see out of his original vision. He'll come around."

"He won't. Don't you see? Nothing I do will ever be good enough. I can't believe I upped and left Manhattan to come back to this shit." He turned to face me fully, his knees by my knees, blowing out one slow sigh. He reached for me and practically pulled me into his lap. "I don't care anymore. It only confirms why I should leave. What I say doesn't matter."

I held my breath, as though he'd slapped me in the face. I mean, I had known this, right? I shouldn't be surprised by any of it. But why did it hurt so much?

It was because there was finality in his tone.

"Listen ... I meant it. I want you to come with me."

His eyes searched mine, and there was this ache so deep that it would've consumed me if I were a weaker woman. I'd do what he wanted, not what I wanted.

"I can't. We've discussed this." And then I straightened, and for the first time, I got the courage to ask him what I'd always wanted to ask him, knowing the rejection would soon follow. "Why don't you just stay?" For me, it was evident, but I bit my tongue before more of my feelings flew out.

"I can't." He blew out a breath, sadness encompassing his features. "I can't be around him. I just need to move on and get on with my life. It's like my whole life is on pause to save this company. And all this work that we did, all the months that I've stayed here, has been for nothing. It's for fucking nothing. I'm done. Anytime I think of Colby's or Chicago, I just get so damn angry. I need out. I'm happier when I'm not here."

I extracted my hand from his, feeling the rejection strong and clear, like a bee sting.

I was going to cry. I could feel it, the warmth behind my eyes, and I hadn't cried over him leaving in front of him because it felt sort of stupid really, knowing this was the end game, this was our deal of sorts.

"I get it. I understand," I said, knowing there was no changing his mind.

His face registered panic for a second, realizing what he'd said. "But not with you, Charlie. Not with you. I'm happy with you." He stood and took my face within his palms. "I mean, my silver lining in coming here was meeting you." His lips touched mine. "Stay with me." He leaned in, kissing me more passionately. "Stay with me tonight."

And I gave in because if this was all I was ever going to get, if I could only get Connor for this short period of time, then I'd take it.

CHAPTER 29

CHARLIE

I STARED at his boxes and suitcases along the wall. His plates and mugs and glasses were scattered all across the kitchen table, and my stomach sank and kept on going.

We were silent as I helped him take out all the pots and pans from the cupboard, wrap them up in bubble wrap, and stack them in the box.

I repeated the motion with his utensils and his mixing bowls, and I could not breathe. Tears welled up in my eyes, and he didn't see me crying because he was too damn busy packing the plates, making sure they were secure in the box.

I hated this.

All this thinking and moping had me coming to one irrational thought: he was leaving me even though he had a choice.

I swallowed back the lump in the back of my throat, but that did nothing to my tears, nothing to stop the stream from falling down my face. It came harder and harder until a sob escaped me.

"Charlie?"

Connor immediately rushed to my side, and I swiped at my tears, ignoring his looming presence above me.

'Cause if I looked at him, met his beautiful face that I loved so damn much, the tears would flow endlessly.

I'd get over this, right?

My father had left, and it had taken me a while to get over that. I remembered the anger at first, as though it were his fault that he had gotten sick, and then the utter sadness that took me under, but over time, I did recuperate. I'd healed.

But this was different, and I knew that. If my father had had a choice, he'd still be here. Connor had a choice, yet he was choosing to leave—leave his company, his legacy, his nana, and more so me.

Connor didn't give me a choice to deny him because he pulled me into him and wrapped his arms tightly around my waist, dropping his head to the crook of my neck.

"Stop crying. I can't take it when you cry," he said, his voice broken.

Even though I shouldn't, even though it would make it harder in the end for both of us, I hugged him against me, feeling his chest rise and fall against mine.

I sobbed into his chest, and he squeezed me tighter.

I loved this man—so damn much. He'd lifted me up in some of the lowest points with my mother, and he believed in me, in my art, in my paintings. He made me want to be a better person, to strive for utter perfection, to believe in myself and my abilities. And he was leaving.

"I love you, Charlie. So much. Maybe ..."

I lifted my head and placed one heavy hand on his chest, pushing him away. I swiped at the tears—angry now. "Don't say that."

His eyes widened, and when he reached for me, I slapped his hand away.

"Don't say you love me because if you did, you'd stay."

Boom.

There it was—my ultimatum—what I really wanted out in the open. Like fireworks on a silent night, clear and deafening. Hadn't he told me to do that—to tell my mother how I really felt, to not sugarcoat my feelings?

"I ... I can't."

My hands fisted at my sides, and I let out a ragged breath. "Why not? Because you have family and a girlfriend in New York? What you're doing here is running. Staying is the easiest choice, and you refuse to do it. You have your family here and your friends and"—I placed both hands over my chest—"me," I rushed out.

I swiped at the last of the tears, and all that was left was this never-ending anger.

"All you have there is a job, a desk you go to every single day." I shook my head. "But here, you have a legacy—your legacy—and I know you don't want to believe it, but it is yours. When your parents leave this world, it will go to you and your brother. Or would you rather it go to some investors who couldn't give two shits about the families Colby's employs and who would rather tear your company apart and sell the different lines?"

He took a step toward me. "You don't understand, Charlie."

I raised a hand. I didn't want him to touch me; it would slay me. "No ... I do. You are resentful. Your parents were never there for you, growing up, obsessed with setting up this company. I get your anger toward them. I get why you feel the need to run away ..."

"I'm not running away," he snapped.

"But see ... you are. You have this underlying bitterness toward them, and because of that, you want nothing to do with anything that they are ever involved with. I get that too. Where is forgiveness and compassion and all those qualities that make you ... you?"

His facial features dropped, and he tilted his head, a frown heavy on his face.

"I can't ... it's just too hard. But me leaving has nothing to do with you, Charlie. I stopped considering this my home a long time ago. When I left, I promised myself that I would never come back, so I set up a life in New York."

"A life? You call a desk at your financial institution, an apartment that's bare, and friends you see every other weekend a life?"

He was unhappy. That was the fact of the matter. He was running away, not setting up a life.

I was done—officially done. He could leave. Fine. I couldn't stop him, and he already knew how I felt. But I didn't have to stand here and help him do it.

"I'm sorry. I just can't today." I averted my stare and walked to the couch to grab my purse.

When he reached for my wrist to still me, I turned to meet his eyes, and his face crumbled.

"Don't leave like this."

I lifted my chin to tell him what I honestly felt in my gut. My voice breaking, I begged him, "Don't leave at all."

"You know it can't be like that."

He made no sense.

"This is your decision, Connor. Single-handedly yours."

When I yanked back my hand, slipped my purse over my shoulder, and walked to the door, he yelled out, "Charlie, I love you!"

I heard the wretched brokenness in his tone, and it hit

me directly in the chest. I gripped my purse strap tighter and turned to face him.

I wanted to tell him that these months had been the best months of my life. I wanted to tell him that he'd made me believe in myself again, in my ability to paint and create and have faith that others would enjoy my art. When my father had died, it'd seemed that all I'd worked hard for and done according to my craft was pushed to the side, where it wasn't admired or sometimes even acknowledged.

I wanted to tell him that I'd never felt a love like his, and I'd never been this in love before, where my insides wanted to burst from elation from being loved by him and able to love him.

But love was unconditional. I knew this. I had grown up in a household that taught me this, and as our eyes locked, a deep, overwhelming sadness began to take over.

"And you know I love you too. But you have to stop saying those things because ..." My tear ducts welled up with tears, and I blinked up to the ceiling, hoping they wouldn't fall. "Because I know you love me, but you, right here, are telling me, *I love you, Charlie, but you're not enough to stay.*"

The tears fell anyway. When I turned and placed my hand on the doorknob to leave, Connor called out to me, and by the choked way he uttered my name, I knew he was crying too.

He'd already made his decision to leave.

And I wasn't going to help him pack up and do it.

I had more self-esteem and self-worth to know that I was enough. I might not be enough for Connor Colby, but I would be enough for someone else. I'd be enough for someone else to stay.

CONNOR

The next day, I was not a joy to be around. I'd packed up my office. Weirdly, being here for only a few months, I had boxes of stuff to bring to New York.

I peeked up when Kyle strolled in.

"Hey."

"Hey."

"I heard World War III happened in the boardroom."

There was an edge to my laugh. "Yeah, not my proudest moment."

Looking back in hindsight, I wished I could have held back my temper a little bit. There had been a lot of F-bombs dropped in front of the other board members, which wasn't exactly professional.

Kyle plopped down in his regular spot in front of my desk. "Mom and Nana gave Dad a little beating with words."

You would think that would give me satisfaction, but it didn't.

"So, you're really leaving." Kyle picked up my stapler, as though he were going to steal it.

And I placed more files into the box. "Yeah ... why?" It wasn't like he hadn't known this.

"I didn't think you could do it. I mean ... not with Charlie here."

At the sound of her name, my stomach dropped. My eyes flipped to meet his, and I swallowed. "She knew I was leaving from the start."

"You didn't see this, huh—you falling for her?"

I shook my head, focusing on the task at hand, stuffing more items into the moving box, but seeing nothing, only witnessing her tears streaming down her beautiful face when she'd left my place.

I could have predicted everything else, like the fact that my father would reject any idea I placed in front of him. But I'd never predicted Charlie.

"I'm going to miss you, big bro."

My eyes met his then. "You need to visit more. I have a few contacts out in New York who own a couple of retail stores. You can always move up there and see where your sock biz takes you."

Kyle tipped his chin. "Nah. New York is way too fast for me. I like slow and leisurely."

Wasn't that the truth? I wasn't about to lecture him that slow and leisurely wouldn't get him anywhere.

"I'll be back," I said because there were always the holidays and Nana's birthday.

"It'll be different. It has been weird in a good way, having you back for a while," he said, his voice quiet. His gaze focused on the stapler in his hand, opening and shutting the top.

I hadn't been back home more than a long weekend since I left for college.

"But I'm not too worried." He stood, placing the stapler back on my desk. "I know you'll be back for good, you big baby."

I widened my eyes, laughing. "What?" I motioned to the boxes in front of me. "Um, moving?"

"Yep. Wanna bet?" His smile widened.

"You're crazy."

"If I am so crazy, you won't be scared of a little wager."

I laughed.

CHAPTER 30

CONNOR

I'D INVITED Charlie to my last family dinner, but she wasn't talking to me.

I hated how we'd ended things, how she'd left crying. I'd been calling her constantly, but once again, her phone was off.

We were at our favorite Italian restaurant, Toressi. All of us were seated there—my father, my mother, Kyle, and Nana.

Since I'd come home, I'd only had dinner with my family once. Oddly, it seemed like a holiday because that was the only way I'd agree to have a sit-down dinner with my family.

I couldn't even look at my dad, still angry for everything that had happened between us.

Small talk ensued. We weren't a family who spoke about anything deep. It was as though we were strangers, though we'd grown up together in one household.

It wasn't until my mother said something after dessert that my head peeked up at my father.

"Connor ... your father has something to say."

She kicked him under the table, and I knew this because he jumped.

"Yeah ..." He cleared his throat. "So, I've set things in motion and have given the marketing team a go with your concepts." Pride was still heavy in his tone. It was the way he spoke in general, voice powerful, booming, even though he'd just admitted I was right.

I perked up in my seat. "Really?"

"Really." He tipped his chin. "Everyone was in agreement that this is the approach we should follow as we take Colby's into the next generation."

I squinted, and the wheels in my head started turning. If this was a ploy to get me to stay, it wasn't happening. "I'm not staying."

"That's not why I approved the plans. I've ..." He ran one hand through his pepper-gray hair. For the first time, he couldn't meet my eyes, and his gaze flittered to the table. "I've been stubborn in my ways. I brought you in to change the direction of Colby's, and I wasn't listening. I know this is the right decision because the vote to use the concept of family was unanimous."

When he finally lifted his head, I nodded, feeling vindicated, confidence filling my shoulders, making me sit up taller. "Well, thank you. I need you to back this. I need you to fund the money to make this Colby's biggest launch ever because I know it'll be the game changer for this company's future."

My father nodded. "I will."

"And Charlie had a lot to do with those ideas. I think she should be recognized at the next board meeting. I think you guys need to approach her about maybe joining the marketing team to lead the efforts of the rebranding."

My mother nodded from across the table. "That's a great idea. She really has an eye for things."

Nana smiled beside me, motioning to me as though I'd won the prize in some game show. "She sure does. And that commercial seemed so real, so believable between you and Charlie. The proposal. The wedding. I'm glad you didn't film what happened after the wedding."

"Mama," my mother scolded, but the whole table laughed.

"Why isn't she here tonight?" Nana raised an eyebrow.

"I invited her, but ... yeah."

"She's salty because Connor is leaving her," Kyle added.

I stiffened. "I'm not leaving her. I'm leaving Chicago."

"I'm sure that's not how she's taking it." Kyle's smirk grated on my nerves.

I had no clue why he wanted to consistently torture me. He knew this wasn't easy for me, leaving her.

"Shut up. You know nothing ... bro."

"Remember our little wager."

I shook my head. "This is one you are going to lose for sure."

"I'm five for five. I doubt my losing streak will happen anytime soon. I hardly make a bet where I have a chance of losing."

"This time will be different."

"We'll see." His tone was confident, so sure.

As dinner continued, all I could think of was Charlie. And I didn't want to leave Chicago, not talking to her.

After dinner, I ended up at the pool house because I needed to see her.

I tapped on the door, and when she opened it, I swore I was almost knocked on my ass, just at the sight of her.

Her hair was up in a messy bun. Only in a T-shirt and shorts, she looked stunning. Her right cheek had a streak of yellow paint, and her paintbrush was in one hand.

"Connor." Her voice was shaky, her face hesitant, but after a beat, she stepped back, so I could come in.

"I'm sorry I haven't been picking up your calls." Her eyes dropped to the floor. "I just ... I wanted to make it easier on both of us."

"I understand."

Silence spanned the space between us, and I looked behind her to see a canvas with splatters of yellows and oranges in abstract form.

"It looks like you're busy, but I couldn't leave without saying good-bye."

Her gaze flicked upward to meet mine, and my fingers twitched.

The need to touch her, to hold her, was unbearable, but I kept my hands by my sides.

"I was just beginning a new piece."

She moved farther in the room, and I followed her in. After placing her paintbrush in a cup, she wiped her hands on her shirt, which was already covered with dried-up paint, and she turned to face me.

"I'm not really good with good-byes." She pushed her toe into the carpet, her gaze flicking toward the floor again.

One.

Two.

Three long beats later was all I could take.

I stepped into her, forcing her to meet my eyes. "I don't

have a hard time usually. But this time is different. It seems especially hard to say good-bye to you, Charlie."

Her bottom lip trembled, and I was determined not to make this a sad good-bye.

"I came to tell you that my father has approved the plans for our concept. The marketing team is working on it."

She blinked up at me, her eyes lighting up, her whole demeanor changing. "Really?"

"Really." My lips tipped up to match hers. "And ... they want you to join the marketing team to make sure that our concepts are taken all the way to the end."

"Wait, what?" She reeled back.

"Yeah ..." I took another step toward her, needing to close the distance. "Why not, Charlie? Computers is not where you need to be. You need to be in a department that will spark your creativity. You're at a company that you already love. Why can't you be at a place where you also love what you're doing?"

Her eyebrows knitted together, and doubt plagued her features. "I don't know."

I placed my hands on her shoulders, peering down at her with a confidence that she needed to feel herself. "What don't you know? You need to have more trust in your abilities. You know that you want to say yes."

She nodded. "I do."

"You do?"

She smiled. "I do."

Her words brought me back to our time on the lakefront, her in her beautiful dress, stunning, and us reciting our fake vows. Immediately, my chest tightened.

"Then, I'll tell my parents you will take the job." I pointed at her when she began to speak. "Don't even try to talk yourself out of this one."

"But—"

And before she got the words out, I kissed her.

Because I wanted to.

She sighed and melted into my arms, right where she was meant to be.

My kiss was soft and sensual, and I threaded my fingers through her hair, palming the back of her neck, bringing her closer.

The feel of her against me was heavenly, and I never wanted to let her go.

But when she placed a hand on my chest, I let her push me away because that was the right thing to do.

I knew it was wrong to want her, knowing I wouldn't be here in the morning.

CHARLIE

We were breathing hard from that kiss. And I wanted to give in to him, but I didn't think my heart could take it, knowing that when I woke up tomorrow and when I went to work, he wouldn't be there. I had to keep part of me intact.

"Thank you." I placed a light hand on his chest, feeling his heartbeat thud rapidly under my fingertips. "Thank you for introducing me to Nui and for allowing me to believe in myself a little more. And for this new opportunity at Colby's."

He tipped my chin with the lightness of his fingertips. "It was really my pleasure, Charlie. And thank you for helping me with this remarketing endeavor and for dealing with my pain-in-the-ass self."

"Yeah, I guess patience is my strong suit." I patted his chest and took a healthy step back.

His smile faltered when I did.

"Connor, I wish you the best of luck in all that you do. No sad tears today because it was great while it lasted." I smiled, but the words felt heavy with a sadness I couldn't shake.

He let out one long exhale, and when he took a step toward me, I took another step back.

"It was more than great. You were my unexpected heaven in a place I like to call hell." The joke was evident, but there was no light or humor in his eyes.

"Charlie ..."

When he reached for my waist, I placed both hands up. "I have a lot to do tonight."

I couldn't let him hold me—unless his hold promised to be forever, which I knew very well that it wouldn't.

Silence stretched between us. It was long and never-ending. My gaze dropped to the floor, and I wanted to cower into the floor and sleep until the morning and forget he had ever been here.

When he cleared his throat, my eyes moved to meet his.

"I should get going."

I nodded, unable to form words, unable to get my next breath out.

I followed him to the door, and when he turned around, the overwhelming sadness threatening to take me under was mirrored in his eyes.

"I'll miss you, Charlie."

There was so much emotion uttered in his words that I had to choke back the sob wanting to escape.

"I'll be back in the fall ... Nana's birthday." His voice was so soft that I could barely hear him.

I forced a smile, knowing everything would be different by then.

"Good luck, Connor."

"Good night, Charlie."

I shut the door and almost ran to my bedroom.

That night, I cried myself to sleep, wondering if I could turn back time and take a different direction in that closet, knowing the outcome of today.

CONNOR

I woke up early, and oddly, the whole family was at my door to bid me good-bye an hour before I had to leave.

Well, shit, I wasn't prepared for that.

Kyle had a box of bagels, and they stepped into my place.

My mother pressed her cheek against mine. "We brought breakfast." Mom lifted some OJ.

"Uh ... isn't there work today?" I said as Nana and my father filed in behind my mother and Kyle.

"There is. But we are here to bid you *adieu*," Nana said, lifting her signature box of cookies.

"There's no need for everyone to see me off. I have a car coming at nine."

"We wanted to see you off, son." My father's words hit me in the gut.

"Thanks." For a moment, my voice didn't even sound like mine, so full of emotion. "All my silverware and cups are packed."

Nana dug in her oversize purse. I swore she had everything in there. "I've got cups and napkins and a knife, so that's all we need."

I laughed. "Did you steal those utensils from Bagel Hut?"

She lifted a shoulder, unaffected. "We bought a box of bagels, so I wouldn't consider this stealing."

They made themselves at home and occupied my rented table.

"Well ... thanks."

"Mom and Dad would like to tell you something," Kyle said, kicking his feet up onto my table.

"Way to make it awkward." Nana snorted, opening her box of cookies and stuffing one in her mouth, crumbs falling down her chin.

"Your father and I have decided," my mother said—but everyone at the table, me included, knew that she'd made the decision for my father and her—"we will ride this new rebranding toward the end to save the company, and if it doesn't pan out, we will sell it."

I blinked and then double-blinked.

"Well, I'm almost positive it won't come to that, not if you put the effort and the money behind this relaunch."

"It probably won't, but if it does, all we will have left is what is in this room," she said, smiling.

My breathing slowed at a memory then, one where I must have been no more than seven years old, where my mother held one hand and my father held the other and we were jumping on a trampoline.

I closed my eyes briefly, wondering if it was a memory or a dream.

My mother stood and extended a bagel that she'd spread cream cheese on. "There's a ton of things your father and I regret. A lot of things we wish we could have done differently." She breathed out a small sigh.

My gaze flickered to my father at the other end of the table.

"At the time ... Connor, we were doing the best we

could," my father added, his gaze flickering from the table and back to meet my face.

I swallowed back a lump in the back of my throat because as I stared back at my father, I realized it was a memory. They'd thrown me a birthday party at one of those trampoline places. I'd dragged my mother out to the trampoline, and in turn, she'd grabbed my father.

Seriously, a man could only take so much. After leaving Charlie last night, all emotional, and then this ...

I could've gotten on a plane this morning and never looked back. But like the saying went, *Tomorrow is never promised.*

"I'm sorry," I said, all this pent-up emotion filling me up and spilling out. "I haven't been the easiest through the years. I've been kind of an asshole more recently, to be honest."

My father stood then. "There's no need to be sorry. All we can do is move forward from this."

His words hit me directly in the chest because he was right. All we could do was move forward or harbor all this animosity and never speak again. But what was the point of that?

As I glanced around the room and caught Nana's eye, I realized that, yeah ... my dad had been a shitty dad, but he had done the best he could at the time. He had given me his time when he had it, like spending my birthday with me in that memory that had pushed to the surface.

We weren't perfect.

My father walked toward me then and patted my shoulder, bringing me in for a hug. "When you come back to Chicago next time, you're staying with us."

I nodded against him, feeling like a teenager again. I couldn't recall the last time my father had hugged me. Just then another memory triggered. It was when I had gotten into an accident when I was sixteen years old. He'd rushed to the hospital, and his eyes had checked for any damages before he pulled me into a hug. The hug was brief because the yelling ensued right after about my reckless behavior, car racing, but the hug had happened. A shallow sigh escaped as the memory surfaced.

In front of me, my mother cupped her mouth, and her eyes shone with unshed tears.

Nana, being the dramatic grandmother that she was, jumped us as though we were in a hug bubble. "See, I knew this would happen. Food always brings everyone together."

I laughed, and so did my father, who stepped back to look at me—for once, pride showing heavy in his irises.

"You did well, son. I know this is the total revamp we need. You did well."

"Thanks."

"We're going to miss you," my mother chimed in.

That was when Kyle added, "He'll be back ... don't you worry."

They drove me to the airport that day. All five of them hopped in the car to drop me off as though we were a family who did that when we so weren't.

I hopped on my flight back to New York, and for once in my life, this dreadful feeling sat at the pit of my stomach. Usually, I was relieved, leaving, but I couldn't place this new, foreign feeling. I got nauseous on the plane as if my body were rejecting the flight back to New York.

CHAPTER 31

CHARLIE

THE NEXT DAY at work was horrid. I couldn't pretend that I hadn't cried my eyes out because I could barely see out of them, given they were so puffy.

Casey brought me my favorite coffee in a venti cup to my desk. She gave me a hug without saying a word, and I was glad she'd said nothing because the tears would have been endless and flowing. If his name were mentioned, it would be game over.

Erica from the marketing team came over just before lunch. "Hey. I just wanted to come over and show you your new desk."

My eyes flew to my hairline, and I cocked my head. "Sorry?"

"We're working on the new specs this afternoon, and Mr. Colby said you'd join us. I think it makes sense to move your desk closer to our team."

"Oh." *Goodness, well, that was fast.*

I'd verbally told Connor yes, but I hadn't had a full conversation with anyone else yet.

"Okay."

"You wouldn't have to move a thing. Just your files. We'll have your computer set ... oh."

She slapped her head because I was the computer tech for this location. Of course, I'd be setting up my new computer.

"We can always have Tony do it. I hear he's moving over after you officially transition to our new team."

I shook my head. That would take days. "I'll do it."

She smiled and patted my shoulder. "What you and Connor have come up with is amazing. The team is going nuts over the new direction this company is taking."

And just like that, the mention of his name diminished the joy in me, the joy of this new job, because without him, I wouldn't have had this opportunity.

His flight had left this morning, but I missed him because his presence followed me all over the office. In the boardroom, in the coffee room, in the break room, especially in the closet.

"I'm excited." I forced a smile to form on my face.

———

It wasn't until lunch when the tears started flowing again.

"He's a fucking idiot. And I told him that," Alyssa said.

It was a simple thing that had set me off. Casey had emptied her bag and belongings, and among them was the book *Sexy Filthy Boss*.

I remembered reading that months ago and Connor catching me reading it. He'd made a flirty comment, and that was the beginning of the end for me.

Casey's arms wrapped around me. "Men are jerks. We can form our own club. The Dickless Club."

"And what a sad and lonely club that would be, and I don't want anything to do with it," Alyssa shot out. Then, she nudged my shoulder. "Seriously? She doesn't have a dick, so she's already dickless. The best way to get out of the broken-hearted funk is to jump on the next guy, get back on the horse."

Casey scowled. "That's so foul. And heartless."

"Call me the lion without a heart." Alyssa smirked. "Let's go to O'Malley's. I'm buying the next few pitchers and you're drinking until you forget your own name. Trust me. In a few days, you won't even miss him. Connor what's his name?"

That night, I got butt-ass wasted, and then I slept over at Casey and Alyssa's place.

But for once, she was wrong. Because even a whole week later, I missed him dearly.

He'd called me and texted, but I needed a clean break. That was the only way I'd get over this, get over him—to pretend like we hadn't ever happened.

CONNOR

Life was different when I went back to New York and continued with my daily routine. It didn't seem like a life at all.

Brad patted my shoulders, welcoming me back to work. "Hey, it's good to have you back." He dropped a stack of papers on my desk. "This is Roastery Coffee. Going under. There's no saving this one. We've tried for the last few months. We're in a liquidation scenario now."

That sucked. My thoughts flickered back to my

company—to Colby's. I hoped they could pull through. I reminded myself that I needed to text Alyssa about seeing last month's financial statement.

As soon as the thought registered, I shook my head. I had meant, my father's company.

"And tonight, we're going out. Do you want to come? Denise has been asking about you."

Denise. A one-night stand that had turned into more than I could handle.

"No, I'm still settling back at my place."

"Come on, bro. You've been back for days now. It's a Friday night. Let's go out."

I huffed under my breath.

Did I want to stay in my apartment and try contacting Charlie, knowing that she wouldn't answer my call? Did I want to watch TV and have every show play, reminding me of Charlie and her love of reality TV shows?

If I wanted to move on with my life, I needed to move the hell on.

I tipped my chin. "Where are you guys meeting tonight?"

"Club Vision."

I groaned. *A club? Oh, hell.*

I straightened, knowing this was what I had to do. "Okay, see you guys there."

It was a slow and agonizing day with figuring out that my colleagues were right about this company. I wished I could prove them wrong and find a solution to save Roastery Coffee, but no, unfortunately, they had been in the negative cash flow for years.

At five thirty, I shut down my computer and took the subway home.

I opened the door, and the atmosphere seemed exceptionally lonely today, so I called Kyle.

"Hey." He picked up on the first ring.

I dropped to the couch, feeling as though I'd run a marathon for the day, absolutely exhausted.

"I'm like your new best friend. Don't you have other people you can talk to?" he said, mocking me.

But wasn't that the damn truth?

I had been calling him as though he were my girlfriend, giving him the lowdown of my every damn day. I'd even called him to ask what he was eating because I could only ask, "What's going on?" so much during the day when the answer wouldn't have changed from moments earlier.

I'd stopped calling Nana because the last few calls had ended with, "Come home already. You know that's what you want to do."

"I'm going out tonight."

"You should," Kyle said. "It'll make you realize how much more you want to be here."

"Shut up."

Because he didn't know shit about it. This was me getting on with my life.

"Where are you going?"

"This club."

"A good lay will mess things up for you; I promise you that. Get drunk. Do whatever you need to do, but don't do that."

I let out an exaggerated sigh. "It's done. She won't even pick up my calls."

Maybe what he was telling me not to do was exactly what I needed to be doing to get over her.

"Well, your choice. But that's one sure way to ruin any chance you have with your perfect girl."

I closed my eyes and rubbed at my temple.

Perfect girl. Because she was. I'd never been turned upside down about anyone else before. If I didn't feel so deeply about her, I wouldn't have asked her to move in with me, knowing we hadn't known each other for a long time.

"I need to eat dinner and get ready."

"Have fun. Even though I know you won't."

"You're an asshole, you know that?"

"That is something I can agree with." Kyle chuckled.

I'd prove him wrong. I was determined to have a good time with the guys tonight.

———

I walked into Club Vision way too early. At ten in the evening, there was hardly any people. I'd been here many times before. The trance music played in the background, and I was already ready for bed, tired of a night that had hardly even started.

I ordered a beer and texted Brad and the guys. After thirty minutes, they showed up, but I was ready to leave.

We got a VIP table where the minimum was a thousand, which was a drop in the hat for us bankers.

They were talking about the deals they'd recently won, the commission associated with the takeovers they'd just closed, companies they'd just liquidated. There was so much joy in helping struggling companies liquidate, and at times, it felt wrong to celebrate that, even with the big commission check on our side.

I kept pounding it back, beer after beer, wanting and needing to feel numb, to force my brain to turn off, to stop thinking about Charlie.

It wasn't until Denise sat by me that I popped my head up.

"Connor." She hugged me, her hand resting on my thigh. "I've been waiting for you to come back home."

Home? It sounded foreign, coming from her lips.

"When did you get back?" She smiled, and I noticed that her bright red lipstick was smeared.

"A week ago," I said, tipping back my beer.

She was beautiful in a way that was over the top—her hair in curls that lay in the middle of her back, her V-neck halter top that didn't hide a thing, and her dark, smoky eye shadow.

This had been my type a few months ago but not anymore.

"I called you a few times." Her voice was high-pitched, almost whiny.

I wondered how I hadn't noticed it before.

I knew she'd called, but I'd simply ignored her.

"I was busy."

Busy working, busy trying to save a company ... busy falling in love.

She leaned in, and her chest brushed against my arm. "I've missed you," she whispered, closer to me. There was a subtle suggestion in her tone.

Her hand made it on my thigh, and I inched away.

But she only angled closer, her lips by my ear. "We're going to have fun tonight. I can tell."

Her fingers made small circles further up my thigh, and I flinched. She smelled of a strong perfume, and I wanted the fresh scent of summer, the ocean ... I wanted Charlie's natural fragrance.

Shit, I missed her.

If I wanted to forget about her entirely, this was the way

to do it, right? Bury myself deep inside Denise and just forget, even for a moment, about the girl I'd left in Chicago.

But then I was smart enough to know that that fix would be a temporary high, and nothing would replace the real thing.

I took her hand and lightly placed it on her lap. All I could think of was Kyle's words—and I didn't want to mess things up.

I'd had one too many beers, and if I stayed here, there was a very good chance that, in the morning, I would regret what I had done.

"Connor ..." she cooed when I stood.

Brad slung an arm over my shoulders. "Hey, bud, where you headed?"

"I'm just not feeling it tonight," I said. "I'll see you at work."

The guys started to protest, but I was out the door, hailing a cab because I already felt like shit from my overhaul of beer.

Once I reached my apartment, I surveyed the area—my home. And I realized this wasn't my home any longer. It was an empty vessel that I slept in. Home wasn't in New York anymore. Home was where my heart was, and right now, my heart belonged to someone in Chicago.

Without hesitation and still half-drunk, I booked the first flight to Chicago in the morning.

CHAPTER 32

CHARLIE

I WAS at my new desk, surveying the layout of the day ahead. We were meeting with the printers to go over the new packaging. This morning, I had gone over the Power-Point presentation a second time. The marketing team had fine-tuned my original sketches, and Mr. Colby himself had cleared them. Now, we just needed to present this to our printers, so they could start printing the new packaging next week.

I stood, stapling my stacked papers, when I turned my head and found Connor. My heart jumped to my throat.

I blinked and then double-blinked.

I was dreaming.

I had to be because there was Connor.

In nothing else but a diaper.

My eyebrows scrunched together, and I rubbed at my eye.

"Charlie."

He pulled me into him, and my whole body reacted.

Good gosh, if this were a dream, then I never wanted to wake up. He hugged me fiercely as though he never, ever wanted to let me go.

And I held him close, equally as hard, until I remembered he was naked, except for an adult diaper.

I reeled back. "For the love of all that is holy, what the heck are you wearing?"

"Adult diapers." He shook his head, searched the vicinity, but I was in the corner office and it was lunchtime. "It's a long story." He reached for both of my hands.

"What are you doing here? Don't you have work?" I asked. *Shoot, should I be concerned?*

I pinched myself and yelped.

"What are you doing?"

"Just making sure I'm awake."

He laughed. "Charlie ..." The way he uttered my name was so reverent, so sweet, that it made my heart turn over in response. "I've missed you."

Self-preservation was a funny thing. I took a step back from him, and it was as if I'd slapped him in the face because he flinched.

"What are you doing here, Connor?" I repeated, my voice soft, almost sounding defeated.

"I came back for you." His voice was firm, his gaze set intent on mine. "This week has been the longest, most dreadful week that I've had in ... in what seems like forever. And it's because I can't stop thinking of you."

He pulled me in by the elbows, and I let him because my body ached for his touch. A stronger woman would have been able to stay away and resist, but I wasn't a strong woman, not when it came to this man.

"Everywhere I turned, I wished you were there, right beside me, but I knew that was impossible because you were in Chicago." He brushed my cheek with the lightness of his knuckles. "And I just decided ... I don't want to put myself through hell anymore. You were right, my brother was right, and Nana was right. I'm tired ... tired of lying to myself. I can live without anything else—because I have—but not without you, Charlie. I can't live without you."

His breath was warm, and it coasted across my face, causing my stomach to flutter.

"Move in with me."

His repeated words slapped me back into reality.

"We've discussed this. I'm not moving to New York."

"No. I'm moving here, moving back, for you." His eyes searched mine, and the intensity in them was so blinding that my breath caught. "Move in with me," he repeated his words slower this time, tender, his gaze all-consuming, his chocolate eyes blazing.

"Isn't it too soon?"

He smiled then, biting on his sexy bottom lip. "I'm a firm believer in the saying, *When you know, you know.*" The smoldering flame behind his eyes was overwhelming.

His words brought me back to weeks ago when we had gone over our original sketches.

He playfully pinched my chin. "We haven't completed our work here yet. I want to finish the last sketch of that commercial—where it's thirty years after they got married. They're at a birthday party of their seventh grandchild. He's holding the love of his life in his arms, so tightly but with the same excitement as though it were the first time he held her. He's watching their grandkids play, the whole while thinking of how lucky he is ... that this is the life they built— a life they built together."

I smiled up at him, my heart fluttering and beating a million times a second.

"Can we do that, Charlie? Build a life together?"

I watched the play of emotions on his face—excitement, anticipation, but most of all, love.

I nodded, so choked up that I couldn't speak.

"Is that a yes?"

"Yes," I said, finally finding my voice.

He closed the gap between us and kissed me, claiming my lips with the full hardness of his mouth. His kiss was demanding, all-consuming, that I nearly fell over from the contact. It had been so long since he kissed me, and in that moment, I knew that I never wanted to be kissed by another man. For the rest of my life, as long as I was breathing on this earth, my lips, my heart, my soul belonged to Connor.

"What the hell?" It was Alyssa.

"Are you in a diaper?" Casey asked.

We both flipped to face them, and Connor turned all shades of purple.

I stood in front of him to shield him from their eyes, but that was all for nothing because Connor was legitimately twice my size.

"We came to get you for lunch and ..." Alyssa shook her head.

"This was Kyle's stupid idea, wasn't it?" Casey asked.

Connor groaned, confirming that it was indeed Kyle's idea.

"Why do you even bet against him when he always wins?" Alyssa deadpanned.

"What was it anyway?"

"He bet me that I wouldn't be able to stay away from Charlie for two weeks. He called me a baby for leaving ... hence"—Connor motioned to his crotch—"the diaper."

Alyssa laughed.

Casey pushed out her lip in disdain. "Your brother is a jerk."

"That he is."

"All you had to do was wait another week, and you would have won," Alyssa said.

"Yeah"—Connor's eyes searched my face—"but one week was way too long as it was." His one arm snaked around my back, bringing me closer. "There was no way I was going to last two."

"Does that mean you are here for good?" Casey asked, eyes light.

"Yep. Forever until Charlie moves to another state."

"I'm not moving."

"Then, I'm here forever," Connor stated.

Voices sounded from the hall, and Connor dropped to his knees, crawling under my desk.

"How long is this bet supposed to last?" Casey asked, pushing my chair in so Connor couldn't be seen, more so that he was blocked in.

"Ten minutes. I had to walk in the office and stay here for ten minutes, and it's been way past ten minutes."

"Where are your clothes?" Casey asked.

"Kyle has them."

Alyssa laughed. "Now, we have to find Kyle, who doesn't work here."

"He's here. Just seriously torturing me. Try my office."

"Come on, Casey. He's afraid of you."

Casey stomped after Alyssa on a mission, and a tiny part of me was scared for Kyle because Casey looked like she was out for blood.

After they were out of sight, I ducked down, tucked myself under the desk, and laughed. It was way too close for comfort.

Connor reached for me, pulling me into him, but it was a tad uncomfortable, given that he was massive and his head was crouched over as though he were in a fetal position.

It didn't stop him from kissing me and making me giggle like a little schoolgirl.

I got on my knees, leaning closer, and palmed his cheeks. "We got interrupted. You didn't finish the story." He quirked an eyebrow, and I continued, "There's another sketch you're missing, the one where their fingers are intertwined, hands wrinkled from the years, as they sit in matching rocking chairs, watching the sunset in front of them ..."

He finished my sentence, as he had done weeks ago when we were brainstorming, "The scene ends when he's feeding her chocolates ... why? Because she can't feed herself because of her arthritis."

When I slapped his shoulder, laughing, he grabbed my hand, locking our fingers together.

I leaned into him, my face only inches from his. "So, you are here for good now?" I asked, my heart full.

"For good. Forever and ever ... until you get rid of me."

I sighed. "That's not ever going to happen."

He kissed me then, speaking as his lips brushed against mine, "So, I'm yours now until the end of time."

"You'll forever be my baby, you big baby," I said, pinching his diaper for emphasis.

THE END

EPILOGUE

CONNOR:

I stepped out of the car, taking in the moon high above in the night sky, illuminating the lake beneath it.

I rubbed my hands together then wiped them for what seemed like a million times down my black slacks.

"Hey." My brother approached, coming to my side of the car. "Don't worry. You got this."

I swallowed. Hard. I didn't understand why I was so nervous.

"I mean, you wanted to do this months ago but you couldn't find the perfect ring so what's the problem?"

"Nothing," I said, smiling. Absolutely nothing.

He was right. I had wanted to do this months ago but was looking for the perfect ring, waiting for the perfect time, plotting out the perfect proposal.

He handed me the black velvet box and I flipped it open, staring down at the internally flawless single solitaire.

Kyle let out a low hoarse whistle. "What did that cost you? Two years of your salary?"

I shook my head and let out a nervous laugh.. "No, but close to it."

He threw his arm over my shoulder and led us away from the car toward where everything was going to go down. "Casey should be here with Charlie soon."

A few hundred yards from the lake, my brother patted my back one last time, lifting what he had in his other hand – a video recorder. "See you on camera."

"Thanks, bro. For doing this."

"Thanks for letting me do this. I told you. You need to record this for your future kids." He lifted his fist and I bumped my fist against his before he walked to the other side.

It was crazy to think that was how we bonded, filming a series of commercials that essentially saved my company.

My company.

Over the last year, my father had finally stepped away from the day-to-day functions, letting me implement my ideas, managing and leading my way.

The past year with my family had been one of my happiest moments. Over the holidays, we went skiing with Charlie's family. I didn't remember a time when we went on a family vacation with everyone.

My pulse ticked up when Casey approached from a distance leading a blindfolded Charlie toward the lake, toward me.

I closed the space between us, meeting her exactly where I needed them to be, in between two trees underneath the moonlight.

"Casey?" Charlie extended her hands, feeling for nothing but air. "Where did you go?"

Casey threw me a thumbs up, smiled, and walked toward the hiding spot behind the tree.

I stepped into Charlie and after I reached for her hand, she pushed back the blindfold and smiled. "Connor?" Her face registered confusion at first. "What is going on?"

Seeing her in the dress I'd bought her, all my nervousness faded away.

She was wearing what I told Casey to specifically pick out for her. It was Casey's birthday last weekend and Casey had made up the excuse that they were going out to dinner for her celebration. Casey had gotten ready for her pretend birthday dinner at Charlie's place and picked out this dress to specifically wear for today—a blue flowy chiffon dress, one that Charlie had drawn out for the proposal scene when we started brainstorming for the commercial months ago.

"Charlie, you look amazing." I pulled her in at the waist and planted a chaste kiss on her soft lips, my one hand heavy on her hip.

She tilted her head, her eyes playful. "What are you up to?"

"Up to something good for once," I said.

"Are we celebrating? It's not our anniversary." She wrinkled her nose in the cutest way and I tucked an escaping strand behind her ear.

The moonlight cascaded a shine across her beautiful features and the sounds of the lake rushing against the shore brought me back to when we had filmed the proposal scene, but now we were at a different lake and under different circumstances. We were no longer playing a part, I was living in the now.

Just then the lights that Kyle and I had strung on the trees lit up.

I knew when she knew, because she stepped back and both hands flew to her mouth. Taking her hand, I dropped on bended knee and that was when the first of her tears began to fall.

"Charlie...."

I whispered her name, getting choked up myself.

"I kind of knew you were meant for me on that very first day I'd met you in front of that candy wall and you told me you hated our signature chocolate bar."

She swiped at her tears and laughed.

"But what solidified my love for you was your kindness in helping me save my company—our company now. Because what's mine is yours." Staring up into her eyes, I knew it was because of her that my life was complete. "I came back for you and got more than I ever wished for. I got you. I got my family back. I am now leading this company where it's never been before." I swallowed down all the emotion bubbling up to the surface. "We didn't finish writing out the commercials. We only finished up to the marriage scene."

Her tears fell harder and faster down her cheeks.

"Will you make me the happiest man alive and finish out the rest of the scenes with me? Where we are gray and old, holding hands and sitting on our porch, watching our grandkids play games in our front lawn. Charlie, will you marry me?"

With a nod of her chin, I was up on my feet.

"Yes! Yes! Yes! A million times yes."

Both of her hands were on my cheeks as she kissed me sweetly.

"I love you, Connor Colby." She pulled back, smiling up at me. "But you are forgetting one part of the story—the part where we are giving out chocolate bars to the grandkids as prizes. Sugaring them up before we give them back to the parents. "

I didn't think I could smile any bigger. "You always complete the start to my stories."

Kyle and Casey emerged, clapping and cheering.

After Casey jumped on Charlie in a congratulatory hug, Kyle pushed the video camera, still taping in my direction. "So, big bro, any words to say?"

I reached for my future wife, dipped her, and my lips descended on hers.

"And they lived happily ever after."

The End.

Again.

STAY IN TOUCH

Here's where you can find me. Join my reader group to stay in the loop about my most recent books.

JOIN MY READER GROUP
WEBPAGE
FACEBOOK
TWITTER
INSTAGRAM
GOODREADS
AMAZON
BOOKBUB

ACKNOWLEDGMENTS

Another book! YAY!

First and foremost—Thank you God for continuing to fill my mind with ideas and giving me this opportunity at this time to write full time.

To the husband who loves me unconditionally—Thank you for taking the kids when I have to write. This book would not be here if it wasn't for you.

To the kids—Thank you for your love of reading. I hope you can read my books one day when you are older and be proud of your mama.

This book is dedicated to my BFFs in my reader group. Almost a year ago to the date, I posted a picture of a candy wall. My brother had just started working as a computer tech at a candy and factory. One of the perks of working at the candy factory is that he gets unlimited candy and chocolates. My six year old has six cavities to prove it.

Who could have guessed that a whole book could come to life from one post.

Thank you for telling me to write this story.

Thank you for the inspiration.

Thank you for the playlists.

Thank you for the names of the characters.

Thank you for it all.

I appreciate my readers so so much.

To my beta readers—Alyssa, Aisha, Elizabeth, Emily & Norma. Thank you for giving this a last look to catch any last minute mistakes.

To my tour groups, Ena and Shauna—Thanks for promoting this book and sharing the love.

To my blogger friends and readers—Thank you for always supporting and sharing the love of my books.

To my cover designer, Najla—You are one talented designer. Thanks for your patience in bringing this cover to life.

To my author friends that sprint with me, encourage me day in and day out, I heart you. You know who you are.

To my sounding board, my friend, my editor—Kristy. I appreciate our late night and weekend calls. Thanks for helping me make each book the best it can be. I heart you big time.

ALSO BY MIA KAYLA

Let me help you find your next read...

THE BRISKEN BROTHERS

Boss I Love to Hate - An Office Romance

Teacher I Want to Date - An Opposite Attract Romance

THE TORN DUET - ROCKSTAR ANYONE?

Torn Between Two - Book 1

Choosing Forever - Book 2

THE FOREVER AFTER SERIES

Marry Me for Money - Forever After Book 1

Love After Marriage - Forever After Book 2

The Scheme - Brian's book -Forever After Book 3

Naughty Not Nice - Forever After Book 4

BILLIONAIRE BROTHERS

Unraveled -The Tattooed Bartender

Undone - The Actor

STAND ALONE

Everything Has Changed - The Football Player